I0577378

Editor: Caitlin Lengerich, @chronicledbycait

Cover Design & Illustration: Bayley Killmeier, @dicebarn

Formatting: Zarin Madiyha, @author.zarinmadiyha

UNFINISHED BUSINESS

———✳———

CARA CALLOWAY

To those with a tough exterior and a secretly soft heart,
and everyone who's ever felt too broken to be worth loving.

I promise you're a storm worth chasing.
But let yourself enjoy the sunshine a bit too.

Playlist

DEATH WISH LOVE | BENSON BOONE

STAY | GRACIE ABRAMS

GRAVE DIGGER | MATT MAESON

BEACON HILL | DAMIEN JURADO

FAST CAR | TRACY CHAPMAN

BLOOD BANK | BON IVER

HYMN TO VIRGIL | HOZIER

HALFWAY TO WHOLE | MATT MAESON

THE ALBATROSS | TAYLOR SWIFT

FAVORITE CRIME | OLIVIA RODRIGO

WORK SONG | HOZIER

NOBODY LOVES ME LIKE YOU | LOW ROAR

LET ME IN | DERMOT KENNEDY

HOPE IS A DANGEROUS THING FOR A WOMAN
LIKE ME TO HAVE | LANA DEL REY

YOUR NEEDS, MY NEEDS | NOAH KAHAN

YOU HAUNT ME | SIR SLY

CURSIVE (FEAT. MANCHESTER ORCHESTRA) | MATT
MAESON

FATHER FIGURE | TAYLOR SWIFT

WALKIN' AFTER MIDNIGHT | PATSY CLINE

I TOLD YOU THINGS | GRACIE ABRAMS

LOVERS | ANNA OF THE NORTH

CARRY YOU | NOVO AMOR

Content Considerations

While this story focuses on healing and love, it also touches upon sensitive topics, including: mention of a suicide attempt (off-page), references to substance and alcohol abuse, a toxic family dynamic, a complicated mother/daughter relationship, and an on-page tense family conflict. Please take care of yourself while reading.

chapter 1

I DON'T BELIEVE in happily ever after.

People lie. Cheat. Slowly grow to disdain you over a twenty-year partnership. They put you on a pedestal you're terrified to topple from, so sometimes you take a flying leap to get ahead of it. They hurt you. They leave. Marriage vows dissolve, and fiery honeymoon-phase passion banks its flames. They say love is a choice, but what happens when the person you promised yourself to doesn't feel like they're even an option anymore?

And if, somehow, you manage to fall in love—and stay in love—well, there's always death waiting to crush that joy beneath its thumb.

Maybe some people are lucky enough to live a Barbie Dreamhouse perfect life. To pass peacefully in their sleep, hands linked with their beloved partner who—miraculously—expires at the exact same moment. It's peak Hollywood romance, isn't it? Taking your last breaths simultaneously after a smitten lifetime together.

That's not in the cards for someone like me.

I'm pretty sure I'm playing a different game altogether. Less Hearts, more Craps.

There's nothing people want to root for more than a love

story. The more tragic and doomed, the better. They want the enemies to become lovers. The grump to soften for their personal sunshine. The exes to realize they made a mistake. They cling to the tiniest sliver of misty-eyed hope for a happy ending that ties everything up in a pretty bow, completely ignoring how unrealistic it is. Thankfully, this proclivity is exactly what's going to save my and my brother's web series from the worst fate possible: fading into forgotten internet irrelevance.

Because what love story is more doomed than one between two dead people?

"Winona? You got the shot ready yet?" River lets out the longest, most tortured sigh of his life, shoulders drooping harder than the force of gravity.

Clenching the stabilizer, I swoop the camera for one last pan of the ominous structure behind him. "Yeah! Got it." Under my breath, I mutter, "Twerp." He'll catch it in post, but maybe he'll also catch the extent of his dramatics.

River tugs at the collar of his oversized faded Star Wars tee where the lavalier mic is hidden, his intentionally-ratty jeans finally looking like they belong in the decrepit scene. If there's anything that never fails to remind me of our decade age difference, it's his fashion choices. Despite all the primping he did this morning, he runs his hands through the black coffee mop on top of his head before flashing a dazzling smile. Butthole got the best teeth in the family.

"In 1952, an unthinkable crime was committed in a formerly quiet East Texas farming community not far from where we are now," my little brother starts. "A young wife and mother, Edith Page Milton, was found murdered on the banks of a river not even a mile from her home. Local law enforcement determined her neighbor, James Dewhurst, was the culprit. He was arrested, and although he originally entered a plea of not guilty, the very next morning he changed it to no contest—not claiming his innocence, but not admitting guilt either. He was quietly sentenced to life in prison, where he eventually met his end due to natural causes."

River spreads his arms in presentation. "Here. At the now-defunct Black Magnolia Penitentiary."

Set against a sinking cigarette-ash sky, it's the perfect shot. The imposing structure looms like a nineteenth century Gothic artifact —Manderley or Thornfield Hall reconstructed in the Red River Valley one limestone brick at a time—and River stands in the center of its stunning symmetry. If it weren't for the clue of a chain-link fence topped with barbed wire and the watchtower past the turret, it'd be easy to mistake for a grand austere estate.

"The case never went to trial, and eventually faded into obscurity. Until now." He slips his hands in his pockets, and I pan the camera as he walks. "A long-time fan who wishes to remain anonymous reached out to inform us that Edith Page Milton's family recently found a series of letters from James Dewhurst to Edith—sewn into an heirloom quilt—that position him not as her killer, but as her lover. The family no longer believes Mr. Dewhurst to be the one at fault."

I don't know how he does it—sticks to his script so flawlessly, delivers it without a single hiccup. Maybe a penchant for performance runs in our genes. But I love seeing his broad confidence, his unabashed spirit, how at home he looks in his own joy.

We've come a long way the past two years.

"The viewer who reached out claims to be a close friend of the family, and said they wished for us to run an investigation here, at Black Magnolia, to publicly exonerate Mr. Dewhurst and try to make contact with his restless spirit. And between you and me, we're hoping to dig up some details on what *really* happened to Edith Page Milton while we're at it. Maybe Mr. Dewhurst knows more than we think."

The corners of my mouth curl despite my initial doubts about this episode. He makes the case sound so compelling when he says it like that. Every guilty man claims he's innocent, and loving someone isn't a preventative measure against hurting them, but the twinkle in River's eye is enough to draw in even a cynic like me.

When I first skimmed the anonymous fan's email in our inbox I flagged it as spam. When River begged me to take another look, I worried he might actually buy that a Nigerian prince needs thousands of dollars to unfreeze his accounts. The email read like it'd been written by an AI bot, and the sign-off name was *Apple*. River insisted that even if it was a prank, it might give us a good idea for a new location to scout.

What we got is a ghost hunt and a cold case in one, and in his words, *True crime is, like, always popping off.* He's convinced this episode will not only revive our stagnating series, but bump our viewership enough to land some new sponsors and solve all of our financial woes.

He's seventeen. Of course he thinks that.

But maybe—*just maybe*—I have a good feeling about this one too. This could be our best yet. I can't explain it; it's my intuition. Or maybe it's River's naive dedication to proving this dead man's innocence that's getting to my head.

"Welcome back to another episode of Halbach Hunts Paranormal Investigations"—River's voice drops with gravitas—"at the notorious Black Magnolia Penitentiary, which is scheduled for demolition next month. This may be our last chance to reach the spirit of James Dewhurst, if he still remains. And if he does, we intend to find out."

He signals he's finished and I cut the recording on our intro, lowering the camera. "Crushing it, Riv. Did you already get the drone footage? You wanna go inside?"

His phone's already in his hands—it's an extra appendage at this point. "Yeah, I did that first thing. I think we can—Hang on, it's Payton."

He turns his back to me as he picks up the call from his girlfriend, pacing a few steps away in the overgrown dry grass. He'd drop anything for Payton. Which would be sweet if it didn't happen at the most inopportune times. Like when I'm serving dinner, when I'm in the middle of a conversation with him, or when we have a ghost hunt to kick off.

Craning my neck, I swallow. Photos online don't do this place justice.

A shroud of fog drifts from the dense tree line of slouching branches, the woods set back from the property, yet completely surrounding it. Dried and dying vines choke the formidable stone walls. Large cathedral windows line the entrance with panes like bared teeth, but I feel it in my gut as I gape up—there's nothing holy about this place. It may be built like a place of worship, but Black Magnolia is the furthest thing from a sanctuary.

No one would ever guess a brutal prison was tucked behind the miles and miles of quaint, pastoral farmland two hours north of Dallas.

Even out here the energy feels heavy. Dense. Restless. More intense than any of the other three dozen or so haunted locations we've filmed at since the show's inception. I can only imagine what it's like inside.

"Shit's fucked." River drags a hand down his face, walking back toward me. Before I can decide if I should say something about his language, he barrels out, "Payton's stuck on the side of the road somewhere. She sent me her location. Her tire popped—she hit something, I guess. She's okay but she wants me to come get her."

"She can't call an Uber?" Him leaving was not part of our plan.

"She was, like, hysterical, Win. Fuck. I'm not telling her to call an *Uber*." His glare is precious—dare I say. His response makes me proud. And they say chivalry is dead. It's not. It just curses like a war veteran and wears clothes three sizes too big.

"What about her parents?"

"She said they're staycationing at Zaza." River groans and I'm tempted to parrot it. Staycationing wasn't even in his vocabulary until I moved him to Dallas. "They'll be pissed if she calls."

For as much as I want to snark at him about bailing on me *again* for a high school girlfriend he probably won't even remember in a few years, I reel it in. He's young. He's still the main character in his world. He's still convinced Payton is his forever.

There's one small corner of my heart not completely dead and iced over yet, that wants him to hold onto that hope for as long as he can. He deserves it—after everything. And an even larger part of me feels a personal responsibility to make sure River grows up to be a *good* male partner.

"Okay." I dip my chin in a surrendering nod. "So, go pick her up."

"But the episode . . ."

Hesitance folds into his features and the war plays out clear as day on his face: help his girlfriend, *orrrrr* hunt ghosts on his most anticipated investigation of the year on the *one* day the historical society agreed to let us in?

I could whack him over the head with the EMF reader. I don't remember ever being so indecisive as a teen—I'm not sure I had the luxury.

I school my features into a flat, I-can't-believe-how-dense-you-are look and angle my head. "Go help your girlfriend, Riv. I'll keep busy and capture B-roll."

"Okay. Yeah. Okay, you're right. I should." He casts one more longing look at the prison. Forget the EMF reader, the camera is feeling more apt. I've never been a good shot, but he's got a big ass head. *Boys.*

"You know how to change a tire?"

His brow furrows. ". . . Yeah?"

I know he'll just Google it, but I can't, in good faith, send him off into the wilderness without a little guidance.

"Break the bolts before you jack it up. Loosen in a star pattern. Don't forget the emergency break. And check the air pressure on the spare if it hasn't been used in a while—might be flat too." I scrunch up my shit-eating grin. "Oh, and lefty-loosey-righty-tighty."

He rolls his eyes. "Yeah. Got that."

Because I'm trying to be a good big sister, I say, "If you really want to impress her, take her to get her favorite treat after." But because I'm more than just his sister now, I tack on, "And drive safer than Payton does. Please."

I underhand him the keys and he catches them.

Standing at the edge of the parking lot, I watch him drive away until the rusted red paint of my shitty old sedan disappears beyond the trees. Seconds later, the bump of the engine is swallowed by the foliage and I'm surrounded by silence. Like the thick summer air has squeezed out even the slightest sounds of nature. I take a slow breath and turn, gazing up at Black Magnolia.

What are the chances I'm *really* alone here?

If there is anyone I will go to the ends of the earth to make happy, it's my baby brother. For better or for worse. Even if that means exploring an abandoned prison with the wandering souls of convicted felons entombed within its walls forever.

chapter 2

LIKE PHANTOM FINGERS, the tall grass tickles my ankles as a gust of wind whooshes past me, the prison letting out a tired sigh as I start recording again and approach.

River handles all the research for our locations, per our agreement, but I try to responsibly skim his notes before driving him into the ghostly unknown. Black Magnolia has a reputation for paranormal activity among the local community, but it's a spec of dander in the universe compared to haunted hotbeds like The Queen Mary, or the Lizzie Borden House. The prison's had firsthand accounts of strange noises, echoing footsteps when no one else was inside, compelling audio captured through Spirit Boxes, that kind of thing.

The front door is something out of a *Game of Thrones* episode —solid wood, reinforced with metal studs and banding, rust scabbing its hinges. It takes my full body weight and three good pushes to shoulder it open, the wood groaning as I cough from all the displaced dust.

The air inside the atrium is stifling. Thick, humid, and so dense I could drown in it. It reeks of mildew and acrid metal as I take a step over the threshold, panning the camera across the entrance. Every hair on my arms stands at attention as my core tenses—the heavy, sinking feeling I always get in my stomach when I'm not alone. The Knowing.

Chills spider crawl up my back and I focus my attention on the viewfinder, like it's digital armor between me and the energy here. Three steps inside and this place is even creepier than the antique dealer's storage attic we filmed at last month, which had *three* separate Ouija Boards.

God, the things I do for River.

If only I'd known this was where we'd end up when I let him convince me to drive him to the abandoned sugar factory back in Kansas—the first time I'd ever believed something like ghosts existed. He'd filmed our visit on his phone and that was the beginning of the end.

He bargained for this show like most kids beg for a dog. *I promise to do all the editing and social media stuff. You don't even have to get me a birthday gift this year—well, maybe a lavalier mic would be nice. I'll do all the research and script writing and boring admin stuff, you just have to drive me places and film with me.*

But watching him in that sugar factory—analyzing every response that came through his app, grinning and gasping when a stray noise jerked his attention over his shoulder—was the first time I'd seen him come alive after I finally came back into his life. I couldn't say no to that.

And, okay, I usually think it's fun too.

When I'm not flying solo.

River and I have a rule—well, *I* have a rule—that we don't investigate by ourselves. Up until a few months ago, when he officially got his license, it was out of necessity. But even after, we kept it up. Too much bias comes into play if you don't have someone to call you on your assumptions. Not to mention the underpinning safety concern of stalking around uninhabited places, typically in the dead of night. He insists he could handle all the recording equipment and tools himself, but as our designated pack mule, I don't think he really understands what all that entails.

The good thing is I'm not *really* investigating. I'm filming. I'm not pulling out a single tool, not inviting anything to communicate with me. It's daylight outside; I have nothing to be concerned about.

Here. Alone. In a haunted prison.

If there's working electricity here, I wouldn't have the first idea of how to turn it on. The historical society that owns this place was no help when we reached out. They grudgingly agreed to a date and made us sign waivers and didn't even supply an emergency contact.

I pan the camera across the sheets of peeling paint on the wall, the towering entrance, the sort of detail shots I know River likes to play with in post-processing. Sunlight falls like snow from the multi-story front windows, dimming the closer it gets to ground level, and I tiptoe across the shadow line cast by the open door, boot by boot, until it ends.

To my left and right are hallways, and in front of me, another imposing door. Focusing the lens on the window at the end of the long corridor to the left, I attempt a shoddy Hitchcock zoom. This downtime is a great opportunity to scope the place out—see if I can make any sense of its layout. Because the lovely historical society couldn't be bothered with a map or schematics either.

A low growl echoes behind me and my hair stands on end as my shoe crunches in something on the ground. I whirl, pulse racing.

The noise grows into a rumble, and I curse under my breath. *Just a car, idiot.* What could River have forgotten? I step toward the window, but this engine sounds far bigger and more grumbly than my Corolla. My heart leaps into my throat.

Is it the police? Did someone call about a trespasser? Even with permission from the historical society, if the cops in this town are anything like the ones in the armpit I grew up in, they'll be frothing at the mouth to write a ticket just to say they did something for the day.

I scramble to put the camera equipment back in my backpack, preparing to book it. But whoops and hollers drop some of the tension from my shoulders. That's not exactly law enforcement behavior. I wipe my sweaty palms on the front of my shorts and peek outside again.

It's a white truck. Big enough to steamroll over me and crush every bone, decked out with what looks like antennae on the roof. And as it peels into the parking lot, tires squealing with the drift around the curve, I can make out the words on the storm cloud wrap clinging to its side doors: SADDLE UP STORM CHASERS.

My stomach plummets to the depths of Hell as my mouth falls open. *You've got to be kidding me.* I pray to every deity imaginable that the last person I want to see isn't riding shotgun in the cab of that monstrosity.

The world is small, but it ain't *that* small.

The idiots do a donut until the truck is facing back the way it came and my teeth carve pleas into my lower lip. *Please don't be him. Please don't be him.*

But a flash of cinnamon hair tumbles from the cab, male voices and laughter bleeding through the open front door. The door thuds closed, he slings a backpack on his shoulder, turns toward the prison and time stops. My blood coagulates into sludge.

It's been two years, but no passage of time could weather away the details of that face from my memory.

Charles Rosenhoth is a ghost, and not the kind I go looking for. He's the kind I run from.

I'm frozen. This isn't real. Is it safe to sprint into the woods? Can I get out of here undetected? Surely River doesn't need this footage *that* bad, right?

This can't be happening.

Two other men hop out of the truck and the three of them start walking toward the front door. I need a plan. Stat.

There's a narrow recess on the other side of the stone archway down the left corridor, which I tuck myself into, pressing as tight to the wall as my backpack will let me. If they come inside, hopefully I'll go undetected until they leave.

I gather my long, dark hair in a ball at my nape, prying it off my clammy neck as I hold my breath. This is so goddamn stupid. I'm *hiding*. My molars clench in protest.

But after the last time we spoke, I didn't think I'd ever see Charlie again.

Heavy footfalls, interspersed with chatter, get closer. And closer.

The goddamn Saddle Up Storm Chasers.

I'd be lying if I said I never watched their videos. The first that comes to mind went so viral, it snuck into my algorithm completely unprompted: *TEAM SADDLE UP INTERCEPTS DANGEROUS TORNADO SHIRTLESS!* Wasn't hard to figure out why that one landed with the masses—three fit, reasonably attractive men putting their lives at risk to drink adrenaline like water and collect scientific data for the betterment of storm tracking while showing off their abs wasn't a hard sell.

"Look. The door's already open. Guess we don't need the crowbar after all," an unfamiliar male voice says.

Crowbar? Because they couldn't bother themselves with asking permission first like we did.

Men.

"Maybe it was the ghosts. I hear this place is haunted," Garrett, another crew member and someone else I haven't seen in years, says in a tone that suggests he doesn't believe a lick of it, punctuated by a *wooOOOooo*. I roll my eyes. How dense do you have to be to not sense you're not alone here?

A familiar laugh curls its ancient fingers around my heart and I swallow. A laugh I used to coax out after he had a bad day. A laugh that would pop out at the most inconvenient of times, like when I was angry at him or when we watched the kindergarteners' charming Swan Lake performance at Colby Theater. A laugh he used to tease me with when he had me naked and desperate beneath him.

Charlie.

I try to become one with the dark corner.

"I'm sure my day here will be completely uneventful compared to y'all's," Charlie says. "And I can take a ghost or two. Might be a nice distraction, even."

"You got everything? Backup batteries? Radio?" Garrett asks.

"Yeah, I'm good. You guys get out of here," Charlie says.

As they exchange their goodbyes, all at once my muscles tighten. Charlie's coming inside. Alone. If he catches me, it'll be just us.

For the first time in two years.

Footsteps echo in the atrium, and with a creak, the front door closes, stealing away some of the light.

Charlie shuffles around the room. I stand, stiff as a board. Their truck engine chugs back into the distance as Garret and the other guy leave. A deep, metallic clang reverberates through the empty space, and Charlie hums in consideration. He must've opened the door across from the entry. Fantastic. He'll head deeper into the prison and I'll head the fuck out of here.

More footsteps bounce off the walls.

Slowly, they fade into silence. This is my chance. It's now or never. I steel myself, bracing to sprint as hard and fast as my body can take me, and pray the damn cartilage in my hip behaves until I make it to the tree line.

I lunge from my hiding spot in synchronicity with another foot fall, except this one's too close . . . and I slam right into him.

Jesus, he's built out of rock. His chin knocks me in the nose as, on reflex, I stabilize my hands on his taut stomach, and he yelps. We ricochet off each other, two asteroids colliding in space.

"What the—"

"Fuck! Ow."

Like dark black pools, his pupils dilate as his chest heaves with heavy breaths, taking in the scene before him. He goes completely quiet. Takes a step back. Gapes at me, his full lower lip parting from his top, mouth a crescent moon as he adjusts his glasses.

He blinks a few times, batting those criminally long lashes framing his cracked ice eyes, like he can't really believe what he's seeing—who he's seeing. He looks the same and yet completely different, or maybe I'm searching for clues he's changed. His tousled hair seems longer. Are those new frames? There seems to be more of him than the last time I saw him, like a fresh layer of muscle's been laid in my absence. The barest glint of metal pokes from his collar—a thin gold chain around his neck.

But he's still tall and slender, still in casual jeans and a tee. Still clean shaven. Still sporting a bruised shade beneath his eyes—still not sleeping enough. Does he still stay up too late reading about other worlds?

"I—" His voice breaks off in a rasp as he shakes his head in slow disbelief and my knees buckle like I'm going to snap in two. "Winona?"

So much for an escape.

chapter 3

"HI," I eke out.

It's the best I can do, given the circumstances. There is no such thing as the right words for our situation. *I'm sorry* wouldn't begin to cut it. And maybe my bitchy side doesn't want to be the first to say it, either.

Charlie's brows pitch, eyes darting over every inch of my face, my body, like he's scanning to see if I'm real. "Why are you . . . what are you doing *here*? And—in *Texas*? I thought . . . Am I seeing things? Is there a gas leak? What the hell's going on? Jesus, you scared the shit out of me."

He's still staring and I don't know what to say, or do, so I let him. It's a strange sort of time warp, standing here with him. Never mind the fact we're in a creepy, deserted prison. We're in the same room. Breathing the same air. I could reach out and touch his heartbeat. Feel the warmth on his skin, if I wanted to.

"What are you doing here?" he repeats, taking a half step closer. The twist of his brow looks like he's worried we *are* suffering from carbon monoxide poisoning and I'm seconds away from kicking it.

Maybe I should speak.

But there's no easy way to explain I've picked up the hobby of communing with the dead since we last saw each other—it sounds silly when you say it out loud. Charlie's all left-brain. The only room for fantastical ideas in his life are the books I got him hooked on back in college.

"Working," I squeak. A normal person, who hasn't been keeping tabs on him since she left, would ask what he's doing here, because she wouldn't already know this from her part-time sleuthing. I say nothing.

"In . . . here?"

"Yes."

The quiet used to be something comfortable we shared. A gentle reassuring reminder that neither of us needed to work to fill the space—we were just happy to be there. Together. But this silence is so awkward, so tense, it winds and winds and winds around my throat, constricting anything else from coming out.

His gaze drops down my body, unfocused and distant, confusion still tugging on his features. Like the snick of a blade on a whetstone, his attention sharpens in the vicinity of my chest and I scramble to cross my arms, but I'm too late. The *Halbach Hunts Paranormal Investigations* logo sits loud and proud, smack dab above my heart—because someone has to wear these stupid branded shirts, after how much money we spent on them—and there's no hiding it.

"Halbach Hunts, huh?"

I could write and illustrate a visual dictionary on all things Charles Anthony Rosenhoth if I had any sort of artistic talent, and a reason to do so. I could ink a star chart of every mole and lingering childhood scar on his body. I could sort and categorize his idiosyncratic reactions by what emotion was percolating in that quiet, locked up brain of his. If there is one thing I know in this world, it's him.

And that feathering muscle in his jaw, that small tic in the twist of his mouth, like a sneer's begging to be set free and he's chewing it back—that's not the hurt, the betrayal, the ache I would've expected.

No.

Charlie's pissed.

Maybe I don't remember him as well as I thought.

"New side hustle," I answer vaguely, shaving back my cuticle with my thumbnail.

"Like . . . hunting ghosts?" He scoffs.

Molten lava spurts from the chambers of my heart to my cheeks. I narrow my eyes. "We prefer the term *paranormal investigators.*"

His dry laugh fires off like a gun. Its echo in the barren room taunts me. Dragging a hand down his jaw, he mutters under his breath, "You've got to be kidding me."

"What are *you* doing here?" I finally shoot back, hands curling into fists at my side.

"New side hustle," he deadpans. "Storm stuff. This area's tornado warned today. I'm on photo duty."

Tornado warned? That explains all the weather alerts I've been swiping away the past few days. "So you'll . . . be here a while?"

Charlie steps out of the thin light and closer to my darkness, bathing the angles of his face in shadows that only serve to make him look sharper—more piercing. His voice drops, gravelly and goading, as he says, "Don't sound so excited, sweetheart."

My eyes flare back at him as I suck in a sharp breath, snorting his bitterness like a drug, letting it consume the festering shame in my gut. "We can't both be here." Not with words like that lingering between us. *Sweetheart.*

"I'll be up in the guard tower." He looks away, shaking his head a little. "Don't worry, Winona, you can keep avoiding me." He says my name with a dark and heavy tone. A practiced curse. Nothing like the way it used to sound like gospel.

We're mirror images of each other, thumbs tucked behind our backpack straps and fat-bellied hurt that's been feasting for years nesting in our brows. I want to shoulder check him and storm out and never see him again—leave our tangled past ground to dust beneath my shoe.

But I'm doing this for River.

This is our one shot at this episode. The one day he secured permission for us to be here—since no way am I condoning a crowbar entry. This time next month, Black Magnolia will be a pile of rubble with the demolition coming. It's now or never. I refuse to let my past be the reason I let my brother down; I promised I'd always put him first.

"Fine," I bite.

"Fine."

"You stay on your side of the prison and I'll stay on mine."

"Of course." He rolls his eyes—just *so* disappointed in me. It turns up the burner on my simmering annoyance. I don't want his passive aggression. I want his rage. If he's going to be mad at me, I want him to at least do it right. None of this pseudo-polite bullshit, dancing around what he really wants to say. The tight smiles, the practiced words. The truth, shackled and barred behind his teeth. We used to be honest with each other.

I need to get out of here—out of this atrium. I'm suddenly claustrophobic standing so close to him. Every inhale is tainted with his scent: sharp and smoky vetiver with the faintest snap of something citrus. Guess he hasn't given up wearing the cologne I bought him for his twenty-fourth birthday.

"So, it's agreed?" I slip my tongue across dry lips, and for some idiotic reason I can't place, I extend my hand. It's out, and I can't take it back now.

Charlie eyes it like he's questioning if he wants to pull the pin on a grenade. Finally, he takes it, his large, warm palm enveloping mine with a firm squeeze. A zing of victory jolts up my arm like a match dropped on a trail of gasoline.

"Okay," he says.

Our shake lingers for a beat too long. I drop his hand like a hot pan, and swipe my palm over my jean shorts to cool the burn. I clear my throat, but Charlie stands there. Staring. Like he's waiting for something else. Some kind of acknowledgment, beyond this strange coincidence we've found ourselves in. And it's a reasonable thing to want, but like hell am I going to give that to him off the cuff considering he caught me off guard like this. I don't even know where I'd start.

"Right. Well. Good luck with your storm," I say.

"It's nice to see you again." His words are rough and rusted over as the front entrance's hinges, like he's been storing them for a long while. Each syllable scrapes me raw—latent venom sinking in to sting. "You look good, Winnie."

It pierces me like a weapon, that old nickname. So soft from his lips, yet sharp enough to draw blood. *That* is exactly why I need to get out of here.

I nod, because my throat's too tight to speak. He nods back, that vague disappointment in me sinking even deeper into the crease between his brows. Then he turns on his heel and carries on down the corridor and I study the shape of him as he walks away. And it hits me—this is a moment he never got to have.

Shaking the thought from my head, I round the corner and head back for the door. I'm in serious need of fresh air.

But I push on the door Charlie closed behind him and it doesn't budge. My brows furrow and I push again, leaning my weight into it. Nothing. I attempt to jiggle the handle, but nothing budges. Shoes sliding on grimy tile, I ram a shoulder into the wood and hold it.

Nothing.

Shit. Shit. Shit.

My chest pinches.

"I—uhm . . ."

With each subsequent shove against the door, my hands grow clammier, my body a million degrees hotter. Thoughts swim in my head. I'm stuck here. There's no way out. What if I die in here? What about River?

"Um. Charlie?" I call, an embarrassing shake to my voice. I don't know what else to do. My hip aches with the force as I throw my body against the stubborn wood. Louder, more frantic— "Charlie!"

Blood's rushing so loud in my ears I don't even hear his echoing footsteps come up behind me until he's suddenly there. "What's—"

"It won't open," I blurt.

"It's probably swollen from the humidity." *Or the pissed off ghost of a felon playing a mean prank.* "Here," Charlie murmurs, right by my ear. "Let me see."

Ridged veins crisscross the back of his hands as he gently pushes mine aside and takes the handle. The muscles in his arms flex as he pushes his weight against it.

I feel silly for calling him for help. But what else was I supposed to do? If we're stuck in here, that's his problem too. Charlie makes another attempt at loosening the damn thing, a grunt vibrating in his chest as he surges against it. The deteriorating metal howls but doesn't move.

"Okay," he pants. "It won't open."

My breaths come out sharp and fast as I rest a hand on my relentless heart, then press the cool back of it to my warm forehead. Nausea roils in my stomach and I brace my other palm against the filthy wall.

Charlie's head tilts ever so slightly, his brows pulling together as he steps toward me, all frustration in his features gone. "Are you okay?"

"I'm fine," I bark and jolt back from him.

His jaw feathers as his eyes narrow. "Didn't know you were so claustrophobic," he grumbles. He eyes me like this is a detail I've changed about myself only to spite him.

"I'm not," I growl.

Or I wasn't. But ever since River, the stakes have felt higher with everything I do. Because if I screw up, I'm not just letting myself down, I'm letting him down. If I hurt myself, he'll be stuck worrying about me. If, god forbid, something terrible happens and I die, he's left all alone in this world.

"Should I call nine-one-one?" My teeth worry my bottom lip.

"That's extreme. This isn't an emergency."

"We're stuck in here."

"We can find another way out."

"Right. Because prisons are notoriously easy to break out of," I deadpan.

"Hey, Ted Bundy did it."

"What a role model. Besides, he jumped from a courthouse window, genius."

He brushes off my biting remark, his light eyes turning pensive behind his glasses as he looks over his shoulder toward the other doorway. "When I checked this place out on Google Earth, I noticed the fence in the yard was partially down. If we can find an exit out back, then we should be good. We can probably walk right out."

"Probably," I echo. "So we should—"

He nods. "Make sure, yeah."

"All right. So we double-check for a way out of this place. Then go our separate ways."

"Right. Yeah." He runs a hand through his tousled chestnut hair, mussing it more than it already is. The way his eyes dart, that sideways pinch of his mouth . . . I know he's going to ask an uncomfortable question—something he's been sitting on. It doesn't take a genius to know what. He clears his throat. "Guess that gives us some time to catch up."

Our shared history beats between us like a pulse, but what's done is done. There are no questions, no answers, no heart-to-hearts that can unplay the cards we've both put down. It's not that I'm avoiding it to be a bitch—although that's probably what he thinks—I just don't see a point in revisiting things. Charlie and I are over. Nothing will change the fact that I don't deserve him.

But if he wants to grill me at some fruitless attempt for *closure*, then he can be my guest.

I set my jaw, wrap my arms around myself and lift my chin. "Sure. For the ten minutes it'll take us to find an exit."

"I think you've forgotten the things I can get done in ten minutes," he quips.

My stomach swoops. He wants to play dirty? I can play dirty. I'm not interested in being the bigger person. "I don't remember things ever *getting done* that fast."

Even his soft *huh* of amusement oozes pretension, needling me without even a word. As if he's silently volleying back *My memory recalls otherwise.*

He looks at me with equal parts resentment and a devilish desire to push every single one of my buttons and see which still makes me tick. It makes me want to lock myself up and throw away the key. This was not how I expected the day to go.

All these years later, and Charlie still has this unruly habit of barging in at precisely the wrong time.

chapter 4

SIX YEARS AGO

IT ALL STARTS WITH A ROSE.

I'm the first one backstage on opening night of *All That Jazz: Swan Lake.* Even with sticky, sweaty palms I raced through folding programs in the front office in record time, and clocked out of my time sheet early. I have an entire hour in the dressing room to myself. To relax. To get ready. To panic-spiral about messing up tonight as I pace the floor.

My first real performance, not just for family and friends, like recitals at my old studio back home. It hit me, the sheer number of people expected to come out for the show this week, when it materialized as a ginormous box of shiny paper I needed to bifold.

Playing over and over like a skipping VHS, all I can picture is botching the timing of the kick section of the opening song. Being the singular screwup who ruins the impressive visual. Being cut. Losing my spot. The driving force behind why I moved to Dallas at all—well, aside from college, I guess.

The snick of the door handle interrupts the tape. I whirl around.

"Oh, sorry, didn't realize anyone was in here yet," a deep, smooth voice says.

It's a moment lifted from a movie as I stare at him. The tunnel of golden light from the bulbs lining the mirrors in the oblong room, encircling him like a halo. The black crate in his arms overflowing with dozens and dozens of lush red roses. The way he adjusts his glasses, the curious corner of a smile coming out to play, when our eyes meet. He's so strikingly handsome my heart pitter-patters for reasons outside my brewing anxiety.

"You're fine. I'm decent." My legs turn to jelly as I tug at the hem of my ratty old T-shirt. Maybe *decent* isn't the best word.

"I just have some deliveries to drop off." He doesn't take his eyes off me as he slides the crate on the counter. "What's your name?"

I squint and cross my arms. "Who's asking?"

He nods to his crate of blooms, one corner of his mouth pulling down like he's trying not to smirk. "Just a guy trying to do his job."

"It's Winona." I drag out the syllables, brows furrowing as he examines his haul. "But don't bother. None of those are mine."

Ignoring me, he bothers. Pastel peach cotton hugs the curve of his bicep as he removes bouquets one by one. *Rosenhoth's Flower House* is centered on his chest in deep garnet serif letters, the 'rose' italicized. His mouth pinches as he double-checks his phone, like there's been a mistake.

I wasn't expecting anything anyway. I doubt my parents even remembered today was opening night. I haven't made any close enough friends who'd drop that kind of money on me yet. It doesn't matter. All flowers do is die.

Flower Boy rests one arm on the corner of the crate, leaning slightly. The protruding lines running across his forearm have no right looking as delicious as they do. His smile tips into caution, a mixture of mischief and curiosity. "I think you need a new boyfriend if he's not surprising you with flowers, Winona."

My name rolling off his tongue sends a pleasant chill down my spine. He says it like a treasured secret—low and intimate, a little delighted.

"I don't have a boyfriend." I haven't had enough positive experiences with males to think they're worth keeping around for long, and regardless dating's the last thing on my mind.

With a confident dexterity, he slips a single stem from one of the bouquets, not disturbing a single other bloom. He extends it to me. "Here. For you."

I eye it warily. "Won't your boss get mad if they find out you did that?"

"My mom owns the shop. I think she'll forgive me if I bring a pretty girl home for dinner."

I stare at him blankly. "What does that have to do with me?"

Ostensibly taken with my confusion, he sighs. "Well. When a man finds a woman attractive—"

"*Oh*," I squeak, frowning. "You mean, like . . . on a date?" An uncomfortable warmth sweeps the back of my neck.

He laughs, like he isn't used to being met with a response like that. Judging by the cut of his jaw, I'm sure he's not. "Right. Yeah. Exactly that. Don't sound so thrilled."

Despite myself, I smile. "Does this sort of thing work on girls often?"

"I don't know. I'm still waiting to see what you say."

Against my will, thousands of butterflies pirouette in my stomach. He's devastatingly attractive—and dammit, okay, charming too—but this chivalrous, flirty thing has to be an act. It always is. A calculated ruse to get me in the backseat of his car in a dark parking lot, his hands pawing beneath my shirt while he molds excuses to my neck about family dinner not working out. I promised myself I wouldn't fall for this again.

"Sorry, Flower Boy. Not interested." I let out a heavy breath and feign like I'm busy, digging through my makeup bag and all its drugstore accoutrements as I sit on a stool.

He lowers the rose, twirling it at his side, but he's not put off by my rejection. From the corner of my eye, I can swear I see him grinning, twin dimples popping in his cheeks. "All good. Figured it couldn't hurt to ask."

"Unless I decide to call the flower shop and make a complaint about the overly forward delivery driver," I quip.

To my surprise, it doesn't even make him stumble. Dare I say, he finds my petulance amusing. "Yeah, that tall, handsome, funny one is a real dick."

A snort makes its escape. "You're not that tall." An even six feet, I'd guess. Only five inches more than me.

"Ah. So you think I'm handsome and funny, though. I'll take it."

I laugh. He's earned it, anyway.

I coat my index finger with concealer and dab it under my eye in the mirror, both a signal this conversation's over and a reminder to him—and myself—I'm not interested in him; I have no reason to try and impress him. Taking the hint, he parses out the bouquets across the counter for the dancers to find later and picks up the empty crate with one hand, dangling it from his thumb.

"Here. For you," he says, and I turn. He holds out the pilfered rose. "Just don't tell Allie Michele one of her stems is missing."

"But I rejected you."

He shrugs a shoulder. "Everyone deserves flowers on opening night, Winona."

My breath catches and I study the delicate spiral of petals, the brilliant shock of scarlet, the way it's only starting to gently open. I take a deep inhale, savoring the sweet, luscious, buttery scent. I've never been given a flower before.

"Thank you," I murmur, taking it. When our hands brush, sparks light in my skull before making a path down my limbs. I quell the blaze with a stabilizing breath, but my skin sizzles all over. September heat's getting to me.

Flower Boy nods in acknowledgment and heads for the exit without another word. No expectant pause, no lingering to see if this last kind gesture is enough to sway my decision. The rose is truly a gift. Not a barter.

He's still a boy, but he doesn't seem all that bad. He's the first person I've made genuinely laugh since I moved to Dallas. And as I watch his reflection retreat in the mirror, my stomach leaps with a desire to stop him.

"Wait," I yelp. He pauses, turning back to me, and I swivel on my stool. "I don't need a boyfriend right now. But I—I could use a friend." Rethinking my offer, I clarify, "As long as you don't do that gross guy thing where you're only being my friend hoping I'll change my mind about you. Because I won't."

He chuckles and looks down at his feet. His chest rises and falls with a thoughtful breath before he meets my eyes again. "Friend. Okay. I can do that."

"It might be helpful if I knew your name. Unless you like being called Flower Boy."

"You can call me whatever you want." One side of his mouth pulls up. Pleased. "But all my other friends call me Charlie."

Flower Boy grows like a weed in my mind. I only last three days before I text the number he gives me. It turns out we both go to Briar College—his junior year to my freshman—and he rents a house with another guy that's only a ten minute walk from my dorm. Both of them are atmospheric science majors. I tease him about being a future weatherman, he corrects me and clarifies *meteorologist*.

Charlie becomes the best kind of friend.

Knowing him is like a portal to normalcy. Like I'm an alien and he's the human subject I'm studying to better blend in amongst the species. He's lived in the Dallas area his whole life. He has a normal, happy family. Two younger brothers. So many friends even the thought of keeping up with them all exhausts me.

It's all fresh, new. And for some strange reason, no matter what I say, he doesn't judge.

Not even when I ask, "How many people have you had sex with?"

What I don't say out loud is I'm curious what a *normal* number is for someone in college. A number I can give people, in case they ask, so they don't immediately categorize me as *Other*. I've been trying so hard to fit into the mold of someone who belongs here; Charlie slots into place everywhere he goes.

"Five." Charlie lifts a brow, silently volleying the question back.

So I tell him, "I'm waiting for marriage," because if he *is* doing that stupid guy thing, waiting around for me to change my mind about him, I figure this will scare him off.

"Religious?" he asks.

"Picky."

It's the closest I can come to explaining how I really feel: sex is the one shred of power I hold over men. I messed around plenty in high school, but this has always been the one line of defense I've never pulled back on. It's the one thing I won't give to someone who doesn't deserve it.

We hang out every time he's on campus.

He takes me to the super-secret-only-STEM-majors-know-it-exists sandwich shop in the basement of Nichols Hall and buys me the best meatball sub I've ever had in my life. I pay him back by buying him coffee. He's so sweet, I'm surprised when he tells me he takes it black. He teaches me to play chess on one of the boards by the campus pond, and his eyes glint when he explains the king is the one you're trying to protect, but the queen's the one with all the power.

I teach him to ice skate on the rink that opens at the park across the street the first week of November, and he executes a perfect hockey stop before admitting he hustled me so I'd hold his hands. On sunny days, we lay in the grass outside the gymnasium and trade memories like Pokémon cards. He tells me he hasn't read a fiction novel since high school, and I threaten to go no-contact on him. His dimples convince me to let it slide. Next time I see him, I surreptitiously slip a copy of Sanderson's *Mistborn* into his backpack that I found in a Little Free Library outside the campus bookstore.

He makes me laugh like no one else can.

It's dangerous, how easy he is to talk to—like no one else has ever been.

Charlie pours the story of his life out and I drink it straight, no chaser. But mine I share slowly, indulgent glimpses here and there, like dipping a finger in the brownie batter for just a taste. And he savors every detail.

There's always a bouquet of roses waiting for me backstage at Colby Theater on opening nights.

The *From* is always left blank.

chapter 5

IT FEELS like something's following us—a spirit or the dredged up memories of our life before, I don't know.

Paint chips and curls off the walls, littering the floor, and busted ceiling tiles cling to the rafters for dear life. With the front entrance shut, it doesn't take long for the air to feel stiflingly thick between us. As Charlie and I wind deeper into the prison, navigating only by soft gray light seeping through the windows, he's determined to root through my life like a raccoon sniffing through the trash.

"What are you doing back in Texas?" he asks, sidestepping a shattered beer bottle. The low timbre of his voice makes me shiver. Not the worst place to start.

Not the best, either.

"I live here. Just outside Dallas."

"Since when?"

"About a year and a half ago." He's quiet so I leap to fill the silence before he can prod any further. "So. Storm chasing. New side hustle, you said?"

"I'm doing it full time, actually," he answers tightly.

A surge of energy rises up my sternum, tightens in my throat, as I blurt, "What happened to the forecasting office?"

"Quit."

Some kids dream of singing on Broadway or throwing a pitch at Wrigley Field when they grow up. Little Charlie only ever dreamed of his name on an employee badge for the National Weather Service. It was one of the first things I ever learned about him. If I close my eyes, I can still picture the look of pure glee on his face in the photo he showed me from seventh grade, holding up his official laminated ID card he got after his dad took him to become a trained storm spotter. The day his internship at the regional office turned into a full time job offer, we went out for dinner to celebrate and he splurged on champagne—the real stuff, not the cheap stuff from California. It felt like magic, watching someone achieve a dream they worked tirelessly toward for years.

And now he's thrown that away?

It's not my business to feel so protective over this. That doesn't stop my jaw from clenching like I'm trying to crunch diamonds. "Why?"

"Guess I needed something to keep me on my toes after you left," Charlie quips, voice flat.

A breath whooshes out like he socked me in the stomach. *This is going well.* "How's that working out for you," I grit out.

"We're on the road a lot."

"Across the country?" He always said he wanted to travel more. Guess he got his wish.

But he shakes his head. "Mostly just Texas. Between tornado season in the spring, hurricane season in the summer and fall, and the crazy ice storms we've been getting in the winters lately, this state keeps us pretty busy. You remember Garrett?"

I angle my chin toward him, glaring up beneath my lashes as my mouth gapes. "Of *course* I remember Garrett."

Those cracked ice eyes don't stray from our path. Colder than ever. "He started letting me tag along on his live-stream chases, helping with equipment and navigation and what not. We were the first on the scene for a tornado that touched down just outside of Lubbock and the channel sort of blew up. All the big names in chasing were talking about us."

We come to a split and without hesitating, Charlie hangs a right, so I follow. He's always been thorough; I wouldn't be surprised if he dug up schematics of this place from a local archive in town and knew its layout like the back of his hand already. The corridor opens up to a multi-level cell block and a chill creeps up my spine. Barred doors hang loose from their hinges as we stride past the tiny spaces where so many men spent the worst days of their lives.

"It's a legit operation," he continues. I can't decide if he's nervous-yapping or genuinely wants to justify his choice. "We brought on a support team, and another guy to chase with us, Chad. We have a decent following"—I swallow my snort so I don't let on I know all this already. Saddle Up Storm Chasers is closing in on 350,000 subscribers, which is a little more than decent— "and we've even been interviewed for a few articles. One lady out of Boston who interviewed us said her fiancé's actually a big fan. He's some kind of . . . fisherman? Farmer? Anyways, he was pretty geeked about the weather stuff."

We're officially in nervous-yapping territory.

My stomach sinks. I used to be the one person he was comfortable being quiet with.

"What about you? What happened to dance?"

"You know what they say," I deadpan. "Those that can't do, teach."

"But I recall you—"

"I'm over at Winslow High School," I cut him off, because I don't want to hear him spout some comforting nonsense about how I *never had a problem with the "do" before*. There's so much he doesn't know. "Assistant dance teacher. The ghosts are just for fun. Got a little web series too."

Silence walks between us a few paces and I can make out the

shape of a door tucked beneath the rickety staircase along the far wall. He rubs the corner of his jaw, like he's been chewing on this next question for quite a while.

"I never realized you believed in that kind of stuff," Charlie says.

"I take it you don't," I volley back, tone sharpening like the thorns of a rose—a protective measure against greedy grazers. The story of how I found myself in this strange new world is mine and mine alone. One question would lead to another and another, until we've wound our way back to River. Everything in me steels at the thought of someone prying into my little brother's life. We're not going there.

"If I could see hard evidence for it, sure," Charlie considers. "But everything seems to be explained away by science. Or humans interpreting what they want to interpret."

A growl threatens in my chest. People believe in plenty of things they can't see—religious deities, good and evil, gravity, dark matter, love. Why is it always ghosts that get shit on?

"You're entitled to your opinion. Even if it's wrong."

His laugh is a shock to my system; I'm used to people putting up more of a fight.

A small window in the heavy metal door casts a dull wash of light across the floor as we approach. "Moment of truth," Charlie mutters as his large hand wraps around the handle. One good tug and it cracks open. Relief surges through my limbs.

"Oh, thank god," I sigh.

The breeze takes the chance to sneak inside as Charlie peers out, cool air chilling my clammy skin. Like a down feather blanket, low hanging gray clouds suffocate any attempt at sunlight—darker than they were this morning. The storm's moving in.

"There." Charlie points out toward the prison yard. "See that?"

As promised, a section of chain-link fence near the back entrance of the property slouches in the overgrown grass. Nothing

I can't climb over. That is our way out of here, and most likely River's way back in.

"Great. An exit." I attempt to dry my sweating palms on the front of my shorts.

Charlie squats and picks up a stray rock nestled in the dirt outside, his backpack jostling with the movement. He positions it in the frame, propping it open as he lets gravity close the door again. "There. Just in case."

"Thanks."

I don't need to look to know Charlie's watching me as I stare at the charcoal sky; I feel it in my skin, like a hum of energy around me. It's what happens when you spend so long in someone's orbit —their gravitational force encodes into your bones. I avoid his gaze.

"I guess that's it," Charlie says, sliding his hands in his pockets.

He's right. That's it. We agreed to work together to find a suitable exit. We've done that. We even made polite small talk, catching up on each other's lives on the way over. This should be the end of the road for us.

So why is something in me so resistant to letting him go?

Maybe Charlie was onto something in suggesting we catch up. What we do for work is barely scratching the surface, and yet we've both been floored by each other's changes since the last time we spoke. What else is there about him I no longer know? What other artifacts of his existence without me can I chisel from the stone, if I only steal a few more moments with him?

I didn't leave because I didn't care; I couldn't stay because I *did*.

"Winona, I—"

"Do you—"

We both talk on top of each other but a thunderous scrape of metal dragging on metal bellows in the cavernous cell block, and every individual hair on my body stands on end. I snap my head over my shoulder looking to the left, then to the right. I check my phone. River hasn't texted—he's not back yet. My chest rises with a ragged breath as I close my eyes, tuning into my body. My senses are dialed up to a hundred—racing pulse, warmed skin, hearing tuned to the sound of a pin drop, my stomach a tight rock.

The Knowing.

Something's here with us.

"You hear that?" I mutter.

"Yeah." Charlie's vowels stretch under the weight of his skepticism. "Probably just a—"

"*Shh.*"

It's dead quiet around us. I yank my phone from my back pocket again, but before I can process what I'm doing, my heart skips. The white rectangle in the top right corner, which was full only a moment ago, sits at the halfway point now.

"Holy shit."

"What? What happened?" Charlie asks.

"My phone! It dropped half the battery."

He hesitates. "Okay? And? Did you forget to plug it in overnight?"

"I checked it a second ago and it was full! Something here drained my charge."

"I'm sure there's a reasonable explanation—"

"*Yeah.* Ghosts," I hiss, swinging my backpack off my shoulder.

"If this happened at home on the couch, you'd be calling the Apple Store. But since we're in this creepy-ass place it's *ghosts*? What does a ghost want with your phone battery anyway, Win? C'mon."

I roll my eyes as I dig through the small front pocket. "*Energy*, Charlie. To communicate. I had a feeling—just a minute ago. Right after that weird sound. The battery draining isn't a coincidence."

"I'm sure it's just—" He cuts himself off, staring at my hand, and blinks a few times. "That's a . . ." He lets out a heavy sigh, dragging a palm down the side of his face. "Yup. That's a cat toy."

But I'm buzzing with enough excitement I'd probably set off an EMF reader myself, so I can't be bothered to acknowledge his snark. Our investigations can be hit or miss sometimes, but the first teaser that something's active in a location and willing to entertain us absolutely never gets old.

I know what I heard. I know my phone was charged. And more than anything, I trust The Knowing I felt in my gut. I've honed my intuition like the cold steel of a blade since I was a girl; it's never steered me wrong.

Now I need to verify it.

The cat ball throws a light show in my hand as I set it on the floor several feet away. When the color dissipates, I jump. It doesn't trigger the motion sensor. Excellent.

A small thrill races up my spine as Charlie stays silent—as he watches.

"Hello? My name's Winona. Is anyone here with us? Anyone who's trying to communicate?"

Silence.

Charlie ruffles his hair. "Is this—"

"*Shh*," I hiss, holding a single finger out in his direction. Tipping my chin up, I say, "You can touch that cat ball if you'd like to let us know you're here. I'm just here to talk."

I pace to the other side of the space, careful not to make eye contact with Charlie. I'm aware how weirded out he probably is right now, and if I catch even the slightest hint of it on his face the embarrassment will only distract me. I'm not doing this to impress him—this is for my brother. River would never let me live it down if I didn't make any attempt to communicate with whatever feels like it's here.

"Is there anyone here named James Dewhurst?" I call into the quiet room.

The next thirty seconds pass like honey, slow and syrupy off the curve of a spoon as I wait. I hear the small pop as Charlie opens his mouth to speak, but he promptly shuts up as colors flare from the toy, dancing across the floor.

Goosebumps prickle my skin.

This spirit wants to play.

Most of mine and River's investigations it takes at least a solid forty-five minutes to an hour to really warm the energy of a space. Most spirits like a little sweet talking before they'll agree to a full on interaction, if they interact at all.

It hasn't even been half an hour since River left me here alone. This level of activity so soon is unprecedented. God dammit, of course he's *not even here for it*. My fingers itch to pull the camera from my backpack. But filming more than just B-roll? Without him? That doesn't make sense.

"This level of activity, so soon, is insane," I mumble out loud, more to myself than Charlie as I pace in front of the cat ball.

"Oh, I believe it," he responds anyway. "So a ghost set that off? Allegedly?"

"Allegedly, yes." I scoop the ball and pop it back in the front pocket of my backpack.

"You said you have a web series. Shouldn't you be recording" —he waves his hand vaguely in front of himself toward the spot where the cat ball had been—"all that, if that's the case?"

I chew the inside of my cheek, wondering how much I should say. "In theory. But my co-host isn't here yet."

Maybe it's my imagination, but his eyes seem to narrow at the word *co-host*. "So you conned another person into chasing ghosts with you?"

He has it flipped, not that he needs to know this—River is the one who conned *me*. Two years ago I was in Charlie's shoes, scoffing as my brother tried to explain how a Spirit Box worked.

I need to call my brother. I hate the idea of not taking advantage of this kind of activity immediately, but we have our don't-investigate-alone rule for a reason.

"Speaking of my co-host, give me a sec." I pull my phone back out and dial. The line trills and I bump the volume down; I don't want Charlie accidentally overhearing anything.

"Yo. What's up?" River answers.

"Hey. When do you think you'll make it back here?"

"Uhh, no idea. We just changed one tire, but turns out Payton popped two? Something about a curb . . ."

Oh my *god*. Teenagers. My eyes flutter shut and I count to three before I speak. "Okay. That's not great. I'm getting crazy activity here."

"Oh shit. No way?"

"Yes way."

A groan burbles across the line. "You can't miss that. Not when *I'm* already missing it all."

"I can't record alone."

"Sure you can. If you don't, we might not get another shot to record there."

"But there's so much equipment. And it's not *safe*—"

"Dude. That's why the good lord made a goddamn tripod. Actually, it was Sir Francis Ronalds. You got this."

I exhale a heavy sigh. He's never respected the don't-investigate-alone rule. Teenage hubris. "Can't you call her a tow and—"

"She's, like, distraught, Win. I don't want to leave her like this. She's really bummed about the curb. Her dad's gonna be pissed."

First, I had to talk him into going to Payton's aid at all, and now I can't convince him to come back? Everything's out of sight, out of mind for him. But I consider how I would feel if roles were reversed. If it was River stranded on the side of the road, I'd want someone to stay with him until he got it taken care of. I wouldn't want him to be alone.

"Okay. Yeah. You're right," I concede. "That's the right call. You stay there. I'll figure out how to film without you."

"I'll get back as fast as I can." His voice muffles as he already moves to end the call. "Script's in the side pocket, if you need it. We can't take another L. Don't let me down."

"Sorry about that," I mumble to the now-ended call on my screen before shoving the device away. "Uhm, I guess this—"

"You need help?" Charlie asks. "Filming?"

Dammit. I should've taken the call in another room.

I'm a deer in the headlights. My gut reaction yelps, "No."

"Are you sure? Because I couldn't help but overhear—"

"*No*. I'm fine."

The bastard laughs. *Laughs*. "I guess it's comforting to know you haven't changed much. Still got your claws out, refusing to ask for help."

I want to yell at myself for flip-flopping, but I can't fight the flicker of intrigue about Charlie, about this happenstance meeting, about what I've missed since I've been gone. Before the ghostly interruption, I was seconds away from asking if he wanted to catch up some other time. But is that really a door I want to open again? Yes and no and yes and no.

And dammit, Charlie reads my mind.

"I really am offering to help, Winnie," he says quietly. "You don't have to make it weird."

"Me? Make things weird? Says the guy who pops a boner over cumulonimbus clouds." Scowling, I jut my chin toward the door he just peered out of.

"Actually, those were stratus." A wide grin splits his face as he removes his glasses and wipes the lenses with his shirt, the edge of the tee lifting to expose the soft fawn of his skin. The line of hair trailing to his jeans I definitely shouldn't be studying.

But when the glasses go back on, he's all business again.

"I'm not going to stand here and act like I don't have a lot of fucking questions, Winona." The weight of his words sits heavy on my chest as he steps closer. "But if you need help, then yeah, Win, I'll be a decent person and offer it."

Every interaction is giving me whiplash. We're bouncing from animosity to curiosity to humor back to animosity—and maybe a tinge of disdain clinging to the phrase *decent person*—every other sentence. I don't know where I land with him. Where he lands with me. Clearly neither of us are fully decided about how we feel about the last two years.

This could all go terribly wrong.

But, good lord, I do not want to film in this creepy place alone. The shit I do for my brother.

I cock a hip and prop my hand there. "You and me? A team?"

I can't decide if it's nostalgia or sadness that clings to his uneven smile. "We've done it before."

What I say out loud is "Fine, okay, you can help" instead of what I'm really thinking—*we did, and look how that turned out.*

chapter 6

MY MOTHER RAISED me to believe nothing in life comes free—it may be the one thing she was right about. Because Charlie has a condition for his help.

"When this is done, do you think we could . . ." His light eyes flash to the right. "Talk?"

The way he says it makes it clear: he doesn't mean to simply catch up.

Every avoidant bone in my body wants to shout back *no*. Wants to beg him to leave the past in the past—insist there's nothing left to say. The truth won't make him feel any better, so what's the point in hashing it out? I try not to think about the last time I ever called him.

But I don't want to film alone.

I'm not sure I believe myself as I force out, "Okay. Sure."

Maybe by the time we finish I'll have scraped up enough dregs of courage to be more honest with him than I was the last time. Hopefully.

Relief melts his features. He swipes a hand over his mouth, wiping away his earnestness. He nods toward the way we came from. "I need to set up my own equipment first, too. Shouldn't take long, assuming I don't run into any more stuck doors."

"You need help?" It tumbles out of me before I can decide if I truly want to offer. My eyes dart to the spot where the cat ball went off as I chew on my lip. I'm nervous to leave whatever wanted to play, as if it might sneak away when I'm not looking, but something about being alone in this room unnerves me to my core.

Charlie watches me for a long, yawning minute, saying nothing. Thin lines fan around his eyes as his brow furrows. Like he's caught in his mind, trying to deduce if this is all real or some dream he'll wake up from, half-remembering, half-wishing it were true.

"Sure," he says.

I brush off the shiver slicing down my arms and charge forward, leading the way out of this cell block. "You know where you're going?"

I look over my shoulder just in time to catch his dimples carving into his cheeks, for the first time in so, so long. My stomach has no right to swoop in the way it does. He's distracted by the strap of his backpack; he doesn't even notice me noticing. "Who do you think I am, Winona?"

I press ahead, fighting a tiny smile. "Let's get moving then. The ghosts get pissed if you leave them waiting," I say flatly.

He catches up to me easily. "Follow me."

I don't bother asking where. We're in a decrepit, abandoned prison. The *where* doesn't matter. It all looks the same as it rots.

We crunch through the filthy prison in silence, ducking under dangling wires and sidestepping shattered glass. Charlie leads us back to the atrium we entered through and across it, turning down the hallway where we originally ran into each other. At the end of the looming corridor is a heavy metal door. I hold my breath, lungs pinching, as Charlie reaches for the handle, only letting it out when it grudgingly opens with a screech. Thick, humid air rolls over us.

I can't say I've spent any time in a prison before, but I have seen *Shawshank Redemption* at least forty-six times. We're in the prison yard. A barbed wire fence sections off the pathway before us from the rest of the outdoor area. Charlie motions his hand, *ladies first*, and as one of my sneakers crushes into the gravel, I tip my head up to the smoky sky.

Standing several yards ahead, is a guard tower. It's nowhere near as sophisticated as they are nowadays, and built directly into a sturdy brick wall. No, this one looks more like a move of arrogant engineering: a stout, top-heavy windowed room balanced on spindly metal legs, rust speckling like freckles coming out with the sunshine. I bet it sways when the wind blows too hard.

Charlie tests the bottom step of the zigzagging staircase with his heavy boot, rocking his weight a few times. When the entire thing doesn't collapse immediately, it earns his stamp of approval and he waves me onward. "Up here."

My pulse takes off but my body refuses to move. It cajoles me: *you're safer here on flat ground where gravity can't take your ass out from one wrong step. What would River do without you?*

The hesitancy must be written all over my face. A smirk curls on Charlie's face. "Don't tell me the ghost hunter's scared of a little height."

"Just wondering when I last got a tetanus shot."

I'll only embarrass myself if I don't go up there. Locking my jaw and breathing evenly through my nose, I take the first step. White knuckling the flaking railing, I take another, and another, Charlie behind me.

Up we go.

"You good?" Charlie calls behind me, strangling a chuckle in his throat.

"I'm *fine*." If I fall to my death, I'll just be leaving my kid brother alone to fend for himself in the world. No biggie.

The breeze kicks up, and *oh my fucking god*, I was right. The structure moves beneath me and my stomach clenches. Like it's angry we're invading its space, the metal squeals and creaks, protesting each footfall. But I keep moving. And I don't dare look down as we crisscross our way to the top.

One more set of stairs. My breathing's ragged, my thighs heavy as lead. Maybe I should jump in with my students during conditioning week later this month. Moving through the burn, I drag my right leg up, but before my foot plants back down on the grated metal, warmth sparks at my side. Charlie's large palm curls around my hip.

"Watch your step, baby," he murmurs.

My eyes drop; there's a hole on the step beneath my lofted shoe. I avoid the obstacle and it hits us both at the same time what he just said—what he called me. That his hand's still cradled protectively over my curves.

"Sorry," he hisses, his hand dropping like I've burned him.

My heart's lodged in my throat, so when I try to brush it off, it comes out more like "I'ssokay" than a real word. The way his hands used to feel elsewhere on my body—it's something I could never forget, even if I wanted to. And Charlie wouldn't be Charlie if he wasn't looking out for those around him.

Muscle memory. That's all. An inconvenient, stupid physiological response. A backslide into an old life. I ignore the question stirring in the back of my head—does he call anyone else *baby* these days? It's not my business.

The phantom of his handprint follows me all the way to the top. And up there, I see exactly why his crew dropped him off here for photo duty of today's storm system.

Standing on the platform, there's a perfect 360 degree view of the area for miles, in each direction. The moisture-bloated sky casts a somber, lifeless filter over the pastoral landscape, the smattering of farm houses, the distant white peak of a steeple in the tree canopy, and over Black Magnolia behind me. Charlie hums, surveying the tower's observation post, and nudges the sagging door open as we walk inside.

There are windows on every wall—they must be thick glass if

none of them have busted all the years this place has sat here, unmaintained. It's empty, save for a tipped-over chair, a rickety table, and a thick layer of grime. Tugging at the frame, Charlie wrestles one of the windows open, then swings his backpack off his shoulder.

His jeans tighten around his thighs as he squats, balancing the bag on one knee as he ruffles through it. The past two years have been generous to him—he's found more places to refine his body, to stack taut muscle. My gaze traces his broad shoulders, the shape of his biceps visible through the thin button up he has layered over his shirt, rolled up to the elbows. He pulls out a folded tripod, and my attention zings.

His damn hand again.

His strange, knobby knuckles I always liked; the way his veins pop and fork across his skin like a topographic map; the analog leather watch his dad gifted him for his eighteenth birthday.

It happens in quick bursts, the way that hand flashes in my mind's eye in reverse: wrapped around my thigh as we drove to his parents' house that last Thanksgiving; holding mine as we whispered promises in the Poetry Garden at the Arboretum; exploring every inch of me as our bodies pressed together and all the other sweaty strangers at Garrett's surprise rager faded into the background.

Charlie turns to me, and a stupid breath catches in my chest. He holds out the tripod. "I take it you know what to do with this."

I wipe my sweaty palms on my shorts then snatch it from him, grimacing. I need to get a grip. "Obviously." I extend the legs and quirk a brow at him. "Posting up here and taking some photos and videos doesn't exactly sound like *chasing* to me."

"No. Mostly sitting and waiting. But it's still important." He sighs and I swear I detect a hint of frustration. It's not my place to pry into details, but he's the oldest of three: he's never liked not being the one in charge. I lock the last joint in place and he hands me a camera to mount on the tripod. "There's a regional severe weather organization that holds a competition every year for best storm photography, and best storm captured on video. Winner gets some serious cash, which we're pretty much always in desperate need of. Chasing's expensive. We've gone through three windshields this year alone."

He slides an iPad from his bag, swiping across the screen. He runs his knuckles across his jaw and turns to look west, a handsome intensity settling in his features, and I notice the faintest trace of crow's feet extending from his eyes. They make him look refined in the obnoxious way aging does for most men.

"This season's been kind of a bust," he mutters. "We pick the wrong supercell to chase, or nothing develops at all. Or the equipment glitches and we lose the recording. Bad luck after bad luck. Conditions today are near perfect for development though, and up here, I should have a good enough view no matter where this storm decides to drop something."

He sets the iPad on a table, balanced on a fold-out stand, and it's open to some sort of radar app—except, as he swipes through pages, toggles layers on and off, I realize it's about a thousand times more sophisticated than the one I occasionally check on my phone. Content with whatever it is he's setting up, he takes the tripod, now situated with the camera, and positions it to face the direction of the darkening sky.

For as ominous as the color is, it looks placid. It's hard to imagine the clouds splitting into chaos. What about *this* storm is so promising for him? My eyes flick sideways. "Remind me. How do tornados form again?"

He clicks his tongue and the tick of a smile is the only small interruption to his downcast focus on the radar. "You grew up in *Kansas*, Winnie. Shouldn't you know that?"

"I know it's something like . . . warm air . . . cold air . . ." I clap my hands together for the final piece of the puzzle. There go those dimples again, and the lines around his eyes crinkle with his chuckle. "But why this storm?"

UNFINISHED BUSINESS

"You're not entirely wrong," he starts, flicking through settings on the camera. "Warm, moist air hits up against cool, dry air. High pressure, low pressure. Then they create what we call a supercell, which is really just a type of storm with horizontal rotation. The updraft creates a *vertically* rotating mesocyclone, and under the right conditions, that gives us funnel clouds, which then give us tornados, if they can drop all the way to the ground. All the data points to this storm having everything it needs to produce."

I only understand thirty percent of the words he said, but if I ask for more clarification I know I'll end up with a full on meteorology lesson like the time I made an off-hand comment about how pretty lightning was while we watched a storm outside, cuddled up in bed. It sparked an intense explanation of how the phenomena forms nitrogen oxides and something about plasma and how lightning strikes heat the atmosphere to fifty-thousand degrees Fahrenheit—fives times hotter than the surface of the sun—and him arguing that if I liked lighting I *inherently* liked chemistry too.

So I stick to a simple, "So, not all supercells form tornados?"

"Only about twenty—thirty percent, maybe."

"Why does one produce a tornado and another doesn't?"

"Tornadogenesis still isn't fully understood," he mutters as he toys with the settings on the camera again.

He's so focused he doesn't notice when my tone drops into sarcasm. "Wow. So there's no real scientific explanation for it yet?"

"Not yet. But we're working on it. In fact, that sort of thing is exactly why storm chasing's so important. We collect data in the field of tons of storms—ones that produce and ones that don't—and then we can take our observations and compare that with—" He pauses when I snicker.

"So you're just going off of *faith* that they exist?"

He tilts his head and looks at me, rebuking what I'm getting at, big hands engulfing the black camera body. "This is different."

"Is it?" I cross my arms, smug.

47

"Yes. Tornados are an observable phenomena—"

"Right. Like how I can hear things through my Spirit Box."

"No. I have real data and variables I can control. Ghost hunters are out here smelling busted natural gas lines and calling it demon farts."

I ignore the offensive fart accusation. "But you can't *scientifically prove* exactly why they form."

"We can prove enough of it."

"But you *admit* there are still some things that aren't understood about it!"

He throws his hands up, but no level of exasperation with me could cover the flicker of amusement dilating his pupils. He's always loved a challenge. "Sure. I guess so."

"Trusting something you can't see isn't the worst thing in the world."

"I trusted you," he says quietly, hosting his backpack up, "and you were about as hard to pin down as one of these tornados."

"I don't recall you ever struggling to pin me down." The words tumble out faster than my better instincts can put a cap on them. It's always been like this between us—I don't know how else to be around Charlie, if not vaguely risqué.

He huffs a laugh, his eyes fluttering closed and decidedly ignoring my quip. "All right, that's it for me, if you want to—"

"Is this the part where you rip your shirt off and run in front of the camera?" God dammit, I can't help myself. My carefully-curated filter's always fallen apart under his gentle attention. And getting a rise out of him—an exasperated chuckle, an eye squint, the holy grail of pinking ears—is as ingrained in me as breathing.

But my tease only conjures a cheeky smirk. "Oh, so you saw that one, huh?"

"Kind of hard to avoid it when it went viral." I dramatize a scowl. "Imagine my surprise when I was simply looking for updates on regional weather and I see *your* face on the thumbnail of a video with over a million views."

"My *face*. Right."

My cheeks heat. "It's not like I went seeking it out or anything."

"Kinda sounds like you did." Curiosity plays in his eyes. "Have you been keeping tabs on me, Winnie?"

I swallow. "Just curious what sort of things you're taking your shirt off for these days."

He snorts and shakes his head as he walks back toward the exit. "Quit flirting, Win."

"But I'm so good at it," I deadpan, at odds with the fluttering behind my sternum. So much for getting a rise out of him; I'm the one flustered.

"Believe me, I know."

I clear my throat. "You ready to talk to some ghosts?"

"Ready as I'll ever be."

I rub the back of my neck, suddenly clammy with sweat, as I plod behind Charlie, heading back down the stairs. This prison is a time warp—that's the only viable explanation.

Why else would it be so easy to step into the shoes of the woman I was before I left him?

chapter 7

SIX YEARS AGO

CHARLIE and I are both raging flirts, which makes being *friends* extra interesting.

I should've clocked it as soon as he gave me the rose. He should've clocked it when I nicknamed him on the spot. I've known him for two and a half months but I still can't decide if this is a universal trait for him, or if he reserves it special for me. For me, it's the latter. There's something about him that makes him so fun to toy with.

It's his eyes that are my undoing.

Muted blue, a teasing gray like the cloudy skies he loves—the color and texture of the well-scored skating rink near campus, the one where he wanted to hold my hands. They find me, those eyes. When he enters a room, when he's trying to measure my reaction to something someone said, over his shoulder when we're trying to sneak a laugh that's only ours.

It's a game we play—who can sneak in the dirtiest innuendo; who can make the other blush first. It's very normal and completely platonic and not at all smudging any of the pencil drawn lines between us.

The men I've known have proven they can't be trusted. Not

my unfaithful father, who felt more like a ghost in our house than a parent. Not my older brother and all his rage. Not the boys back home I went to school with who saw me as nothing more than a little bit of fun.

The way I feel so safe with Charlie can't last forever.

Can it?

At night, sometimes I think about him. But the apparition of his mouth at my throat, the way it feels in my imagination, is as close as I'll let myself get. Being friends is less risky.

Friends.

It's the word I asked for, and the one he agreed to, months ago. But the ink around its letters has this way of blurring when we're alone together. So we keep playing somewhere in the gray.

We talk on the phone every day I'm back in Kansas for Thanksgiving break. I tell Charlie it's lame and boring, being back in this tired town. I tell my family I'm working with a partner on a group project so they don't ask questions. But really, his voice is a balm. A reminder that this life, sinking into my sagging mattress while Dad and my older brother Patrick fight in the other room, isn't where I have to stay. I have something else to return to.

I don't get around to calling him until late Thanksgiving day. I tell him we had a modest, uneventful holiday, then listen to him detail the litany of sides his mom cooked and the depths of football rivalry that splits the entire Rosenhoth family in two—Cowboys fans versus Eagles, a hold-over from his dad's north eastern roots.

I don't tell him how whatever stupid bullshit Dad and Patrick have been fighting about all week finally boiled over and my brother backhanded a pie plate off the table, shattering it before he stormed out. I don't tell him how we carried on, pretending nothing happened, until Officer Cahill called to report they'd picked up Pat for driving drunk. Again. I don't tell him how Mom found a way to make it all about her, curling up on the couch with the TV blaring at three in the afternoon and didn't get up. I don't tell him how I microwaved bowls of cold macaroni and cheese for River and I to eat on the back porch while Dad went down to the station and the turkey sat raw on the counter.

I don't tell him the only thing that made this trip worth it was finding the perfect finishing touch for his birthday gift.

The Saturday before classes start back up, Charlie and his roommate, Garrett, have friends over at their house. Something small, he says. But nine minutes into the ten-minute walk from my door to his, I hear the party before I see it. Bringing his present was a stupid idea. Who walks into a college party with a *gift bag*? I bite my cheek and tuck my embarrassment behind my back.

A pretty, petite blonde with huge boobs lets me inside, and when I don't spot Charlie immediately, I hang a right, moving down the unlit hallway and find his bedroom at the end, avoiding the need to make polite fake smiles to any other unfamiliar faces.

Slipping inside, I half-close the door behind me. In here, the noise dulls. It smells so much like him. Fresh and earthy and sharp —an apple I want to sink my teeth into. Like dozens of suspended fireflies, a string of Christmas lights snakes through the wooden spindles of his headboard, casting just enough light for me to navigate. I set the gift bag down on his rumpled green checkered comforter.

"If you're trying to rifle through my underwear drawer, jokes on you, they're all dirty." Soft and sweet like sun-warmed honey, his voice trickles down my spine as I whirl. Charlie's leaning in the doorway, arms crossed, cinnamon hair messier than usual, like he's been manhandling it all night. "You'll have to get me out of the ones I'm wearing."

I transmute my snort into a look of intrigue, one brow raised. "Bold of you to assume I want a clean pair."

We stare at each other for the length of several quick heartbeats.

He breaks first.

His laugh cocoons around me as he drifts closer. Charlie's not a big drinker, but his eyes are a little glassy, his smile looser and more generous than usual. His gaze rakes down my body and my stomach takes flight as I smooth my fitted oxblood corduroy skirt.

"You look . . ." He bites down on his bottom lip, head lolling to the side as he smiles.

"Like I could crush you alive?" I grind my Doc Marten into his carpet for good measure.

"Like you could absolutely crush my heart." His grin goes full tilt. "Fuck, I think I'd even thank you for it."

"Stupid." I laugh, flattening my hand on his chest to push him back. His heartbeat careens under my touch. My body's a million degrees and we're alone in his bedroom, basking in the perfect makeout ambience lighting, and for the life of me, I cannot divorce the thought from my mind.

"So'd you come in here to hide, or—what's that?" His attention flicks to the bed and the corner of a smirk lifts as I take the break in the moment to swipe my hand back. "Did you . . . buy me a gift?"

The warmth in my body surges up and concentrates in my cheeks. "No. That was some other weirdo digging through your dirty laundry."

He clicks his tongue and grabs the bag. "Neighborhood's really going to shit."

"It's, uhm, nothing really—small thing. Belated birthday gift." I wring my hands like rags at my bellybutton as he reaches past tufts of white tissue paper.

"You didn't have to get me anything," he says quietly, glancing up at me beneath his lashes. I shrug in response. As he slides the

53

frame from the bag, I hunch my shoulders to my ears and curse my past self for doing this at all. It's stupid.

"An altocumulus standing lenticular cloud," he mutters, amusement and a touch of bewilderment pitching his words. His smile stretches so wide it makes my heart ache. He tucks it between his teeth and for a split second I'm jealous of it. Tenderness reflects back at me in his gaze, and my limbs tingle. "I can't believe you even remember I said these were my favorite. Thank you. Seriously. I love it."

"Good. I'm glad. Yeah, good," I eke out, eyes wide and glued to him as I fidget with my hem. "They really do look like alien space-ships, like you said. I just thought—you know, your decor situation in here's pretty sad. So . . ."

"It's okay to admit you were thinking about me, Win," he teases, lids drawing heavy over his eyes.

Considering humans are something like 70 percent water, I'm about to start evaporating from whatever heat is growing between us. It's irrational, but the thought of him knowing how much he means to me makes me want to hide under his bed. "Gross. You're projecting. Everyone knows *you're* the one obsessed with *me*."

"Oh, deeply."

My breath catches. Humor has always been my favorite hiding place for things I'm scared to admit. Is it his too?

He clears his throat, shattering the strange tension I'm sure I'm imagining, and sets the frame on his dresser. I force my stupid, horny body through the door before I can make any mistakes.

His body heat trails me down the narrow hallway, following the din of chatter and music back to the throng of mostly strangers. The kitchen already reeks of stale beer, the counters littered with red cups as Charlie hands me a sweating Lone Star from the fridge.

I went to a handful of house parties in high school, meaning everyone knew everyone at least by name and reputation and we rationed a warm 24-pack in someone's basement while their parents were out. But between dance, work, and school, I haven't bothered with parties in college. This is all new to me.

As someone drags Charlie away, howling with laughter, I plant my roots near the sink. I won't burden him, following him like a shadow all night. I clear away the used cups, rinse and recycle abandoned bottles, and help a drunk girl fix her busted zipper with one of the stray bobby pins that are always lingering in my pockets. All things preferable to trying to act like a chameleon around a bunch of strangers.

I thought tonight was going to be a few drinks and a bad horror movie with friends. Good news is I already gave Charlie his gift and it should be easy to sneak out early; there are so many people here, he won't even notice I'm gone.

As I pour out the dregs of the beer I've been nursing all night, Charlie reappears, leaning against the counter. He blows out a breath. "I feel bad."

I side-eye him. "For what?"

"I had no idea Garrett was planning . . . all this." He gestures vaguely toward the chaos. "I can tell you're not having fun."

It's embarrassing how much his observation impacts me. There weren't many people in my life who paid that close of attention before him.

My voice wavers as I insist, "No, I'm fine. This is great."

"You're *cleaning*, Win." He snorts.

"I'm fine, Charlie. Really. Don't worry about me." I force a smile as I rinse my bottle. After the week I've had, I'm too drained for small talk. For people to ask me where I'm from, what it's like back home. I wanted to spend time with *him* tonight.

"Have you met my friend Malcom yet? I think you'd like his girlfriend. They're just in the—"

"I guess I'm not really in the mood to be social." I move to toss the bottle but Charlie intercepts me, warm hand covering mine, and a gasp pops in my throat at how good even that small touch feels. My eyes flick up.

"What are you in the mood for then?" he asks, voice low.

It must be a trick of light on his lenses, the way his gaze drops to my parted lips, then darts away. My honest answer flashes in disjointed scenes in my head, but they all start the same: me and Charlie, alone. Turns out even four-and-a-half percent alcohol by volume is enough to make bad ideas tempting. I let go of the beer bottle like a hot pan, all the words in my head melting together.

He pivots and tosses it. "You want to get out of here? We can do something else. Or I can walk you back to your dorm if that's what you want."

My dorm. Alone. The two of us. My roommate's in Austin until tomorrow. My thundering heart's loud enough to drown the party noise in my ears.

I trace the intrigued angle of his neck, over his shoulder, his arm, and pinch my thigh so hard it might bruise in an effort to muster the courage to say a single word.

We shouldn't. Right? Would he even *want* to?

I swallow.

Could one kiss be so bad? Would it ruin everything?

Excited cries echo from the other room, pulling me from my wild imagination like I've been dunked in ice water. The new Beyoncé song follows, and Charlie's still watching me expectantly.

I'm not great with people. Or feelings. But dancing has always come naturally to me. When my brain, my body, and my heart are all on different pages—like I've been Frankensteined together with parts that don't match—it makes me feel whole again. The world quiets until all I am is music and movement, tuning everything else out so I can just *be*. It's the one time I feel in control.

I grin because I have a feeling I know what Charlie's going to say to this. "Dance with me."

He winces. "Ah, but I don't—"

"Of course you don't." Before he can finish his protest, I grab his hand and drag him from the kitchen. "*Everyone* dances, Charlie."

The living room is packed. There must be a window or two cracked, because over the tang of sweat and alcohol I can taste crisp fall air. Multicolored lights flash around the dark room as I squeeze us through moving bodies, the music so heavy it rattles my bones. I let go of his hand and I move.

The precision, the refinement, I've spent years honing in front of studio mirrors is nowhere to be found. This is all instinct, moving in whatever way feels good. Looser, more fluid, weightless —a call and response as the syrupy rhythm rolls through me.

Charlie hardly sways.

He turns down the corners of his smile and shakes his head, silently reiterating this isn't his thing. I take his hands in mine and guide him like a marionette doll, raising them as I twist serpentine closer to him. He rewards me with the barest of grins. I drop one hand and send myself in a spin with the other, keeping my back to him, before finally releasing him.

"It's not illegal to move your hips," I yell over my shoulder as mine lead by example. "You've seen *Dirty Dancing*! Don't overthink it."

His mouth drops close to my ear, keeping his words quiet, just for me. "You make it look much better than I could."

A wild thrill races through me and I smile. "Don't play like you don't know how good you look."

"Thanks for the compliment." An arrogant laugh caresses my neck and a shiver slices down my spin. "I still don't dance."

Packed in the sweaty drench of nameless bodies, lit only by flaring LEDs, this moment feels anonymous. Like we're background filler in someone else's main character moment, to be forgotten as soon as the director calls cut. The perfect mask to hide behind.

"Why do you have to be so *boring*, Charlie?" The ravenous

pounding in my chest screams he's the most interesting person I know, as my nerve grows a few more teeth. "If you don't want to dance with me, I'm sure someone else will."

I peel away only a millimeter before he reels me back.

"This what you want?" he murmurs, bringing his hand to the front of my hipbone, his fingers curling into my flesh.

"Yeah," I gasp, layering a hand over his. His grip tightens. My eyes flutter shut as I tip my head back, smirking. "Does that make you jealous? The thought of someone else touching me?"

His other hand comes to my stomach. It burns a trail as it inches up, following the dip of my body as I suck in a breath. "Yeah," he growls, "that makes me fucking jealous, Winona."

"What?" I breathe.

"Don't sound so surprised. I've wanted you since the first time I saw you." His words ghost against my charged skin. "*Fuck*, Win. These mixed signals are killing me."

Hearing it out loud dazes me—like waking up and seeing a daydream come to life.

Charlie wants me.

The song slows and I roll the delicious, indulgent rhythm back against him, my free hand winding up to delve in his hair. His touch goes rigid, like he's fighting to restrain himself. I swallow the growing pressure in my throat and act like I know how to play this part. "Friends dance, Charlie."

"You're so full of shit." He huffs a laugh, sounding so fucking tortured my heart races, then snaps me back against him until our bodies are flush. Every inch of him against every inch of me. His hands comes out to play, roaming my stomach, my hips, my thighs. "You think I touch all my friends like this, sweetheart?"

"Maybe for a night," I say, breathless.

"I'd want you for more than one."

The sparking, electric fire between us consumes me, hot and fast and uncontrolled. *Charlie wants me*, I repeat in my head like a prayer. I arch against him, against that hard strain fighting in his jeans, as we burn together on the dance floor. We're in the middle of the pulsing crowd but it feels like we're in our own world. No one but us knows what's happening. The overtuned string of tension in my body snaps and I spin.

Violet and crimson and aquamarine lights flash across his face, and I want to know what each color tastes like on his skin. Under the glow, his heavy-lidded eyes are dilated so wide they look infinite, like the dark depths of the ocean. And, good god, I'm drowning. Splaying wide on the small of my back, his hand pins us back together, my small breasts brushing his chest as I wind my arms around his neck.

"You're drunk," he rasps, eyes darting across my face like he's searching for evidence.

I shake my head. "I only had one."

"What're we doing, Win?" His thumb traces up and down my spine and his gaze homes in on my mouth. My head's too woozy to come up with an answer.

For a moment, we both stare.

It is me who breaks first this time.

I slip and fall into a trap of my own making, winding my fingers through his thick, lush hair as I kiss him. With instant ferocity, he kisses me back, one hand cupping the side of my face. His lips catch against mine again and again, and as I part for him, inviting him deeper, I can't hear his groan over the din of music but I feel it vibrate against my mouth. That hum travels straight through my stomach and drops between my legs.

His tongue lashes against mine, hungry and demanding but dizzyingly indulgent. So controlled it makes me moan. He cups the back of my neck, drawing me impossibly closer, and I tilt more, giving him complete access to me. It's hot and sweaty and I don't know where I end and he begins. He tastes like the sharp sweet of bourbon and feels so much better than I ever let myself imagine.

He jerks back suddenly, but before I can ask what's wrong, he takes my hand and tugs me back through the crowd.

Back to his bedroom.

He closes the door behind us, muffling the bump of music. I press a hand to my sternum, like the pressure might tame my galloping pulse, as I pace to his dresser. My skin's stretched too taut over my bones, my feet too big for my shoes. Every inch of fabric on me is suffocating. I need to lose some layers.

"Jesus, Winona. What was that?"

A half-laugh, half-pant whooshes past my lips. "What? You never kiss a girl before?"

Two fingers apply gentle pressure to my shoulder, urging me to face him. I do. And my stomach bottoms out. God, he's gorgeous. I want to trace the angle of his square jaw with my teeth. His mouth slants with soft awe, like he's amazed I even exist. "No," he murmurs. "Never like that before."

My molecules have been rearranged by his tongue, deep in my mouth. I've been permanently altered, turned from solid into liquid, by the way this man *looks* at me.

We move at the same moment, our mouths colliding in the middle. His hands frame my face and twine in my long hair, mine brace against his hard stomach, mapping out every line and divot I can make out through his shirt. He kisses like someone who knows how to fuck—like he knows exactly where he wants to take me, and he's in no rush to get me there. Like he's savoring every stroke of my tongue.

His grip drops to my ass, drinking in all my curves along the way, and my skirt rides up my thighs as he picks me up and sets me on his dresser. My knees open for him and he steps into the V of space, fingers skimming my thighs as he brings his mouth to my throat. I suck in a shuddering breath as his lips part and he presses a kiss there. And another. My skull bumps his mirror as I crane my neck and a sharp moan escapes when he sucks and bites my delicate skin, then swipes his tongue over it to soothe.

He tucks the stray strands of raven brown hair over my shoulder then lets his fingers linger at my collar bone, the only thing between his touch and my skin a creamy white fitted knit top. "You're so fucking gorgeous it hurts to look at you sometimes."

I crush my mouth against his again as I fight to hold back the shuddering breath in my chest. He says it hurts to look at me, but sometimes it feels like he's the only one who does. The only one who really sees me at all.

"What're we doing?" he murmurs, hand tangled in my hair, our noses pressed together.

"Thought you aced biology." I huff.

"Not what I meant—"

"Charlie—" His whispered name breaks off in my throat as he looks up and meets my eyes, and fireworks pop in my chest. My thighs tighten around his hips. I know what he wants: hard lines and clear definitions and a tidy list of control variables he can rely on. But I can't give it to him. Not yet. It's too much. "You ask a lot of questions, Flower Boy."

I don't know what else to say, so instead I show him. I peel my top over my head and toss it on the floor. His chest rises and falls, his breathing kicking up a notch as he takes in every new inch of me not covered by my lace bralette like he's not really sure this is real. His Adam's apple bobs with a slow swallow.

But he's too damn polite for his own good. Frustration knots low in my belly. Why won't he touch me? He wasn't nearly so hesitant with his tongue.

I take his hand and flatten his palm between my breasts, letting him feel my raging heart as I quietly beg, "I want this, Charlie."

His brows pitch as he slowly shakes his head, but his body betrays him as he crowds closer, thumb sweeping across my skin. "But you're waiting."

A lump swells behind my collarbones. Never have I ever had a boy fight so hard for my boundaries, instead of against them.

My smile slants as I cup the back of his neck, lips grazing his as I say, "There's other stuff we can do."

The magic words to break the spell.

His mouth's on mine again, starved for my taste as he jerks my hips forward, closing the last of the space between us. The dresser shakes beneath my shifting weight, and something crashes to the floor, but neither of us stop to see what. Damp and desperate, he mutters something like *tell me if you want me to stop* against my throat as he kisses his way down, licking, sucking, biting. I nod feverishly as I arch against him, lost in the feel of it all.

"Fuck, Win," he groans. "I want to get you off so bad."

My neediness shrinks to the size of a pinhead as his mouth closes around my nipple, sucking it through the thin lace of my bralette. He lowers the other strap, letting it fall slack on my arm, and cups my exposed breast with his hand, squeezing my other nipple between his thumb and forefinger. In one quick move, he unsnaps the clasp at my back and the flimsy fabric falls away.

His hand disappears beneath my skirt, following my inner thigh all the way to the crease of my hip where I crave his touch most. "Hands okay?" he mutters against the swell of my breast, and I nod. With dizzying warmth, his lips close around my nipple again, the tip of his tongue teasing and swirling the peaked flesh. "And my mouth?"

Oh god. I melt into a puddle on his dresser as I gasp, "Yes."

He jerks me up again, palming my ass. I kiss and nibble his neck, stealing reactions of my own and filing away every single strangled sound he makes in my memory, before I'm falling back and his soft mattress catches me. I ratchet up on my elbows as he hovers over me and I reach between us to tug up his shirt. He helps me the rest of the way, removing it in one smooth motion from the back of his collar. I run indulgent fingers along his abs, letting my nails skate across his skin, and he shivers.

I bow under his careful attention, every inch of me desperate to feel every inch of him, and I can't believe it took us this long to do this. Dulled by the need aching between my thighs, the reasons I had for keeping him at arm's length seem inconsequential when he feels so much better up close. He places the gentlest kiss above my bellybutton, toying with the zipper at the side of my skirt, and pauses.

He brushes the fawn spots to the inside of my knee. "What's this?"

"Just dance bruises."

"And you didn't ask me to kiss them better?" he teases, but I stare at him, perplexed. "Just something my mom used to say when I got hurt as a kid," he explains.

"Oh." I've never heard that before. Not that I'm surprised. My mother cared more about her own wounds than she ever did mine. "Now I know for next time."

"Mhmm," he hums. He presses one, two, three tender kisses on my leg.

One for each tiny bruise.

"You sure about this?" Charlie peers up at me beneath the long curtain of his lashes, hair a mess, and a current jolts up my spine as his free hand links with mine. I nod and his smile is all soft wonder. "How'd we get here?"

My words come out soft, unguarded, maybe even a little bashful. "I kissed you."

"Right. You did." He lowers the zipper and I lift my hips as he pulls the fabric down. "You stole my thunder."

I tilt my head. "You weren't going to kiss me."

His fingers hook into the elastic of my underwear as a smirk tilts on his face, and I am made of jelly. "I've thought about kissing you every day since we met." My insides pirouette and his voice drops. "And I almost did earlier. I thought about it, at least—after you gave me that gift."

"Really?" I whisper.

He keeps his eyes on mine as he lowers the last scrap of clothing from my hips, distracting me from any insecure thought that attempts to spiral in the back of my head. "You act like you're so aloof, all sarcasm and deadpan jokes. And then you go and do stuff like that." He kisses my inner thigh and slings it over his shoulder. "I'm the only one who gets your soft side."

The cool air of his bedroom meets my exposed center and the breath he exhales is so heavy it weighs over my whole body. My eyes squeeze shut as I collapse back on the bed and he sinks to his knees on the floor. Nerves light like kindling in my stomach, burning fast and hot. I've never done this before, though I've been curious ever since I learned what a blow job was when I was thirteen and immediately wondered if there was an equivalent for girls, and if so, why did no one talk about it?

Charlie's warm, wet mouth answers all my curiosities and I suck in a sharp breath. *Oh.* My hands fist his comforter, a small cry leaking out as his tongue slides against me. For a flash of a second, our eyes meet and I melt into a puddle under his ice blue gaze—the hunger brewing there, the satisfaction flecking in his light irises. My next moan builds deep in my chest as my fingers thread through his hair. His hold on my hips tightens, bringing me closer to his mouth, and I arch up against him, my body already knowing the choreography to this dance.

Maybe for a night, I'd said.

Charlie's right. I'm so full of shit.

There's no way this will be the last time we do this.

chapter 8

I'M CRASHING and burning so spectacularly this whole prison's about to go up in smoke.

"Hello," I blurt, drawing the 'o' out like it'll buy me time to get my shit together. "I—uhm, welcome back. To another episode. Wait—no. Let me try again."

Dammit. I'm already regretting telling Charlie to keep the camera continuously rolling. My mind's completely blank in the face of that stupid lens. Soothing the heat, I press a palm to my forehead and ease out a breath. I swallow my frustration, which settles in my stomach right on top of my embarrassment. Not only am I screwing everything up, I'm doing it in front of Charlie.

I pace to the other end of the cell block, glaring at the spot where the cat ball flared earlier. Whatever set it off is what got me into this mess in the first place.

Why did I think I could do this? I'm the behind-the-scenes equipment mule. The off-camera quippy sidekick. Nothing that ever comes out of my mouth could hold a candle to River's natural charisma. Not to mention the "script" he said was in the backpack is a few vague, high-level talking points, most of which are dubbed voice over for B-roll. He left me to the wolves.

"Walk me through your setup," Charlie says, panning the camera after me. "Can't say I've ever ghost hunted before."

"Yeah, you just chase clouds and pray they bless you with something interesting," I snarl, arms crossing.

His tongue clicks. "Ouch. Claws are back out, I see."

Rolling my eyes, I tip my head back and gather my tangles, furled and frizzed under the weight of moist air, then cinch them in a sloppy bun. The back of my neck is still too hot, burning with the familiar ugly discomfort of feeling like there's been a chip in my armor. I've shown too much.

I'm being a bitch. I know I am. If River wasn't so damn fixated on this Dewhurst story, I'd have thrown in the towel three screwed up attempts ago.

I can't do this.

"You're not usually the one in front of the camera, are you?" Charlie asks.

"Actually, fifteen straight minutes of fucking up is a recurring bit on the show," I growl.

"Then you're killing it." A grin splits his face. "Keep going. Five more and we're there."

I pinch my eyes shut and—god help me—tuck my amusement between my teeth. "Ass."

"I'm trying to help, Win." He takes measured strides across the room, watching me through the viewfinder. "You're just a little stiff. Get out of your head."

I pulse my temples with the heels of my hands. "I don't know how—"

"Walk me through your setup," he repeats. Slower. A little more patient. "What did you ask me to do first?"

"Put your phone in airplane mode and turn off unnecessary electronic devices." I tug at the straps on my backpack as my body rotates on its own accord, following the path he cuts across the cell block.

"Keep going," Charlie says.

He'd been obedient as a Boy Scout, meticulously addressing everything in his backpack that was a risk of tainting this investigation. "Then I asked you to check the cells for drafts while I took a baseline EMF read of the room. There was a hotspot"—I point to the wall by the exit—"right there. Probably old electrical work."

He gives a small, approving nod, the corner of his mouth tweaking up. "And I didn't notice any drafts."

"Then I had you help me set out the tools."

Charlie pans the camera toward the REM Pod on the floor. When I told him the antenna on the short cylinder detected fluctuations in the electromagnetic field to let us know if there were spirits potentially nearby, to his credit, he didn't even twitch a brow.

"This is perhaps the most sophisticated of them all," he says, sounding far too stoic for me to take him seriously. He crosses to the far side of the room and squats. "The cat ball."

I snort. "*Motion sensor.*"

I'd tasked him with finding a nice, flat surface to set it. Despite the *are-you-kidding-me* look he'd shot me, he did a fantastic job. I watched with rapt interest as he dragged the toe of his boot across the floor, checking for unevenness. Presumably satisfied, he set it down. He studied the ball as it threw lights in every direction, like it was the latest run of a weather prediction model and he was trying to analyze what it meant for the DFW area.

His brain—the way it works—has always entranced me. Thoughtful. Always problem solving. Never works in half measures, even for things he questions.

Just like now. How easy it would've been for him to make me feel small over all of this. The ghosts. The tools. The way I'm failing spectacularly on camera. Instead, he's helping and knew exactly what to ask to get me to stop fixating on the intro I was bombing.

"You're good at this." I scrunch my nose and wave vaguely toward the equipment in his hands.

Charlie shrugs. "Picked up a thing or two working with Saddle Up. Chad freezes up too. If I don't prompt him with questions he'll sit there with a thousand yard stare."

"So you're the designated camera guy?"

"More like I'm the only one who took the time to figure out how to get good at it," he mutters.

The shadow of disdain in his voice piques my interest. That, coupled with the frustration I picked up from him in the guard tower, has me stalking the meaning like prey. I circle around it, from all different angles. Trouble in paradise with the guys at Saddle Up? Is he clashing with Garrett? What about this new guy, Chad?

I used to be the shepherd of all his secrets. Now I have to pull them out with my teeth.

I lay bait instead of going for the kill.

"You sound a little bitter."

"Just prefer being out on the chase," he says.

He doesn't bite. And I forfeited the right to be upset over being denied access to his every thought when I packed a bag after Thanksgiving at his parents' house two years ago, but that doesn't stop my spine from stiffening. Like my vertebrae are still convinced he's mine.

I grind the thought to dust beneath my shoe as I pivot, pacing away. "I put out two audio recorders, to try catching some EVP, like voices or sounds. And that's—*oh*. Wait."

How could I possibly forget River's favorite part of any investigation?

"Last but not least, the Ovilus 5." I palm the small device from the side pocket of my backpack.

Lowering the camera, Charlie squints at it. "What's that?"

"A communication tool," I say. He gestures for me to pass it over, and I do. "We usually use dictionary mode, which translates environmental disturbances to words in a pre-loaded dictionary."

The compact device looks like a doll's toy in the palm of his large hand as he scrutinizes it. He taps one of two stout antennae, traces the red border around the touch screen interface. "So, it's a random word generator."

"No." I hold my hand out and he passes it back. "It's—it's legit."

He levels the camera back up, pointing it right at me as his head tilts. "How do the ghosts know what disturbance correlates to what word? Do we get a manual for this thing when we die?"

I won't even dignify that with a response. "A good investigator never uses a tool in isolation. That's why we have all these other devices to cross-reference our data points." I plant a hand on my popped hip. "Very *scientific*, wouldn't you say?"

He snorts. "Not the word I was thinking of."

I conjure the flattest death-stare possible. "Another key to a successful investigation is shutting the fuck up."

Charlie lifts a hand in surrender. "Wow. Okay. I'll behave."

The words don't bite on my behalf. The fangs are all for River, the true brains behind this operation. Never mind the fact *I* used to tease him about his obsession with ghosts before he dragged me to the abandoned old sugar factory on the outskirts of our dumpy hometown. He's my brother, it's my job to tease him. Anyone else, though? They don't stand a chance.

I feign like I'm messing with the Ovilus so I don't have to meet Charlie's gaze. I take no issue with skeptics. Some of our most dedicated viewers fall into that category, tuning in only to push the boundaries of their beliefs. But what I don't have patience for is when someone acts like this is all . . . silly. Stupid. Like River shouldn't be wasting his time with this kind of fantasy.

"Sorry," I force out, fighting my instinct to shut down entirely. "You're allowed to question this stuff, I don't care, I just . . ." I trail off, words failing me. Per usual.

"All good," Charlie says quietly. He moves the camera stabilizer to the side, no longer hiding behind it. "I took it too far. I'm sorry. I wasn't trying to be a dick. I'm trying to . . ." He exhales a slow breath. "Understand."

Understand. It's a loaded word. Like he thinks the smoking gun of exactly what went wrong between us lies somewhere within the walls of this prison, tucked behind explanations of what I'm doing here and why.

In a way, I guess it is.

Finally, I deign to meet his eyes, which are already on me. Long lashes curl around the galaxies, swirling in light blue. Supermassive black hole right in the middle, tugging me toward its all-consuming center of gravity.

I swallow and whirl, freeing myself from it.

"If I'm being completely honest, I have no idea how the Ovilus really *works*-works. And not everything it spits out feels legit, but sometimes it has uncanny responses that are more than just coincidence. And outside of all these novel devices, I trust my *gut* more than anything else. Sometimes information feels right. Sometimes it feels wrong."

"Fair. I respect that."

His tone is nothing but earnest and I'm reminded Charlie doesn't have a malicious bone in his body. He always used to give me the benefit of the doubt. Clearly, that hasn't changed. He's not some internet asshole looking to spoil the thing someone enjoys. He's a skeptic, cursed with a brain that never stops hungering for answers, trying to learn. My shoulders loosen.

"I think I want to try again." My teeth worry my bottom lip as I run my hand around my shirt collar, checking to ensure my mic's still in place.

I take a deep breath, center myself, and try to channel my inner River, minus the stupid clothes.

"Welcome back to another episode of Halbach Hunts. Uh, you might know me as . . . *Winona*." I say it like I'm not convinced I'm telling the truth, still stumbling and awkward. "Today, we're investigating Black Mag—*fuck*. He already covered that."

I drop the Ovilus.

Charlie's staring at me. Brows drawn. Shoulders sagging. Lips parted.

"*He?*"

chapter 9

EVERYTHING STOPS. My breathing. My pulse. The rotation of the earth.

It's clear as day in the haunted expression on Charlie's face: that wasn't the pronoun he was expecting. We're standing across from each other in an empty room, but it feels like a fresh divide rose up between us, a towering rampart—mortar still wet—bolstering what was already there.

"Charlie—"

But he shakes his head, and his voice flattens, like he's trying to smash the melding hurt and anger in his throat. "That was better. Try again."

I duck to pick up the Ovilus off the filthy floor, and consider giving up and lying down myself. Burying myself in a shallow grave. Leaving myself to rot under this decrepit place. The punishment should fit the crime, as they say. And hurting Charlie is the worst thing I've ever done.

"It's not what you think—"

His nostrils flare. "Can we stay focused?"

I open my mouth to explain, but nothing comes out. Why is it so goddamn hard to just be honest with him? I clench my molars, squeeze my eyes shut, try and brute force the truth out of myself. It would fix this.

But this life I've carved out for my baby brother and I . . . it still feels fragile. It feels like something that needs to be fiercely guarded. Mentioning River would fall the first domino of many. It would lead to another question, and another, and another. None of which I want to answer right now.

But I trusted Charlie. Still do.

He's never given me a reason to doubt him. Every time I drew a line in the sand and told him not to cross it, he never did. Why would I think this would be any different?

"It's my little brother," I say quietly to the device he loves so much, brushing dust off the antenna. Saying it out loud drops a boulder low in my gut. "River."

When I look up, Charlie's forehead pinches with confusion. "Your . . . brother?"

"Yes," I say, offering nothing else. He doesn't move to ask any follow-up questions immediately, even though I see them puckering between his brows, so I close the door before he can. "I just thought you should know. That's all."

He presses his lips together and dips his chin. A wordless *thank you*, and not a single prying question. His relief mirrors my own.

But the energy between us has shifted. The rapport we'd been rebuilding fizzled. He's drawn into himself, subdued like he always got when he was dealing with something challenging at work, or was working through a tough conversation with his parents. Is he ruminating? Is he embarrassed he shared that flash of vulnerability with me? Whatever the reason, now he's the one who needs a little help getting out of his head.

"I'm shit at this," I say, redirecting us as I rub the back of my neck. "I keep screwing up."

He shakes his head. "Try again. You love to perform."

"This is different," I challenge. If there's anything that'll bring Charlie back to himself it's a friendly spar. And this *is* different.

When I was on a stage, I didn't have to be myself. I was movement and timing and practiced choreography and counts of eight droning like a drum beat as I aligned each muscle exactly where I wanted it. "I don't have the personality for this. I'm not likable enough. Too bitchy."

"You can be very likable . . . when you want to be." His mouth twitches. *First signs of life.*

"You just assume everyone likes the same things you do." I cross my arms. "Like when you tried to convince me I liked chemistry because I said lightning was cool."

He rolls his eyes. "You *should* love chemistry. Chemistry's sexy—"

"Oh god," I snort. *Getting warmer.*

"—it's literally the science of combining things and seeing what happens. Why do you think *chemistry*'s the word we use to explain attraction?"

Discussing *chemistry* with my ex, a man I have it with in spades, is not where my head needs to be at right now. "I'm not funny enough."

"You don't think you're funny? Seriously?" Charlie glares at me from beneath his lashes in exasperation.

"You were the only one who ever laughed at my jokes."

"Because you were usually leaning over and whispering them in my ear." He points to a spot near the door we propped open earlier. "Lighting's better over here. I'm giving you three more tries, Win. You can do this. And if you can't, well, you'll have to figure out how to film without me. So make them count."

There he is. All he needed was a different problem to solve than whatever was tangled in his head. I twist my grin so it looks more annoyed than smug as I cross to where he told me to stand. "Fine."

The camera goes back up. My stomach drops right back down.

Oh no.

"Hi. Winona here. I'll be tackling this prison investigation myself, to start." Tugging at the hem of my shirt, I glance at the row of cells to my left.

"Eyes on me," Charlie murmurs.

My eyes flare like a lens aperture as a flush warms every inch of me not already sweating with nerves, and my legs soften into jelly. He didn't say those words in the context my traitorous body wants to think he did, but that spot low in my belly tightens all the same. How embarrassing—it's been so long, all it takes is a few choice words to elicit a response.

Even worse, Charlie clocks my reaction immediately.

"Head out of the gutter, Win," he huffs, attention focused on me through the viewfinder. "It's distracting—the way you're looking around like that. Fidgeting. Try staying focused on the camera. Like in dance. Spotting. I'm your spot. Use me."

More heat crawls all over me. That wasn't any better than *eyes on me*. I shake the thought from my mind.

"Okay. Sure."

Be yourself. His advice echoes in my head. At this point, I have nothing to lose.

I take what feels like the thousandth deep breath of the day. When I focus again, I lift my gaze a smidge higher. Not on the convex glass, but on two familiar eyes slotted beneath dark brows, drawn in focus. I'm not talking to thousands of people I don't know. I'm talking to him.

I'm talking to Charlie.

"Unfortunate news—my cohost is indisposed for the moment," I deadpan, tucking my trembling hands in my pockets. "So, you're stuck with me today. If you're new here, I'm Winona. If you're not new here, I'm offended if you didn't know that already."

I can only make out the top half of his face through the camera set up, but the lift of Charlie's cheeks washes sweet relief over me, tingles rushing from my scalp through all my limbs. It's silent encouragement—*Good. Keep going.*

"I have a special guest working this investigation with me today. If you're into extreme weather, he might have a familiar face. Familiar abs, too." I roll my eyes. "Yeah, he's one of the guys from that viral video about tornado chasers running around shirtless. Charlie, you want to say hi?"

He flips the camera around, waves, then focuses it back on me. I walk a few steps for dramatic effect, mirroring River's move from this morning's intro.

"We're set up in one of the cell blocks here at Black Magnolia Penitentiary, trying to make contact with the spirit of James Dewhurst."

I nail the intro for the segment.

It's the ghosts who drop the ball.

It doesn't matter how much history I recount on Black Magnolia, how much legend and lore of the people once imprisoned inside its walls, not even the cat ball flickers. I meander inside a cell, sit on one of the dilapidated bunks, and call out to its former occupant.

Nothing.

Most of our investigations start this way. A lot of them even end this way—a complete bust. But this place felt different. I wouldn't be going to the trouble of parading myself in front of the camera, or working with Charlie, if I knew this would be a failed mission. But I felt the heaviness that sat in my gut, the pressure in my low back, the chill creeping up my spine. All the tell tale signs something is *here*.

And yet . . .

"We're not here to judge." I exit the cell and stare up at the open walkway on the second floor. "We just want to talk—get to know you a little better. Could you tell us your name?"

I pace to the far end of the block. No strange smells. No cold spots. No tension pulling like a taut bowstring in my stomach. I'd been so caught up with tackling my episode-hosting debut that I completely forgot to tune into my strongest tool: my intuition. The energy here's gone flat. Burnt off like an open Coke can left out too long.

"Earlier, someone here seemed to enjoy that light up cat ball on the floor over there. Would you like to touch it again?"

Apparently not.

I run my tongue along the back of my teeth and look anywhere except Charlie's face; I can't handle the possibility of a smug smile, or god forbid, sympathy.

"GENDER," the Ovilus finally spits out in its robotic monotone.

A thrill radiates in my chest. Yes. River's notes said this was an all-male prison, back when it was functioning.

"It must be funny, seeing a woman in here, right?" I say into the quiet. "You see that antenna on the ground over there? If you get close to it, it'll make a sound. That'll let us know you're there."

No response.

"We're trying to connect with James Dewhurst. He used to be an inmate here. Do you know him? We have some really interesting news for him."

Nothing.

It's one thing when an investigation is a dud; it happens often enough. It's another thing to fail miserably in front of someone I so desperately want to impress. I don't know why I feel the need to prove to Charlie this isn't child's play, but the feeling scrapes at my ribs.

"Can I ask a question?" Charlie lowers the camera so I can clearly see his face.

"Sure."

"That thing—"

I dip my chin. "The Ovilus."

"Right. That." He scrapes a hand over his jaw. "If you didn't know the background of this place, you would've equated the word *gender* to something else entirely. Right? It's pure conjecture."

"You say that as if every human on earth doesn't operate with a bias." I tilt my head, not shirking from his critique. "But we do have a few methods that aim to eliminate as much bias as possible. We do something called The Estes Method, where—"

A loud clang echoes above us and my heart leaps into my throat as I jump.

"What was that?" Charlie hisses, camera angling toward the noise.

"Are you seriously asking that?"

"Had to be the building settling, or—"

I squint at him. "Ghosts, you moron."

"But—"

"*Ghosts*. This building's over a hundred years old. I think it's thoroughly settled by now."

He frowns. "That's definitely not how old buildings work. There has to be a reasonable explanation."

"It could be pressure changes from the unstable atmosphere outside. Maybe there's a raccoon in the vents. Could even be structural instability. But it could *also* be ghosts. That's why we never look at a single piece of data in a vacuum. We went over this, Charlie."

His face twists with what looks like concern as he glances at the camera equipment then back at me, like he's worried this conversation is ruining the episode. Or will at least be a pain in the ass to edit out. What he doesn't realize is attempting to debunk strange happenings is part of what River and I do when we film.

I crane my neck. "If you'd like to communicate, could you touch one of our devices?"

The answering silence squeezes like a band around my head and I pinch the bridge of my nose. This cell block's as good as drained, as far as the energy's concerned. I face the camera again.

"I think it's time we try a new location," I say to both Charlie and the lens. "Before his death, James Dewhurst was said to have worked in the kitchen here at Black Magnolia Penitentiary, sometimes even spending up to twelve hour shifts there. Perhaps his spirit is still alive and well down there."

"You want me to cut?" Charlie asks.

"No, let it roll. Don't want to miss anything." I swipe the REM Pod and return it to my backpack, then scoop the cat ball.

"Here." Charlie holds out the stacked audio recorders, his fingers brushing mine as I take them and a dangerous heat following suit. After throwing them in the bag too, I shove my hands in my pockets.

He lets me lead the way as we wind back through the prison in search of the kitchen until we come back to the original atrium and the forking hallways. I glance left, then right, then over my shoulder at Charlie. "Which way do you think?"

"Your guess is as good as mine."

Without overthinking it, I hang a left.

Walking in step, we pass under the gridded shadows of two towering cathedral windows and the hairs on the back of my neck stand on end—like we're being watched. I open my mouth to ask Charlie if he feels it too when a low whistle howls behind us.

I suck in a sharp breath, my fingers curling around the soft skin of Charlie's bicep on instinct. "Shit."

"Probably the wind—"

I can't explain it, but everything in me says to *run*. And not the way we're headed. Letting my grip fall to his wrist, I break into a jog in the opposite direction. "This way."

Together, we zip through the atrium down the other hallway, chasing whatever is causing this vibration in my bones—this frequency shift. At the door that leads to the guard tower, another hallway breaks off, and I take it, Charlie close on my heels. The wall is full of grated windows, offering glimpses to what's on the other side, but I don't pause to check what it is.

"What's going—" But Charlie shuts up as we clear a broken metal door and come to a sudden stop.

It's a large, rectangular room with cinderblock walls and high-set windows filtering meager light in. Long stainless steel tables are bolted to the floor with attached stools on either side, stretching nearly the length of the space. A pair of swinging metal doors bookend what looks like it used to be a serving counter, enclosed by a battered rolling metal window on the far wall.

"The cafeteria," Charlie mutters, the thinnest undercurrent of awe lifting his words.

"And I bet that's the kitchen." I jut my chin toward the doors. "We were headed the wrong way. Whatever made that noise led us here. Whoever's in this room wants to communicate with us. It doesn't matter what you believe, Charlie. *That* was real."

He resists the tug of a smile, but I glance at him in time to catch the barest of movement. "Right. Convenient."

His hand gives mine an absentminded squeeze and we both look down at the pressure point; I hadn't even realized our fingers had intertwined. Like flint and kindling, something dangerous sparks between us, and I drop his hand immediately.

I rub my sweaty palms on my shorts and pace a few steps away. "The cell block was a warmup. I have a feeling this is where the real fun begins."

chapter 10

SIX YEARS AGO

I HAVE A SIXTH SENSE.

It's this little spark I get, somewhere deep in my gut. A flare sent up in the dark wilderness. A warning sign.

Like a deer in the woods can sense danger from the snapping of a single twig a hundred yards away, all it takes is one twisted facial expression, one broken-off laugh, and I can tell my family's about to shatter.

It's Christmas Day back in Kansas, a paltry snow falls outside, and my mother looks beautiful as she bends to pull the ham out of the oven—the one she bought at the store and is trying to convince everyone is homemade. Her long, dark hair is coiled in a bun at her neck, she's wearing the same diamond studs she's pulled out for special occasions for decades, and she even put on a slash of crimson lipstick. She looks perfect.

Except for the faint red wine stain on the collar of the burgundy dress she wore to Mass. It wasn't there this morning.

My stomach sinks.

This is what starts the ticking countdown in my head. I don't know when, but I'm certain: Christmas dinner is not going to end well.

Mom only drinks on bad days.

The five of us gather around the oval dining table for dinner. It's dressed with a tablecloth and set with real, porcelain plates. No paper in sight. We pass bowls and casserole dishes around, serving ourselves, as Mom pours another glass of wine. I lost count of which she's on—I'm too on edge, waiting for shit to hit the fan.

Did she fight with Dad? Patrick? Is something going on with River?

Dad smears butter on his roll and glances at Patrick. "How's that new gig going down at the warehouse?"

I catch it immediately: the feathering in Patrick's jaw as he cuts off his laugh.

Tick. Tick. Tick.

"Really, Dad?" Patrick scoffs.

"What?" Mom asks.

"Can we not do this now?" Patrick asks.

"Why don't you want to talk about it, son? Oh, right." Dad snaps his fingers. "I forgot. You got fired, didn't you?"

"Fired?" Mom balks. "It's been two weeks—"

Patrick's silverware clatters on his plate. "Why'd you have to go and bring that up? Mom, I was going to tell you—"

Dad's voice inches louder. "Would you like to tell your mother *why* you got fired?"

"Why do you have to be such a fucking prick—"

"C'mon, son. Say it. Let's hear it. Tell your mother how you fucked up this time."

Patrick is four years older than me, but he looks haggard, slumped down in his chair, his feathery hair a mess and dark circles cradling his eyes. His expression flattens as he mutters, "It was—"

"HE WAS HIGH!" Dad cheers. "On the job! Can you believe it? Coked out of his goddamn mind, from what I heard." He snorts a jagged laugh and shoves a bite of stuffing in his mouth. "It's really something, isn't it?"

I hold my breath and don't move a muscle. Next to me, River does the same.

On my other side, Mom starts to cry.

"It's not what it—" Patrick reaches for something across the table, and his wine glass topples over, spilling dark red liquid across the table.

"Jesus Christ, Pat." Dad's arms fly wide, exasperated.

My shoulders pinch beneath the weight of the thickening air. I spring up, reach across the table with my napkin to sop the mess, desperate to stop this before it gets worse. "It's fine, Dad—"

"No, Winnie. Don't clean up your brother's messes. He needs to learn to do that on his own," Dad snarls. "Sit down."

I wipe faster, pressing my thumb down hard to pull out as much of the stain as possible. If I can just fix this, then maybe—

"I said *sit down*, Winnie," Dad repeats, sharper, more charged, and I freeze.

Clenching my teeth, I sit back down. There's no saving it now.

Dad turns to Patrick, narrowed gaze cold as stone. "Clean it up."

"Fuck you," Patrick shoots back.

"That's your mother's good tablecloth. You know that? Huh? You the one who's going to fucking ruin it—"

"Don't bring me into this, Mark," Mom says, her words fraying at the edges. She gulps her wine.

"—like you've ruined every other good thing in your life? Huh, son? Is that what you want? You must really like being a fuck up, don't you?"

I stare down at the scrolling design on the handle of my fork, memorizing every curve, as my pulse thumps in my ears and no one dares say a word. It's instinct, the way my body tenses, bracing for what comes next. What always comes next.

Patrick jerks his chair back with so much force, it falls back as he stands. He kicks it, and it goes flying across the linoleum. He hurls insult after insult back at our father, his guttural yells ricocheting off the walls. Dad gets up too, shouts back at him, herds him toward the door, screaming at him to get out. River takes off down the hallway. Patrick rips an ornament off the tree, sending it flying like a grenade. I flinch as it pops against the wall, shattering into a thousand pieces. Mom snatches her empty wine glass off the table and makes for the kitchen. I follow.

This is our standard choreography. While Dad and Patrick snarl at each other's throats and River locks himself in his bedroom, I'm the one left to pick up our mother's broken pieces.

She's standing at the sink, refilling her glass, crimson liquid nearly kissing the rim. She peers at me out of the corner of her eye. "I'm *fine*, Winnie. I'm fine."

"I was just—"

"You have a problem with this?" she snaps, jerking her wine up. It sloshes over the top, splattering on the linoleum floor. "Shit. Another fucking mess."

"No, Mom," I say softly, moving to grab a rag.

"Leave it." She takes a swig. "I do so much for this family, and no one cares—"

"Of course we care—"

"They had to go and ruin it. *Fucking* ruin it! Ruin everything! This beautiful dinner. All that work. All that time. And for what? Why do I do any of it?"

"They didn't ruin it, okay?" I say gently. "Dinner's still on the table. Let's go sit back down—"

"Your father doesn't love me anymore. If he did, he wouldn't pull that shit."

"He always gets like this—"

"*None* of you give a shit about me." She tips her glass back and drinks.

"No. We all love you, Mom." I take her hand, but she doesn't look at me. "Let Dad and Pat cool off. The three of us can still eat. This doesn't have to ruin anything."

She jerks her hand back, eyes thinning like the blade of a knife. "Don't coddle me, Winnie Jean. You think I need you to take care of me?" She huffs a dry laugh. "If I did, I'd be screwed now, wouldn't I? How's *college*, darlin'?"

I stay silent because we've done this dance enough times that I know there's nothing I can say that she won't twist. When she gets like this—when they all get like this—it feels like I stop existing. I end where all this ugly hurt begins. What I want, what I *think*, doesn't matter anymore. All that matters is diffusing the bomb.

"I asked you a question," she spits.

"It's good, Mom." I blink rapidly, a lump swelling in my throat. "It's good."

"Good." She takes another long pull from her wine, draining it, then wipes her mouth with the back of her hand. Lipstick smears across her knuckles. Tears glisten in her eyes when she turns to me, her expression splintered in two. "You love me, Winnie, don't you?"

"Yeah, Mom," I say, voice breaking. "Of course I love you."

It's all I say because it's all there's room for in this house. Every other square inch has already been consumed by the incessant conflicts between Patrick and our dad, by my mother and her mood swings, the way she falls apart when she drinks and needs me to clean up the mess. I clench everything I can't share between my teeth—my worry, my shame, my frustration, my rage, my heartbreak—and I swallow it.

This place makes me feel so small now.

Maybe it always has. Maybe getting out of here, seeing it doesn't have to be this way, has made it clearer to understand.

Mom abandons her glass and carries the bottle to the couch; she watches *Miracle On 34th Street* twice, lost in a daze. Patrick's gone. River's locked in his bedroom. Dad's in the garage, downing a beer. I sweep the shimmering glass from the broken ornaments, tuck all the untouched food away in the fridge, and clean the wine off the kitchen floor.

The next morning, no one says a damn thing about any of it.

I can't keep doing this. Can't keep shrinking myself to fit. Can't stomach watching my family destroy themselves and pretend like everything's fine.

Winter Break isn't even halfway over, but I can't stay here any longer.

River is still in his *Toy Story* pajamas when I hug him goodbye, after my bags are packed and in the car. I don't bother with the rest of my family—it's not worth risking another fight. I put the crumbling rambler in my rearview mirror as quickly as possible, tires chasing down the damp country road. Even the snow didn't bother sticking around this place.

The girl I was, when I used to stand barefoot in the gravel driveway looking out over nothing but fields as far as the eye could see, haunts me all the way back to Dallas.

Campus is a ghost town when I return.

Not that I care. Charlie is the only person I want to see. He's been so busy with family plans, I've hardly heard from him all week. He's the first person I text once I settle back in my dorm.

> **Me**
>
> No one told me campus would be apocalyptic this week. I had to scavenge for supplies today. Now all I need is a crossbow.
>
> **Flower Boy**

> You should be fine. Most of the zombies are skiing in Breckenridge or Aspen this week anyways. Bunch of snobs.

One perk of going to a small, private university is the healthy endowment, stretching far enough to fill the gaps my federal financial aid doesn't. One huge, annoying downside is a student body that vacations in places like Breckenridge.

A photo loads in our chat.

It's Charlie, set against a backdrop of glittering white snow draped over rocky peaks and a dusky lavender sky. He's in full winter gear, goggles pushed up to show off his brilliant eyes and wide smile. His caption reads: *Everyone knows the real ones go to Vail.*

I flop down on my bed, tucking my embarrassingly smitten grin against my arm. Only Charlie can pull off something as obnoxious as a family ski trip. I don't even know where Vail is. Stupid endearing snob.

ME

> You're a zombie too?

> RIP Charles Anthony Rosenhoth. Gone but definitely not forgotten.

> He was far too short to be forgettable.

FLOWER BOY

> I'm 6'1" :(

ME

> Right. Not THAT tall...

FLOWER BOY

> Damn. If I wasn't undead before, I sure am now.

ME

> I didn't know you skied.

FLOWER BOY

> Whoa, whoa. Don't insult me. Snowboard, Win. C'mon.

> I thought you were home for the break?

I stare at his question, willing it to disappear. That is a box I don't want to unpack yet; I want to leave it taped shut under the drooping pine needles of my parents' tree back in Kansas. A little white lie won't hurt.

ME

> Last minute work thing at the theater. No biggie. When are you back in town?

FLOWER BOY

> Not until New Years

My heart sinks. Almost a full week. And surely he'll spend New Years with his family. I shove my phone under my pillow, leaving his message on *Read*, and sigh. It's strange for me, missing someone so much. I'm not sure what to do about this ache blooming right behind my sternum, or what exactly it means.

The next few days blur together. I spend so much time in the studio my joints ache, I run through my DVD collection like they'll deteriorate if I don't watch them—a comfort I inherited from my mother that I hate myself for still craving—and figure out that Vail is in Colorado. Aside from a few breathtaking photos and a midnight text on New Year's Eve, I don't hear much from Charlie. I spend the first day of the year in ratty sweats, hair unwashed, ignoring calls from my mom.

The sun's long past gone and I'm on my third rewatch of *The Family Stone* this week when someone knocks on my door. Strange. There's hardly anyone on campus. Maybe building maintenance? Peeling myself out of bed, I cross to the peephole.

A breath lofts in my chest.

Charlie.

I yank the door open.

"What are you doing here?" I ask, laughing. "Who let you in?"

"Janitor." He shrugs. "Guess she thought I looked trustworthy." To send the point home, he flashes a smile, dimples and all. It would be unfair to blame the janitorial staff for falling prey to his radiant charm.

I close the door behind us as he walks into my room. In one hand, he's holding a plate tented with foil; a bottle of champagne dangles from the other. He offers me the plate. "Here. Courtesy of my mom. I know the dining hall's closed today and friends don't let friends microwave lasagna for New Year's dinner."

"Lasagna? Sacrilegious." The porcelain bottom's still warm against my palms as I accept it. "I'm not a heathen, I was planning on the frozen Alfredo." Lies. I was planning on smashing the rest of my Nature Valley bars, crumbs and all. Alfredo sounds more dignified. I nod toward the bottle. "Did you swipe that from your parents?"

"Actually"—he slips his shoes off and sprawls on my bed—"bought it with my *own* over-twenty-one ID. It has bubbles and everything."

"That is so unbearably sexy of you," I deadpan as I slide into my desk chair and set the plate down.

"I was hoping you'd say that."

"You're wearing glasses and a cable knit sweater, talking about being a law-abiding citizen. Women everywhere are drenched."

"Fuck off." He ducks his chin as a nervous chuckle pops in his chest and the most beautiful, delicate shade of strawberry scales his ears like the pink honeysuckle vining the fence outside the campus library.

He thinks I'm teasing him, and yes, I am, but not like that. It's embarrassing the things that happen between my legs when he adjusts his glasses—when he carefully folds them after taking them off whenever we start kissing. When I can't help but notice the way his clothing hugs his tight body. He looks like he came from a nice dinner—navy chinos, and I spy the points of a white shirt through the collar of the cornflower blue sweater. His hair's tousled in an intentional way, unlike his usual fresh-out-of-bed look, and his scuffed white sneakers are replaced by a clean pair of chestnut loafers. He is so deliciously everything I want.

And I look like I've been couch surfing in a sewer.

"If I'd known you were coming over, I would've showered at least. Changed clothes. Trimmed my nose hairs." The foil crinkles as I unwrap the plate.

"No, no. I like those long. It suits you."

I ball the foil and chuck it at his head. Laughing, he swats it back. But I'm too entranced by the plate to defend. I could drown in the savory, buttery aromas, the fresh snap of rosemary and garlic. Taking up most of the plate is a generous cut of prime rib with a rosy center and peppery crust that makes my mouth water. Verdant green, thick-stemmed asparagus is topped with finely-shredded parmesan, a lemon wedge to the side, and a whipped, creamy mound of mashed potatoes that looks too good to be instant.

"Your mom *cooked* this? After you flew home *last night*?" I pick up the silverware he so thoughtfully included on the rim of the plate.

Charlie snorts. "Yeah, she's intense like that. You'll see one day, if you ever meet her."

Intense is an understatement, from what I know about Katherine Rosenhoth. A thriving floral shop. A family ski trip. A Martha Stewart meal when most people would be sleeping off travel exhaustion. *How functional*—I catch the dry joke in my throat, chasing it with a delicious bite of potatoes.

As I eat, Charlie tells me all about Vail, and how he's not sold on his brother's new girlfriend, and how his mom scheduled him double the amount of shifts running deliveries across town for her shop over the break. But when I cover the leftovers halfway through the plate and swallow my last bite, he asks how my trip back home went.

"It was fine. Pretty boring." I'm an expert at dodging these sorts of questions—all it takes is some sleight of hand. A small dose of the truth, a little redirection. "You know, everyone back there still calls me Winnie." I scoot onto my bed and sit facing him with my legs crossed, one knee resting on his thigh. "When I moved here, I thought Winona sounded more mature. More adult."

It felt like a fresh start.

"Winona's sexy." Charlie studies my face, like he's reconciling me with the names, and hums in thought. I fight a blush. "But Winnie's cute. I like Winnie." He flashes a dorky grin, like the double entendre isn't obvious enough on its own.

I like Winnie. It sends something reeling in my chest.

Hearing it roll off his tongue in the gentle, low timbre of his voice is the first time I like being Winnie. Because *he* likes Winnie. And if someone as kind, and smart, and funny as Charlie likes Winnie, then surely she isn't all that bad.

He grabs the bottle of champagne from my end table and wraps his hand around the mouth. The cork releases with a *POP!* My stomach tumbles. I've done a good job of forgetting Christmas, forgetting the wine stain on my mother's collar, until now. He tips the bottle toward me.

"Happy New Year"—his smile slants—"Winnie."

My brows pitch as a tender laugh slips out, fizzy bubbles spreading through my limbs. And I clutch the neck of the glass because my mother only drinks on bad days, and with Charlie there is no such thing as bad days. And because I am not my mother.

"Don't tell the Champagne region of France all I have is coffee mugs to drink out of," I say.

"As long as you don't tell them this is the cheap shit from California." His gaze flicks down to the bottle. "I'm good like this if you are."

In answer, I tip my chin and take a sip, then pass it back. "Thanks," I say softly as he drinks. I don't specify for what, because I mean for it to encompass everything: for dinner, for splitting a bottle of cheap champagne with me, for thinking of me at all.

We haven't seen each other in almost two weeks. Even longer since we've hooked up, since I was on my period the last time and all we did was cuddle. Sitting so close like this on my bed, I don't know why he hasn't kissed me yet. An antsy, eager energy buzzes through me. I'm in the mood for some fun.

"Let's play Truth or Dare." I waggle my brows as I grin. "If you bail on the round, you drink, and the asker gets to go again. You first."

"Okay," he says, stretching the vowels like he's not sold, as he eyes me with skeptical amusement. "Guess I pick Dare."

"I dare you to take your shirt off," I say immediately.

"You're such a perv." Charlie rolls his eyes in good humor, pulling the sweater over his head. His scent, baked into the fabric, envelops me as he tosses it in my lap. He pops the first button of his collared shirt, then the second. He gets all the way to fourth before prodding, "Win?"

A flush rises on the back of my neck. "Oh. Uh. Truth."

"What would you do if you knew you wouldn't fail?" He shrugs out of the shirt and tosses that at me too. I slip it on.

My gaze falls to his chest as I hum, thinking. "I'd be a professional ballerina."

He lifts a brow. "I think you have a decent shot at that?"

I shake my head. "Even people who've spent their whole lives training don't always have a decent shot at making it. I didn't start young enough. I never even trained en pointe."

We couldn't afford the classes on their own, not to mention a new pair of shoes every six weeks. I was fortunate the studio director let me exchange labor for lessons at all.

"Don't get me wrong," I continue, "I really enjoy the jazz I get to do at the theater, but ballet's always been my favorite." The precision. The control. The way every movement is articulated down to the toes. "Plus, dance in general isn't exactly a safe career choice. I wouldn't be double majoring in communications if it was."

"Fair enough." He dips his chin. "I'll take Truth."

"Have you ever been in love?" Curiosity over his romantic past has been gnawing at me since the first time we kissed. The topic of other partners—past or present—just never comes up, and I'd rather suffer in uncertainty than look clingy and ask directly. This is the perfect cover.

"I thought I was once. For a while, actually." His gaze lifts, finding mine. "But now, I'm not so sure."

I swallow. "Dare."

Charlie tips his head, studying me as his eyes narrow in thought. "I dare you to tell me about the most embarrassed you've ever been."

"Easy," I say flatly. "That'd be in high school, when I let a boy take naked photos of me and he leaked them to all his friends almost immediately. By the next day, everyone at school knew what great tits I had."

His brow furrows so deep, I wonder if it's making his head ache. "That's fucking awful. I'm sorry, Win."

I cock my head. "You're not going to ask why I did it? Let him take the photos in the first place?"

"No? I'm not sure that's any of my business. And regardless of why you did it, it doesn't make what that kid did any less shitty." His voice smooths out. "But if you *want* to tell me, I'll listen."

Running my nail along the jagged edge of a cuticle, I look down at my lap. It goes against all my usual instincts, but I do want to tell him. Like my ugly secrets are a litmus test for how much he'll put up with and still want to keep me around.

"I had a crush," I say. "And I was stupid. And I thought he

93

meant it when he said he liked me. It's fucked, I know, but I thought doing that might make him stay."

"You weren't stupid," he says softly. The corner of his mouth twitches. "And if it makes you feel any better, I think you dodged a bullet when he didn't. I'd bet a lot of money that a guy like that can't even make a girl come."

"Charlie!" I squeal, clapping a hand over my mouth. I double over, howling with laughter, forehead against his hip. He laughs too and his hand brushes my thigh. Even as I sit up, catching my breath, he leaves it there, thumb wearing a tiny path across my skin.

"I'll take Truth," he says around his shit-eating grin.

I bite my bottom lip and tilt my head, matching his smile. "Have you ever thought about me while you jerked off?"

His eyebrows fly up and a delicious color blooms all the way up to his ears; I've caught him deeply off guard. Gaping at me, he levels me with a dubious glare and I suck back a giggle. But his gaze darkens as he tips the champagne to his lips. Eyes on me, he drinks. Molten heat pools low in my belly, sinking further south as my pulse skyrockets.

He wipes his mouth with the back of his hand. "I'll take another truth."

"Why haven't you kissed me yet?" I breathe, my lips parting.

He scrapes a hand over his jaw. "Herculean self-control."

"No, but . . . why?"

"You really want the truth?"

I stare at him, because we both know I already know.

"I want a lot more from you than just a hookup, Win."

My stomach tightens. "C'mon, Charlie. This is fun. It's working."

"Until it's not," he mutters. "Someone always ends up hurt."

A stuttered beat echoes behind my sternum. "You think you'd hurt me?"

His thumb stops tracing my skin. "No, Winnie. I think you'd hurt me."

I push the sleeves of his button-up to my elbows, suddenly hot. "The real thing never ends well."

My parents had "the real thing" once upon a time, from what I've been told. That didn't stop my dad from sleeping with a teller at his bank; it didn't stop my mom from revenge screwing my eighth grade math teacher, either.

"That's not true," he challenges.

Maybe not for people like him—people who come from beautiful, successful, well-adjusted families who fly across state lines for ski trips. But for me? For the trash from middle-of-nowhere Kansas whose nudes are saved on the phone of every jock from high school, and whose screwed-up family couldn't even make it through Christmas dinner without cracking right down the middle?

"You want too much, Charlie," I whisper, tucking my shaking hands beneath my legs.

"No. I want you to want me more than you're scared of whatever this is between us." He leans forward, pushing a stray hair out of my face, and our eyes lock.

There's pure, unrestrained desire flaring back at me. Electricity prickles up my spine as he grabs my wrist, thumb covering my pulse point. Can he feel how wild I am for him? Is he counting each tortured beat? Time thickens, slow and syrupy and sweet, as he brings my hand to his parted lips. I exhale a whimper as he leans into my palm and his warm mouth meets my skin, right at the heel of my hand. My whole body pulses as he draws in a long breath and kisses me.

"God, Winnie." Another kiss. "You try so hard to come off like you don't give a shit, but I see past it all. I think you do want more. You're just scared to let yourself have it."

I blink away the stinging threat of tears. "How do you do that? See right through me?"

In answer, he plants another kiss on my palm wordlessly. I stretch my thumb to caress his cheek.

"No one's ever wanted me like this," I murmur around the swelling lump in my throat.

Not my parents. Not my big brother. Not Sam Wheeler or the boy on the football team who passed around my photos. Not Denny or Bryce or Michael or the other jerks who thought I only existed when their tongue was down my throat.

It's proof miracles exist when he understands me—*truly* understands what I said. When he stills his kisses and looks up at me and whispers back to the quivering artery in my wrist with so much tender, earnest acknowledgment, "I'm sorry." As if he heard the twang of painful truth in my voice, knew I meant more than this explosive chemistry between us.

He tugs me closer, his other hand moving to my hip as I straddle his lap. Delicately, I slide his glasses off, fold them, and set them on my end table.

"I want you so much it makes me think I'm losing my mind sometimes," he murmurs. "I can't imagine how anyone can look at you and not see something incredible. But, Win, I—I can't do casual. Not with you."

How strange it is to feel so special to someone. I don't know how I did it, how I tricked this boy with cracked ice eyes to see so much good in me—more than I see in myself. But the way he looks at me, the way he touches me, the way he treats me . . . it makes me want to see it too.

When I packed my suitcase on my bedroom floor before I left for college, I told myself I would never let a boy hurt me again. But for once, the sixth sense sparking in my gut isn't a message to run.

It's telling me to stay.

I left Kansas for the last time the day after Christmas, and it hits me now, clear as day: I don't ever want to go back. I want to leave every ugly piece of me back home, and be the girl he sees in me instead. I want to trust him.

His anxious eyes are searching mine for an answer, and maybe a better girl would put him out of his misery quickly. But Charlie likes *me*. And I like to play.

I delve my fingers into his hair and kiss him. He groans, hands tightening on my hips, and parts for me immediately. His tongue caresses mine and a small, desperate sound pops in my throat. Jerking me closer, his fingers curl even deeper into my flesh, and I pray his touch leaves a mark. An artifact to prove I meant something to someone once—meant something to *him*.

His kisses trail my jaw, then lower, his warm, wet mouth worshiping my throat. Closing around a spot that makes my toes curl, he sucks on my sensitive skin, sinking his teeth in enough to make me gasp before soothing it with the glide of his tongue. And it feels so fucking good, not just because of the sensation, but because he does it all with so much pure, aching want. Like he'd take his last, dying breath if he didn't get to put his mouth on me again and again. Like he'd cease to exist if it weren't for the choked moans I catch in the back of my throat as he tugs at my collar with his teeth.

His voice is gruff as he asks, "Is this going to be the last time?"

"That depends, Flower Boy." I drag my hand down to his bare chest, flatten it over his pounding heart. "Are you going to be my boyfriend or not?"

It takes eons for him to process. It's a beautiful sight, watching it bloom on his face.

His grin is infectious; I feel it down to my toes. Warm and sturdy, his arms wind around my waist. "You have this nasty habit of stealing all my best moves right out from under me."

"Yeah, well." I shrug. "I think you're kind of into it."

"So very disgustingly into it."

He moves to kiss me, but I stop him. "Promise we won't hurt each other?"

"It's a deal."

When we seal it with a kiss, I really believe I will keep my end of the bargain.

chapter 11

THE ENERGY HERE IS HEADY, drumming. Alive. The leaden boulder in my gut, the awareness stretching across my skin like something's watching me.

This is exactly what I need.

Together, we run through the equipment setup all over again, scattering devices across the built-in tables. Again, I watch as Charlie applies a charming amount of thought and logic to assisting me, spacing things equally apart without needing to be directed. As he sets the Ovilus 5 down two tables over from the REM Pod, I pull out two more tools.

"Spirit Candle," I explain before he can ask as I palm what looks like any standard short, chunky LED candle. "It's an EMF sensor—triggers when the electromagnetic field fluctuates." I set it on the table closest to me. "And this is a Paranormal Music Box. It detects motion through temperature changes." I calibrate the coffin-shaped wooden device and it cries out its eerie tune. It takes its place a foot over from the candle. "We like setting these together to vouch for each other, so to speak. Capturing both EMF fluctuation and movement at the same time."

"Why didn't we use those in the other room?"

"More space in here. Overloading your investigation with trigger devices just increases chances for false positives."

"Thorough," he mutters, adjusting his glasses as he crosses back over to me.

I flash a smirk as I strip my backpack off and set it on one of the table stools. Charlie mirrors my action. "Watch it, Charlie. You're sounding a little impressed."

He snorts, panning the camera as he looks around, and a growl sounds from his stomach. "Wonder what the food's like in prison."

"You can try asking. I bet you could easily charm a ghost." My brows arch in a dare.

Warding off the idea, he lifts his free hand. "Talking to an empty room? I'll leave that to you."

"Specialty of mine," I deadpan.

We take our positions at the far end of the room in a corner enclave so we have a clear view of everything. Sunlight bleeds in through the barred windows and tallies itself on the floor, eight individual slashes of hope. I wonder if the reminder of the world outside ever felt like a sick tease to those imprisoned here.

Charlie peers out the glass dripping with dusty cobwebs, looks toward the sky, and hums.

"Mind if I check the radar really quick before we start?" But he's already drawing his phone from his back pocket.

My gaze lingers a beat too long on how the moss green fabric conforms to his ass. "Sure. Yeah." Pulling my attention away, I grab my own phone. I absolutely should not be checking out my ex. What I *need* to be doing is checking in with River.

I swipe off Airplane Mode, and when my service reconnects, a series of texts from him flood through.

RIVER

why'd no one tell me tow trucks take for fucking ever

> they should teach us how to change tires in school. no offense to pythagoras but shit's stupid and not real-world applicable

> bro delete your instagram story that's so embarrassing

> you better be capturing some sick ghost activity

> when they take her car away, if dude ever decides to show up, then I'm gonna take P home. then it's ghost time

I blow a quiet laugh through my nose and shoot him back a quick message about the new entrance at the back of the prison. I have no idea what his ETA is, and if I ask I'll probably just get "no idea" in return, and that uncertainty sours in my stomach. After everything that happened, I can't help but worry too much.

Deepening my voice, in a perfect rendition of the classic, smooth, news anchor voice, I return my phone to Airplane Mode and mock, "And now, back to Charlie, with the weather."

"System's setting up nicely," he mumbles, not looking up from the screen. "But we still have a few hours until it reaches the DFW area. Two . . . two and a half."

Perfect timing. We'll finish our ghost hunt, part ways, and he'll set up shop in the guard tower in time for River to show up.

From the middle of the room, the REM Pod buzzes. A pleased chill climbs up my spine. I glance at Charlie, full attention on the camera and phone out of sight. "Did you catch that?"

"Think so."

I nod and look directly into the lens. "We're here in the dining hall of Black Magnolia Penitentiary, which is rumored to be the place James Dewhurst spent most of his days. Unfortunately, the doors that lead to the kitchen where he worked are stuck and won't open for us. But we're hoping we can still catch some activity here. The energy in this room is . . . I wish you could feel it." I rub the back of my neck, looking over my shoulder. "But it's *intense*. We just set everything up and the REM Pod over there has already gone off."

Charlie follows as I start down the aisle between table rows.

"Thank you for touching that device, whoever you are. And thank you for leading us here." I roll a cheeky smile between my teeth. "I think my friend here has a question for you, if you don't mind answering it."

I stop short and turn around to find Charlie's eyes wide behind his round-framed glasses. "Uh . . . no, I actually . . ."

A full grin forces its way on my lips. "Can you do something to let him know it's okay to ask? I think he's nervous."

"*Winona*," Charlie hisses, as if he thinks the ghosts won't be able to hear him if he's quiet enough.

"Maybe set off that cat ball on the floor? Try to turn on the candle? Or touch—"

"SMOKE," the Ovilus monotones.

Adrenaline dumps in my stomach, surges through my limbs, and I laugh. *Smoke*. Like . . . cigarettes—they're traded like currency in prisons. If Charlie wants to ask something, he needs to give something in return.

"I'm sorry, I don't have any smokes. But I do have a bottle of moonshine. Would that work?" I call into the empty space above us.

"*Moonshine*?" Charlie sounds even more exasperated, which only ratchets up my amusement. His gaze darts around the room, like his hackles are raised and he senses exactly what I do in here.

I pull the clear jar-shaped bottle from the front pocket of my backpack and lift it in the air. "If I give you this, will you let my friend ask a question?" Coming up from behind it so as to not set it off, I set the bottle between the Paranormal Music Box and the Spirit Candle. "I'll leave it right here for you. If you want to come get it, this thing will play some nice music for you." I wave my hand in front of the music box's sensor and the chilling, tinny tune rolls until I pull back. "Nice, right?"

"Right. *Nice*," Charlie grumbles under his breath.

I swallow my snort. I sincerely hope he's shaking in his storm chaser boots right now.

"Can you set something off to let us know you're here and willing to communicate with us?"

"DRINK."

My chin whips toward the Ovilus, heart rate building speed to a gallop. Such an intelligent response—that can't be coincidence. "Yes! Yeah. Go for it. Have a dr—"

"TOGETHER."

I look toward the camera, amusement tangling in my expression. "You want us to have a drink with you?" Silence. "How about if you set off one of these devices—*any* of them—Charlie and I will have a drink with you. Deal?"

His head tips sideways, boring holes into me with a fierce glare. He willingly seeks out some of the most violent storms known to man, but imbibing with the dead is where he draws the line? Silly.

The REM Pod squeals, alerting to the highest degree, and my stomach drops as we both whirl to face it.

"Thank you for that. Well, Charlie," I say, a little too loud. Just enough to be extra obnoxious. "A deal's a deal."

Crossing back over to Charlie, I hold my hand out for the camera setup, which he passes over. I reach into the side pocket of my backpack and extract a tripod, swapping the stabilizer for the stationary mount. I place the setup off to the side of the corner brick enclave, the perfect spot to capture the room as well as me and Charlie.

"Grab the moonshine?" I call as I fiddle with the light attachment, until it illuminates the spot we'll be standing.

With a heavy sigh, Charlie does, muttering something like, *This is absurd.*

He tries handing it to me but I smirk. "You're the guest of

honor, and this ghost seems fond of you. You go first." His gaze flicks to the jar of liquor, then to me, then back to the moonshine. I click my tongue. "Don't worry, the guy I bought it from was only blind in *one* eye. You should be fine. Bottom's up."

His eyes narrow on me, the corner of his mouth twitching. "You absolutely owe me a storm chase after all this."

He opens the jar and takes a swig. His brows tense, wincing as the burn of it hits. Features twisting in sheer disgust, he holds the jar out to me, dragging the back of his hand over his mouth. The edge of his bottom lip catches, just barely, against his knuckle.

I take a vile, burning sip of my own and pound a fist against my sternum as I cough. "Okay," I rasp. "We had a drink with you. My friend's going to ask his question now."

Charlie stares at me, utterly unamused, the faintest shade of rose spreading on the peaks of his cheeks. The humid heat, maybe. Or the alcohol. Or perhaps I still possess the ability to make this man blush. I nudge my head toward the expanse of room where this unseen entity possibly lurks, flashing an encouraging smile like a mom trying to convince her kiddo to tell the nice lady in the apron what they'd like off the menu.

Voice flat, devoid of any enjoyment or pleasure, purely in service of getting me off his back, he asks, "What kind of food did you eat in here?"

After a beat, the Ovilus says, "DOG."

Charlie snorts. "*Dog*? They did not feed you dog."

"Did that ghost just get you to laugh?"

"No, it—"

"NAME."

Charlie grimaces at the Ovilus and shifts imperceptibly away from it, closer to me. *Man of science my ass.* Everyone's a believer when the paranormal's staring them dead in the face.

"I'm Winona," I say. "And this is Charlie. We introduced ourselves earlier. You must be someone different than who we spoke to downstairs. Can you tell us your name? Do you see that recorder on the table? That little device with the red light? Can you go up to it and say your name?"

While I give the spirits a few moments to gather the energy to fulfill my request, I push up on my toes, bring my mouth to Charlie's ear, and murmur, "You nervous?"

"What? No."

"Your knee's bouncing."

Grimacing, he stills it instantly. It's written all over his well-carved features: I'm getting under his skin. That, or Mr. Skeptic is scared. My teeth sink into the bottom curl of my smile as I look up at him, our faces only inches apart, and his gaze drops to my mouth.

Clearing my throat, I back up. "I'll grab the audio recorder, see if we caught any EVP."

I retrieve it, rewind, and let it play, closing my eyes as I listen. My voice echoes back to me, and then it's a wave of static and white noise. A gasp sticks in my throat as a disturbance interrupts the monotony.

"Holy shit. Did you hear that?" I rewind and play it again. "Tell me what you hear."

"Nothing, I—"

"Shh. Listen again." I rinse and repeat. "You don't hear that? At the end there? It sounds something like . . . *I see*?"

His brow furrows as he leans a little closer to the the audio recorder I hold between our heads. The corner of his head grazes mine as I play it yet again.

"Lindsay," he says, matter-of-factly, pulling back to look at me like he's proud he figured out the answer first. "It sounds like . . . Lindsay."

The realization drains all the way down his body—from the widening of his eyes, to the parting of his lips, the slumping of his shoulders, and I bet even his knees buckle. He heard a spirit speak.

I chew the bottom of my lip as I replay it again. "But . . . this was a men's prison. Lindsay? That's a woman's name. I know there were female medical staff, but in the cafeteria?"

"Lindsay can be a man's name. Historically, I think it actually *was* a male name."

"GEEK," the Ovilus monotones.

Damn. Roasted.

I look at Charlie and burst out laughing, snaking my fingers around the curve of his bicep without thinking. "Hey! Be nice. He is sort of a geek—"

"*Am* I?" Charlie whisper-chuckles. His pupils—close enough I can see even in the low lighting—are blown wide, drunk on the adrenaline of what's happening. And maybe a little moonshine, a fresh hit to his bloodstream.

"—but he . . . he's really smart. And for a geek, he was very popular in college. Everyone liked Charlie." It's indulgent and irresponsible but I graze the side of my thumb along his warm arm. My attraction to him is still loud and clear even through the chaotic noise of our past.

"Everyone except *you*," he murmurs, his mouth brushing the top of my head. If he's put off by my touch, he's going above and beyond to hide it.

I roll my eyes. "I think I liked you the *most*, idiot."

He draws back and there's such a soft curiosity pulled taut between his brows it aches behind my ribs. So many questions flicker in his eyes. Questions he has every right to ask, and ones I'm not sure if I'm ready to give the answer to. It's not even the alcohol going to my head—it's the pure adrenaline rush of the investigation. But I'm walking far too close to dangerous territory.

In saving grace, the REM Pod shrieks across the room. I drop Charlie's arm, jump back, creating space between us. Inhaling long and slow, I try steadying my pulse. Charles Rosenhoth isn't the man I'm here to talk to.

"All right, Mr. Lindsay. We have a few questions for you."

chapter 12

I SMILE BOLDLY toward the light-capped camera setup and flick my eyes up, ready to commune with the dead.

"Were you a prisoner here, Mr. Lindsay?"

Silence.

"Maybe an employee? Here at Black Magnolia Penitentiary?"

Silence.

"Did you spend your days in the cell block we visited earlier, or—"

The REM Pod squeals.

"Thank you for that response. Did you—"

"MURDER," the Ovilus drones. Every hair on my body stands on end.

Charlie drops his mouth to my ear. "What the fuck are we talking to, Win?"

Apparently, a murderer. I swallow and redirect. "There was a man locked up here for homicide. His name was James Dewhurst. Did you know him?"

Colorful lights throw as the cat ball signals.

I'll take that as a yes.

"Wherever you are, is James Dewhurst there with you?"

I glance sideways, expecting to find the soft, young face of my little brother, umber eyes matching mine and a mop of dark hair on his head. Instead, I see Charlie. Piercing light blues. The small divot between the peak of a cheekbone and strong angle of a jaw. A square chin. A shadow cast on his nose, pronouncing the delicate bow left from when he broke it playing hockey at fourteen. Ears that stick out just a little too far from his head, but are wonderful for balancing the arms of his glasses.

"WATER."

I gasp, shoulders lurching, as I'm yanked back into the moment. I clear my throat. Water . . . water . . .

"We're not far south from the Red River. Is that what you're referring to?"

"CLOCK."

I slip my phone from my pocket enough to check the time and roll my eyes. "About a quarter past three, since you asked so nicely."

Charlie frowns. "Should you really be getting snarky with a ghost, Winona?"

Smug delight lifts my cheeks. "So it *is* a ghost?"

He shakes his head, eyes flicking toward the ceiling, but I know him. I know the way the corners of his mouth are turned down means he's holding back a smile.

I meander around the cafeteria, asking questions, receiving only silence in return for several minutes. None of the devices trigger. Not unheard of in an investigation, but not ideal either. However, I still feel the sense of presence in this room—the energy hasn't drained away. Maybe Lindsay's feeling shy.

"We want to hear your story, Lindsay," I say. "We're not here to judge you for what you did or didn't do when you were alive. For what put you behind bars."

Charlie's unconvinced expression wordlessly communicates,

Speak for yourself, this dude was a murderer. I turn on my heel, prying my attention from him, and pace a few steps.

"You were still a person. You still deserved love and respect. I can't imagine spending my life locked up in a place like this."

Silence.

"Did you have a spouse? Children? Family you left behind?" My throat tightens. "Do you miss them?"

I strain to listen. For something. For anything.

"I'm sorry if you're alone, wherever it is you are. I'm sorry if you're lost, or scared, or lonely, or confused. No one deserves to feel that way."

More. Damn. Silence.

Charlie clears his throat. "Scientific leanings aside, I can get behind whatever that just was. Even if there's nothing listening. On the off chance something *is*—"

"There *is*, Charlie. He told us his name. You heard it yourself."

"Pareidolia." He waves me off.

It's the go-to debunk for most—*your brain is tricking you into seeing and hearing what you want to see and hear*—and roots frustration in my gut like a weed. Such a convenient way to explain away anything we don't understand. Maybe if people weren't so obsessed with hard and fast answers, black and white rights and wrongs, we'd know more about the world around us. My world made a lot more sense when I made room for gray.

"It was kind of you, Winnie," Charlie says quietly. "It's a rare novelty, seeing you be so vulnerable." His mouth slants with faint nostalgia. "I usually only got that side of you in the middle of night, after I'd just made you—"

Eyes widening, he glances at the camera. Like he just remembered it's still recording everything we say, and little does he know, *usually* River edits our episodes. Jesus Christ. I'm going to have to take one for the team and handle this one. A breath catches in my throat at the flood of sweaty, tangled memories reeled in by his words. Like a true gentleman, he feigns a cough, displacing the conversation enough to change subjects.

"It's quiet in here," he says. Nice save. "Should we try another location again?"

Determination tightens in my fists. "No. I still feel something here."

Maybe I need a new approach. Something that might entice a restless spirit, hungry for closure. For redemption.

"Whoever you are, Mr. Lindsay or someone else, did you know the family of Edith Page Milton no longer believes James Dewhurst murdered her? They found letters—from James to Edith." The muscles in my throat resist my swallow. "Edith Page Milton's family believes they were lovers."

Charlie's brows lift in interest. Right. I forgot to fill him in on the backstory.

"But what they still don't know is who did it, then. Was it her husband? Did he catch them in an affair? Was it purely an accident that Mr. Dewhurst was blamed for?" I pace down the aisle between the tables again, glaring at each device as I pass. Willing something to react. I rack my mind, trying to recall specifics from River's research. "The Dewhurst family didn't come from money like the Miltons. Or the Pages. James Dewhurst was known to be a recluse, a black sheep." Muttering under my breath, I add, "A death sentence in a small town."

None of the devices trigger. Not even the Ovilus makes a peep. But the energy in here still sits like a sheet of pure lead on my chest. A tense restlessness. A deep sorrow. A twist of rage. A spark of The Knowing, deep in my gut. I take a slow breath in, then out.

There is *someone* here. And I won't let them play games with me any longer.

"Fine. You don't want to talk to me?" I stalk over to the jar of moonshine and snatch it. "We can wait."

Charlie's mouth falls open, gaping at me. "What are you

doing? Did you just steal that moonshine from your ghost? Do you think that was a good idea?"

"Yes," I say curtly. "Spark of intuition."

"Intuition," he mutters. "I don't think I have that like you do."

"Yes you do, Charlie. We all do." I take a swig of the moonshine; it burns all the way down. "Some of us are just better at listening to it."

He wears his curiosity like some people wear their hearts on their sleeve. Being on the receiving end of it now makes me squirm. With a heavy sigh, I blow the loose strands of hair around my face and lean back against the wall next to Charlie, extending the liquor toward him. He stares at it, then with a resigned what-the-hell shrug, takes it from me and sips.

"And now, we wait," I grumble.

I don't turn to meet his gaze, but I feel Charlie watching me. From my peripheral vision, I see the intrigued quirk of his mouth, and another intuitive spark lights in my gut: he's been waiting for an opportunity like this.

"Why don't we play Truth or Dare?" he asks, like we're in college all over again. But there's something sharp behind his eyes. "You know, kill a little time. If you skip, you drink. Asker gets to go again."

My throat constricts. I don't need any special sixth sense to see right through what he's getting at: Charlie wants answers. He wants to know why I left—the paltry story I gave wasn't enough. But I've wound this truth so tight around myself, pulling a single thread will unravel the rest. Giving him what he wants means giving him everything.

The thought of telling him . . . it feels like being deep under water. The growing dark. The mounting pressure. The more I speak, the more air I lose, and the further down I sink until I can't kick my way to the top again. Until I'm drowning.

My skin's too hot. My heart's too fast. My leg starts to bounce. We're in this godforsaken prison together and I know he won't stop wanting this. I can't keep running, even though I want to. It'll only hurt him more if I do. I have to do this. I have to give this to him, even if it makes me want to crawl out of my own skin. He deserves it.

I pull myself together enough to flash him a bored look. "Fine. I'll take Truth."

"Why'd you come back to Texas?"

My shoulders sag with relief. Softball question. "I never meant to leave forever. Job offer helped too. You're up."

"Dare."

Because I'm a coward deep in my core and desperate to delay the inevitable, I bat my lashes at him and provocatively deadpan, "I dare you to take your shirt off."

He scoffs. And drinks. "Try again."

"I dare you to tell Mr. Lindsay you think he's funny."

"I think Mr. Lindsay is—" he says, facing me.

"No." I motion vaguely above us. "Tell *him*."

Charlie presses his mouth into a chagrined line and looks up. "Mr. Lindsay, I think you're very funny," he says flatly.

My snort eases some of my tension. Makes it easier to repeat, "Truth."

It's already darker in here than from when we first set up, the clouds outside the barred window growing denser. The pitter-pattering rain is a steady droning now. Tipping my chin up, I spot a shattered window, high on the opposite wall, where the sound leaks in. The damp smell of petrichor and rust swirls around us.

"Are you seeing anyone?" It's so quiet, it's almost covered by the murmur of the storm.

I swallow. "No."

He's silent for a beat, and I can almost hear him working this out in his head, stress testing hypotheses to see what holds up. "Truth," he says.

He's being so open, so earnest. It's not fair of me to keep

treading in the shallows. No more jokes. "What did you think when you first saw me today?"

"It felt like I was seeing a ghost. Pun absolutely intended." His uneven smile is twinged with sadness. "I was . . . relieved," he drags out, like he's trying to taste if it's the right word. My brow furrows. That's not what I expected. "It was nice having proof of life." Lower, he adds, "It's been over a year, Win. I've been waiting. For something. For anything."

"I know." I glance away, picking at my nail beds to distract myself from the sting in the tip of my nose.

"How honest do you want me to be?" Subtle harshness edges his words and I stumble with how to respond. "Because if you're gonna do that thing where you act like nothing's wrong here, or you'll just avoid it because it makes you uncomfortable, I'll leave it surface level and save my energy."

It's a knife twisting in my chest, wounding because each word hits true. But I promised myself I'd do better. If not for me, for my brother. I brace for every biting word coming my way. "Tell me. I can take it."

"I was pissed." His jaw feathers. "And I was confused. And I wanted to force you to *stay*, and listen to all the shit you put me through these past two years. And I saw that fucking *name* on your shirt, and I—"

He drags a hand over his mouth, taking a deep breath. But the tension radiating off of him deflates as he turns and meets my eyes. It's not rage I see there. It's hurt. I don't wear it on my face—a lifetime dreaming of dancing on stage helped me build an impenetrable facade—but I break under the weight of what I did. The place that filled with butterflies the first time I met him backstage of Colby rings back hollow. Scooped out by my own damn claws.

"Winnie," he whispers, pivoting his body toward me. "*Fuck*, Win. I missed you. I was mad at you, but I missed you. And I was *happy* to see you. And that made me hate myself a little. Because when I look at you, I want to see someone who ruined every good thing we had. But all I saw"—his Adam's apple bobs and my skin shrinks tight around my bones—"all I *see* is a woman who meant the world to me."

My heart beats outside my chest. If I wasn't so practiced at keeping my shit together, I'd have tears in my eyes. They're threatening my lash line with unbearable heat.

I open my mouth, with no idea what to say. Raw, honest vulnerability has always made me freeze up. But backing down from it is exactly what he expects from me.

A light in the corner of my eye makes me jump. The false flame of the Spirit Candle flickers, sending amber light dancing around the dimly lit room. My mouth falls open and eerie, tinny music tinkles out from the music box.

"What the—" I whisper.

The Ovilus, in its unnerving robotic voice, spits out, "KISS." Charlie and I both let out strangled, awkward half-laughs, the interruption bursting the tension between us like a pin to a balloon. The sheer strength of the reprieve I feel in my chest is an embarrassment.

I wish I was better.

"Are these ghosts trying to set us up?" Charlie huffs. His head dips as he rubs the back of his neck. Like the weight of everything he'd been holding in left his muscles aching.

"Or they felt left out of the game." My heart pounds a million miles a minute as sweat dews on the back of my neck.

"Horny little shits," he mutters.

"They spent a lifetime locked up in an all-male prison. Can you blame them?"

His lips twitch. "Guess not. Dry spells are tough."

God, we are standing far, far too close. "Sorry, Mr. Lindsay, try again. That's not happening." I reach for the jar of moonshine in Charlie's far hand, letting my touch linger irresponsibly long. "Guess we both have to drink on that?"

His chuckle is a low, smooth thing tingling across my skin as he takes a pull from the jar, swallowing without a wince, then lets me take the liquor. "Never knew you to back down from, well, anything, really."

"Me? This is for your benefit." Quirking a brow, I tip the moonshine side to side in front of him, then toss back a harsh sip.

He scoffs an incredulous laugh as his brows pinch like he's confused. Mirroring the looming clouds above, his eyes darken on me. "You think I'm scared to kiss you, sweetheart?"

"Shouldn't you be?" I whisper.

"Maybe," he concedes. But he doesn't back away.

Of all the things he excels at, one thing Charlie's never been very good with is banking the flames of whatever it is that's burned between us for as long as I've known him. It melts down his pupils into wide, black tar full moons. It echoes in his body language as he shifts almost imperceptibly to face me. It bottoms out in my stomach as his gaze falls to my mouth. We're both inching closer to a blurred line we really shouldn't cross.

I let out a weak laugh and bite down on my lip. I want to say, *This is a reckless idea* so badly, but I can't find it in myself. My logic, running on the fumes of the lust coursing through my veins, is looking for any reason to rationalize this. To convince me it's okay. Because, god, I want him so bad. I've wanted him since the very first time he handed me a rose.

"This okay?" His voice is a low, smooth rumble as he traces the bottom curve of my mouth with his thumb. I let out a shuddering breath and nod.

Tipping my chin up with his knuckle, his lips meet mine. Soft. Gentle. Chaste. My hand flies to his chest, eager to test if his heart's as off the rails as mine is. It thuds back to me affirmatively beneath his clothes. This is the most innocent kiss we've ever shared—far more contained than even the first, that night Garrett sprung a surprise rager on us—and yet, it feels the most sinful. It is a tease, a taste, not even close to being enough. He pulls back, rests his forehead against mine, exhales like the weight of our past is forcing every oxygen molecule from his lungs.

It's a familiar comfort, kissing him. And I knew I'd miss it when I left—it was part of why I kept so far away, so out of reach. Because he's intoxicating. My own personal catnip. Part of me always knew colliding with him again would mean opening the door to asking why I even gave up on this in the first place. I can't even blame the moonshine; I'm drunk on him.

And he said it himself: I've never been one to back down.

Reaching past him, I set the open jar of moonshine on the sill of the barred window, sliding my other hand around his neck, grazing the cool metal chain he wears, toying with the curling hair at his nape. The confusion, the hesitancy, the desire, it all blurs together on his face.

It happens so fast neither of us has time to think. To second-guess.

His mouth crushes against mine in a kiss that's more practiced than testing. Like it's only been a few weeks since we did this last. I'm an explosion of cataclysmic size. It's been so long since I've been touched, I'm starved for anything he'll give me.

Cupping my face with one hand, his other arm laces around my waist, corseting us together as our kisses make up for so much missed time, both of us clearly too caught up to worry about how we lost it in the first place. I wind my arms tighter around him, drawing him impossibly close, and my back hits the stone wall behind me as his leg wedges me there, tucked between my thighs. I shamelessly run the tip of my tongue along his bottom lip, begging for more. And he gives it to me. Angling my head exactly how he wants, his tongue slips into my mouth, my stomach drops, and I am on fire.

I whimper against him and my hands knot in his hair as his hips pin me tighter against the wall and I feel how much he needs this too. How he strains against his pants. Blown off the rails by how familiar yet new this all is, a desperate desire aches in my core.

His lips move to my jaw, racing back toward my ear, then down the side of my neck. With a mind of their own, my hips roll against him, searching for any kind of pressure I can take. When they rock again, his muscular thigh presses back firmer, hitting everything just right, and pleasure tingles up my spine as I press my fist to my mouth to muffle the embarrassing sound coming from my kiss-damp mouth.

Charlie pulls my hand down, dragging it slowly across my throat, my breast. "Let me hear you. It's just us."

I stifle a laugh because I want to remind him it's *not* just us, not to mention the camera's still rolling, but it's not the time or the place and I'm too desperately focused on this feeling we're chasing to remember how to say words—his hold on my hips, his knee between my legs, his body wrapped around mine as he kisses, sucks, and bites the skin he can reach.

He finds the spot where muscle curves into my shoulder, the spot that's always been the exact right shape for him. Like it'd been crafted specifically for his mouth, or like he kissed me enough there I simply molded to fit him. I moan again, louder. He responds with a low, gritty *fuck*, tucked against my raging pulse point. Loosening the tucked-hem of my shirt, his fingers slip beneath the fabric, grazing the dip of skin that leads to my spine. The pressure builds and builds between my thighs, and he hitches my leg higher around his waist as his mouth meets mine again.

A crack echoes through the building and thunder bellows overhead, so loud the earth shakes beneath our feet. The vibration extends, the wall behind me still trembling, even as the rumble fades. And it keeps—*oh*.

Oh god. Oh no.

That shaking is *me*.

The sensation overwhelms me, my legs clenching around Charlie as I tuck a series of bitten off whines between his teeth and my nails curl into his strong shoulders as the release washes over me.

Fuck. I just—

He pulls back, panting. "Did you . . . you just—"

"*No,*" I hiss.

"I know what you sound like." A swallow rolls down his throat. "How your body tenses—"

"I didn't." Oh god. I did. I made out with him and orgasmed from . . . what, exactly? The simple pressure of his *leg*? *Get a grip, Winona.* Two years is a long time to go without a man's touch, but it's not like I haven't been getting myself off in the meantime. This is absurd. And mortifying on a soul-deep level.

"You did." An arrogant little smirk unevenly pulls at his mouth. He quirks a single brow. "A bit quick on the draw there, huh?"

I tip my head back against the wall, exhaling a single laugh. "Jesus. You really think I'm that easy?"

Lust still heavy over his gaze, his brow twitches, a cheeky, silent, *Well, clearly.*

Dammit. I am that easy.

And I may have made the biggest mistake I could've possibly made.

What felt good—*incredible*—in the moment is taking a wrecking ball to all the careful walls I've constructed between me and Charlie. My skin is cool and clammy but this time it's nothing paranormal. No, that's the sweat of pure regret. I wasn't even supposed to stay here with him. I was supposed to never see him again.

I dig deep into my psyche, searching for the right words to get me out of this mess, specifically the narrow space between Charlie's warm body and the wall.

Languid and hungry, Charlie's palm slips further beneath my shirt, coasts over my ribcage, and *shit* I'm running out of time before I lose myself to him all over again. He's too studied with the curves of my body, too skilled at taking the turns just right to send me reeling. "What was that?" he murmurs against the edge of my jaw.

He doesn't mean my orgasm from hell, fresh from the pubescent experience of fourteen-year-old boys everywhere. He means the kiss. The so-intense-it-felt-like-fucking make out session I instigated.

"A mistake," I grit out, pushing his wrists away.

He takes his hands off me, but braces one against the wall as the rest of him stills, ices into pure, chilled stone. His eyes level with mine as his jaw sets in place. And in his fallen expression, I think I see the part of him that hates himself for still wanting me. The part of him who should hate me instead. It's not like I don't deserve it.

"What?" he growls. "*You* pulled me in for more." His palm slashes against the stone as he lowers it and steps back from me. "Jesus, Win. What kind of game are you playing with me? I can't— I'm not sure I—*fuck*. Why would you *do* that?"

Because I'm selfish and stupid and the taste of mint on his breath from his toothpaste has always left me weak in the knees. My molars clench as I blink back the threat of tears.

Why can't I just let him go?

Shoving my shirt back into the waist of my shorts with shaking hands, I avoid the burn of his gaze. "If you want, you can check your radar app again. Storm's overhead."

"We're not done with our game." His voice is low and so tight it sounds like it may snap.

"Yes. We are."

"We aren't. It's my turn."

"Charlie—"

"Truth or dare, Winona."

My hands ball into fists at my side as I slump back against the brick and Charlie paces like a feral lion a few feet in front of me. There's no escaping. I'm the prey here. "Truth."

He exhales his breath, nice and slow. The bastard's making me wait on pins and needles. The least he could do is make this quick and painless.

"Why have you never served me the papers, Win?" He asks this quietly, like his voice is a little broken and each word is hesitant to find its answer, all traces of his rage dissipating like fog under the heat of late morning sun.

It's a good question, really.

Because despite the screen printed *Halbach's Hunts* on the chest of my shirt, legally I'm still Mrs. Rosenhoth.

chapter 13

SIX YEARS AGO

THE DAY HE PROPOSES, a spring storm capes Dallas. We lay tied around each other like ribbons on his couch, watching it roll in. He draws tingles up and down my forearm, currently lolled across his chest, with the tips of his fingers.

I'm not sure I've ever been happier. The slow moments, when we laze in each other's arms, are my favorite.

The world outside the window lights, a crack splitting through the showering rain. *One. Two. Three. Four. Five.* A deep growl of thunder rolls overhead.

"The storm's five miles away," I whisper to his heartbeat, tucked beneath my cheek.

A soft chuckle answers back, his thumb brushing against my skin reassuringly. "One mile, actually. You count the time between the lightning and thunder then divide by five." His mouth presses to the top of my head.

Yesterday marked four months of being his. And for the life of me, I can't recall why I'd been so scared of being his girlfriend. It's not much different to how things were before. We still grab lunch together on campus, taking turns with who pays. He still sneaks into the studio to watch me practice, and I still third wheel on movie nights with Garrett at their place. He still kisses all my dance bruises better, and there's still always roses waiting for me in the dressing room at the theater, although, these days, he signs his name. But beneath it all is a patient, understanding current of stability, the promise we will do it all over again tomorrow and the next day and the day after that. He is the even-keel constant I've always craved.

"Hey, Winnie?"

"Hm?"

His sternum rises slowly as he inhales the sort of breath that precedes something important. Brows knitting, I lift my head and look at him, stomach fluttering. He is so unfairly handsome. With the barest touch, he caresses the backs of his fingers against my cheek, his thumb taking a detour to trace the peak of my cheek-bone. Maybe for the first time, he looks nervous.

"I love you," he murmurs, his throat bobbing. "I'm in love with you, Winona."

I'm weightless. My heart's outside my body, leaping through the air. I search his face for a catch, for some evidence I'm dreaming or he's playing a joke on me. I find only his wide antici-pation staring back at me.

I gape. "You . . . what?"

His smile softens as he tucks my hair behind my ear. "I love you. You don't have to say it—"

"I love you too, Charlie." The feeling surges through me, a relentless energy, as I inch closer, clutching the collar of his shirt.

"You're going to think I'm crazy," he says, still playing with my hair as his grin widens, "but I think I've been in love with you since the day I met you."

I lean closer, our noses brushing. "You're right. I do think you're crazy—believing in something with no hard evidence? No tried and true data? No measurable variables? No application of the *scientific method*? Who *are* you?"

He clicks his tongue. "Ah, see, there's where you're wrong. I have plenty of data. Mounds of it, really." His hand slides to cup the back of my head. "I've been testing this theory since the day I met a very beautiful—*very* snarky—girl in a dressing room and she brutally rejected me, threatened my job, and then asked if I wanted to be friends instead."

I roll my smile between my teeth. "You should've told her to get lost. Sounds mean."

"Meeting you just clicked for me," he breathes, fingers clenching in my hair. I'm so full of joy it's threatening to leak out of my eyes. "In a way that nothing really has before."

He closes the distance between us and kisses me. I never want to leave this bubble of warm shared breath and love confessions. Sliding my leg over his hip, I move to straddle him. "You're the best friend I've ever had, Flower Boy."

His palm molds to the dip at the small of my back as we kiss again, our sharp inhales syncing, and my body aches for his. Garrett's out all weekend. We have another hour before we both have to work—Charlie running deliveries for his mom, me on ticket box duty at Colby Theater. That's plenty of time. Like his mind's exactly where mine is, his hands slip down to my ass.

"Hey, Charlie?"

"Hm?"

"Remember when I said I was waiting for marriage?"

He stills beneath me, suddenly alert. "Yeah?"

"Funny story, that actually isn't true." I bite my lip, searching his face for signs of disappointment in me. All I find is confusion. "This. This is what I was waiting for."

All other forms of intimacy—with him, with anyone before—had been moves on a board, an exchanging of pawns and knights to keep the game going. Only for love, only for *him*, will I risk the king. It's not any more valuable or powerful than any of the other pieces, but it's something I've wanted to protect, wanted to withhold, simply because I could. Because I only wanted to let my guard down with someone who was worth it.

Unfortunately, his greedy touch backs off my ass, his attention tuning into what I said. "Really? Why didn't you just say that?"

It's one of my favorite things about him, the way he has no reason to keep parts of himself hidden. Not really. He doesn't spill his guts to just anyone, but I know the way he talks to me. I've witnessed how he talks with Garrett. To his core, Charlie believes the best path forward with anything is honesty.

"I was trying to scare you off," I admit. "And if I said I was waiting for someone I loved . . ."

He sucks his teeth. "You were worried I'd use that to my advantage."

I nod and kiss his jaw, dotting a line to his ear. "I got lucky with you. Turns out you don't scare easily. And you have an astonishingly upstanding moral character."

"Did you lift that line from my college recommendation letter?"

I slide my hands along the warm skin of his taut stomach beneath his shirt. "Your high school chemistry teacher was as shocked as I was to find a little threat of temporary celibacy didn't keep you at bay."

"I think my high school teachers would be more shocked I was getting any at all."

"Late bloomer?"

He cracks a smile. "Still waiting."

"You don't have to anymore," I purr against his throat. His lips part as a breath hitches in his chest.

"You want to? Right now?"

"We have a whole hour," I mouth against his skin.

His hands brace the tops of my shoulders. "But it's your first time. *Our* first time. I want it to be special. Not on this shitty old couch."

I nip his chin. "You can carry me to your bed if you want."

He frowns. "Sheets are in the wash. Mattress is bare."

"That's fine."

He scoffs. "That's the vibe you want?"

"Sure." I shrug because I don't know how to articulate that compared to the bed of a pickup truck on a dark country road or a musty basement at a house party, this couch is a Hallmark moment for me. Because the man touching me cares about me. He loves me.

He rolls on his side, pinning me against the back cushions. Hooking beneath my knee, he hitches my leg over his hip and my blood soars through me as his erection presses along my inner thigh. Is this really going to happen? His mouth drags along my jawline, pausing at my ear. His lips catch against my ear as he murmurs, "This whole time, I've been picturing a fluffy hotel bed and ripping a white dress off with my teeth."

A thrill races through me, winding tight circles low in my belly. Does that mean he's thought about . . . marriage? My heart bursts.

He presses a soft, open-mouth kiss beneath my ear. "The tables have turned, sweetheart. I think it's my turn to make you wait now."

I roll my eyes, like this is the most annoying, absurd thing a man's ever said to me. "*Fine.*"

He grins and kisses me. "That's my girl. Just until tonight."

I'm not sure what lucky penny I picked up that granted me a life so sweet. But I hope to god I never lose it.

There are rose petals everywhere.

Everywhere.

"Charlie," I groan, covering my grin with my hands.

They litter his bedroom floor, the duvet cover, the end table I bullied him into buying. A full bouquet, still in its wrapping and still unplucked, sits next to the framed cloud photo I gifted him for his birthday on top of his dresser. He didn't spring for candles, but the string lights looping his head board cast a saccharine honey glow across the sheets. For once, his bed is perfectly made, and an unopened box of condoms sits on the end table. I can't even name the feeling buzzing electric through my body, it's a combination of too many things.

"Too much?" He laughs, slipping a hand around my waist from behind.

I twist to face him. "Mortifyingly romantic."

A satisfied noise hums in his chest. "Good. I live to embarrass you, Winnie."

"Yeah." I work my fingers into his hair, gaze dropping to his mouth. "I know."

"I love you," he murmurs against my mouth. "Fuck, it feels so good to say that finally."

I smile back against him. "Can you believe I was a stranger just a few months ago?"

"I can't explain it, but you've never been a stranger to me, Winnie. Not really."

Hungry for bare skin, my palms slip beneath his shirt. "I never thought I'd find someone like you," I admit, pressing my shaking hands to his stomach.

His gaze drops, clocking the nerves I'm trying to hide. I see the silent question pulling taut between his brows. Before he can ask if I'm second guessing this, I lift his shirt and he helps me pull it off. Lit only by the ambient glow of the string lights, all his shadows and hard edges are sharpened, looking even more tempting than usual. And he's all *mine*. I can't figure out how I swindled my way into this life. His chin dips as he watches me run my hands along his abs, tracing behind the elastic band of his underwear under his jeans. He unzips my dress and I slip out of the straps, letting it fall to my feet. I'm wearing nothing underneath.

We've been in various states of undress around each other before, yet doing this now feels different. And it's not about the sex, but the magic word that prompted it. He loves me. I love him. I have never felt so safe.

"You're sure?" He presses this question just beneath my ear, then kisses down to my collar bone, hands pressing to the small of my back.

"Absolutely positive," I gasp as his teeth graze my throat.

He walks me back until I hit the edge of the mattress and I fall back against it, the sweet smell of roses wafting around me, and at first it feels like any other night together. But this time, we drop our love confessions like bread crumbs so we can always find our way back to them. Whispered to my heart rate thumping between my breasts, panted in his ear as his hand slips between my thighs and teases me slowly, punctuated with a row of kisses down my stomach, desperately moaned as he makes me come with his mouth between my legs, and echoed between us as he looks down at me, arms braced beside my head, before he presses inside me. *I love you, I love you, I love you. I love you.*

I suck in a sharp breath, nails digging into his shoulders as I adjust to the sting of the unfamiliar pressure.

"You okay?" he asks, stilling. "Does it hurt?"

"A little," I say on an exhale.

"You're tense."

"Just nerves," I admit. I've never done this before. What if I do something wrong?

So much affection draws up the corner of his mouth, I feel the warmth down to my toes. "You have no reason to be nervous. I've got you, okay?"

The way he says it, the way he's looking so deeply into my eyes, makes me believe it to be undeniably true. I nod.

He strokes his thumb across my cheek. "Now try and relax for me, sweetheart. It'll feel better if you do."

I consciously loosen all my rigid muscles, taking a steadying breath. *He's got me.* When I exhale, he moves again—deeper, which

I didn't realize was possible—and my body arches up to meet him as I moan. *Oh*. Much better. He must feel it too, see it written on my face, because he doesn't ask how I'm feeling before he thrusts into me again, and a sound, almost like a whimper, breaks off in his throat. He keeps his cadence slow and controlled—the focused pinch of his brows says this restraint is all for me—and I do my best to match each measured movement.

"You feel so—" He pants, eyes fluttering shut as he swallows. He drops his mouth, presses his next words to my throat. "So incredible."

"I'm doing okay?" I manage to ask breathlessly, hands tangling in his hair, holding him as tight to me as I possibly can.

His damp lip snags on my skin as he says, "You're doing so fucking good, Winnie." I feel his smile, the way his cheek lifts against my neck, and it tops up the thrill I'm already drunk off of.

My ankles lock behind his back, urging him in closer as my hips roll up to meet his, and he moans. It sparks desire low in my belly; I'm desperate to make him do it again. I want to drive him wild.

My teeth catch the first inch of skin I can reach, and I tug on his earlobe, then kiss down his jaw. His lips finds mine, greedy and determined as his tongue slips against mine, and our bodies crash together harder, faster, more frenzied. I draw my nails down his back, etching my pleasure along his spine, and he moans into my open mouth. I drink up every last vibration as our teeth knock together.

It's sweaty and wet and uncontrolled and intense in such a beautiful way, I can't even tell that we're two separate people anymore. He is me and I am him and all we are is this want, this *need*, pulsing between us.

He pants that he's about to come and I nod, unable to speak from the overwhelm of it all. Pulling me tight, he drops his head, nose pushing up against my jaw as his body stutters, muscles going rigid, then relaxing all at once. His weight collapses on me, breathing still ragged as I stroke his hair. I'm already addicted to holding him while he falls apart.

He finally moves, kissing my collar bone. "I love you, Winnie," he rasps, and I melt all over again, the happiest tears I've ever known beading along my lashes.

"I love you too, Flower Boy."

It's everything I never imagined for myself. It's so perfect, guilt gnaws in my stomach. Who am *I* to deserve something so good?

I am bliss incarnate as Charlie drags his fingers up and down my side, cradling me against his chest.

"What if we do it?" he murmurs, sounding distant, like he's accidentally said a thought out loud.

A ridiculous little giggle slips out. "I was hoping we could get more than one in tonight."

"No, I meant—" A breath lofts in his chest, his volume dropping as he says, "Get married."

My eyes flare, my heart skipping a beat. I shoot up on my elbow and look at him. "What?"

His grin is soft and loopy. "You think that's insane, don't you?"

"I—I . . ." My gut pings with something I don't expect at all: I *don't* think that's insane.

His hand slips around the back of my neck, looking me deep in my eyes as he says, "I love you. I can't imagine living without you. I've never felt this way about anyone before. You're sharp and witty and you have this softness beneath it all that I think, honest to god, I'm addicted to. *This*, what we have, is what I've been looking for."

I'd never even considered looking for something like this before

—it never felt like it was in the cards for someone like me. I was fortunate it barged right into my dressing room instead.

But maybe this is my chance to rewrite everything.

To spend forever with someone I couldn't have even imagined, had I tried. A man who loves me. A man who's my best friend. A man I see a different sort of future with than the place I came from. To erase the last name that cuts like a scar and replace it with something sparkling. A marriage that's more than just obligation and security.

I rake my gaze over the sight of our tangled bodies, then pin it back to his face. This is exactly how I want my forever to look.

I sink my teeth into the bottom curve of my grin. He expects me to say no, to tell him he's being ridiculous, lost in the post-sex glow. But I love throwing him curve balls.

I love how effortlessly he catches them even more.

I splay my hand across his chest, anchoring against his heart rate. "Marry me, Charlie. And yes, I am so incredibly serious when I say that."

He gapes at me, his brain buffering to process what I said. Tightening his grip around my wrists, he flips us so he's hovering over me. "Oh no you don't. I'm not letting you get away with this again." His face searches mine for any last doubts. "Jesus," he hisses. "I didn't think you'd . . . Hold on."

He rolls off me, and rustles the plastic wrapped around the singular untouched bouquet on his dresser. I push up on my elbows as he turns, holding the delicate pink ribbon that was tied around the stems in his hand. I sit up, both of us laughing like we can't believe this is real. He drops to one knee to the side of the bed, still tying the ribbon in a knot, still swallowing his nervous laughter.

"Marry me, Winnie."

I cup the side of his cheek. "You think this is all some kind of big joke?"

He bites down on the bottom of his grin and shakes his head.

"This is possibly the most serious I've ever been about anything in my whole life." Throat rolling, an intensity settles in his eyes and sobers his tone. "Winona Jean Halbach, will you marry me?"

I'm no longer tethered by gravity. I could listen to that on perpetual loop. My fingers push into his hair. "This is stupid."

"Completely idiotic."

I scrunch my nose. "I think I just want to be friends."

He huffs an exasperated laugh. "And I really desperately want to marry you, woman."

"All right." I glance at his ribbon ring. "Let's do it."

"I knew you'd say that."

I snort. "As if *I* didn't ask *you* first."

"No way in hell am I letting you claim this one." His hands shake the slightest bit as he slides the ribbon on my ring finger. Damn near a perfect fit. When it's seated in place, the tails of the ribbon flowing over the back of my palm, he looks up at me and our eyes meet.

"I love you," I murmur, before leaning in for a kiss.

"I'm really looking forward to hearing that for the rest of forever."

His parents aren't as sold on our engagement as we are.

Katherine and George Rosenhoth are traditionalists in that they don't think their son should be marrying a girl he's known for nine months, without even a real diamond to show for it, before he's even graduated college and started a career. Not to mention the fact he didn't even ask my father for my hand. As I stab the prongs of my fork into a green bean at their dining table, I hold my tongue and keep from slipping the truth: if Charlie *did* ask my dad for permission to marry me, my dad would probably laugh in his face and say, *You can have her, and hey, you want to take her mom too, while you're at it?*

"It's rather quick," Katherine says, her smile a well-worn mask.

"What's the point in putting it off?" Charlie argues.

"If you really think it'll last *forever*, what's a few more years? You should focus on finishing school first."

George grunts from the head of the table. Charlie's younger brothers, Luke and Max exchange *Oh shit!* glances as they keep their heads bowed and their wily grins hidden. My body heats to the surface of the sun and I wish I could melt into Katherine's expensive upholstered dining chairs.

"I never knew you to be so . . . impulsive." Katherine's peaked-brow concern slides to me at the word *impulsive* and her eyes squint, as if it was a poison I slipped beneath her son's tongue the first time we kissed.

Charlie's fork clatters as he drops it on the plate, voice sharp as a knife. My body goes rigid and I remind myself this family is nothing like mine. "We didn't come here asking for your blessing, Mom," Charlie says. "This is between me and Win—"

"A marriage might be between two people, but a wedding is about *family*, Charles," Katherine slices right back.

The blood drains from my cheeks as it dawns on me. I've been mentally toying with a few ways I could get away with keeping my family separate from this—my mom's ill or a nervous traveler, dad's overseas for work—but Katherine is nothing like her son. She pushes and pushes and pushes until she gets what she wants. If she wants my family there, she would find a way to make it happen. I can't risk that. This life I've built for myself out here is too sacred to spoil with my ugly past.

From the first time I met his parents, the sixth sense in my gut that reads people before my brain can has whispered that they don't approve of me. Their opinion of me will plummet if they meet my family. My parents, who most certainly haven't kept their marriage between two people, and who are all rough edges compared to the smooth veneer of the Rosenhoths. Katherine and

George will take one look at us and determine the thing I've been trying to hide the most: we're trash. And their son only deserves the best.

And for as ashamed of my family as I am, I am equally protective of our shared imperfections. The thought of watching the perfect Mr. and Mrs. Rosenhoth inspecting my parents like frogs on a dissection plate, trying to determine what makes them tick, makes me nauseous.

The rest of dinner is tense. I keep quiet until I'm forced to say polite goodbyes.

"I'm sorry about that," Charlie mutters, knuckles white around the steering wheel. "I had a feeling they wouldn't be exactly thrilled, but I thought they'd at least trust my judgement."

A buzzing tension radiates off him as he shakes his head, still in disbelief—the tortured look of the fallen golden boy. I reach over and squeeze his shoulder, letting my hand rest there, grazing my fingers up and down the back of his neck in a soothing gesture I know he loves. "It's okay. I'm sorry too," I whisper. "I get it if you don't want—"

"Don't even go there." He brings my hand to his mouth, kissing it intently. "Nothing's changed. Not for me. I'd marry you tonight if I could."

My eyes widen as my shoulders lift with a sharp breath. That's the solution. "What if we do?"

He snorts. "Get married *tonight*?"

"No, I mean—elope. Just you and me. Our families don't have to be involved."

A slow smile spreads on his face. "You know, Garrett became an ordained minister when he lost a bet. Long story. But I mean, if you're serious . . ."

"I am. I don't care about a big, fancy wedding. All I care about is you."

We roll to a stoplight and he looks at me with overflowing tender adoration, utterly pleased to hear me say that. "Okay." He nods once, decisively. "Let's do it. I don't care what my parents think. Every day I don't get to call you my wife feels like a goddamn waste."

Garrett agrees to take part in our scheme. We buy a matching set of gold bands at a local jewelry store—his thicker than mine. Charlie promises to buy me something sparkly when he's had a chance to save up. I tell him his last name on my license is all I care about. I find a simple white silk dress with thin beaded straps and a cowl neckline and match it with an old pair of flats. Naturally, Charlie already owns a deliciously well-tailored navy suit. For a steal, we hire one of his friends who does photography on the side to take photos. Three weeks after he proposed, we secure a slot in the Poetry Garden at the Dallas Arboretum for a few hundred bucks on a Tuesday.

Everyone around us, even Garrett, thinks this is a rash move. We're so young, how can we possibly know ourselves well enough to choose who we want to spend forever with. *Hasn't it only been four months?* And *isn't that sort of quick?* But to every wide-eyed reception, Charlie—no, my fiancé—smiles and says, *When you know, you know.*

We both skip class to attend our wedding. He realizes we have no flowers first—typical florist's son. But the Texas wildflowers are in bloom so I beg him to pull off the side of the road and let me pick a few. He insists it's illegal, but I tell him that sounds crazy and besides, there's no cops around. I palm a handful of Bluebonnets and some vibrant vermillion Indian Paintbrushes for contrast.

Under the warmth and rain of late May, the gardens at the Arboretum are back in bloom after a chilly winter. Verdant vines set back against the white stone castle-like walls cocoon the space, bursting with colorful florals even Katherine Rosenhoth would be impressed by. Music plays from a Bluetooth speaker as we walk, hand in hand, into the small space. The garden is small and intimate and somewhere birds are chirping and everything inside me bursts with joy. We exchange our vows, and I don't even make it through two sentences before tearing up. The line we both say, which engraves itself directly on my heart, is: *I choose you today, and for the rest of forever, as my best friend, my love, my partner.*

He gets his wish of taking off my white dress with his teeth in a fluffy hotel bed.

chapter 14

I DON'T COME from a family of talkers. Halbachs have always been sweepers. We lift the corner of any old rug and tuck everything we don't want to acknowledge beneath it.

I thought I was ready for this conversation. Thought I was ready for the truth. Thought I was ready for his vitriol, his rage. It's not side of Charlie I've seen often, but facing it head on, studying the hurt in his eyes, strikes a new kind of fear in me.

I was wrong. I'm not strong enough to confront the ways I've destroyed him—the way I destroyed *us*. The anguish in his voice the last time we talked on the phone tortures me on a loop in my head. I guard my heart so fiercely only because it's so goddamn weak, and I'm certain it'll split in two if I'm forced to reckon with this right now.

"You haven't served me the papers either." I'm a creature of habit, doomed to grind my heels into the mud, carve the ruts I'm stuck in deeper and deeper.

"*You're* the one who left!"

I flinch. He's right. I'm the one who started all this; I should be the one to finish it. But what I can't bring myself to say out loud—

because I know exactly what road it'll lead us down—is every time I've tried filling out the paperwork to legally sever us, bile creeps up the back of my throat. My stomach twists into knots. Every atom making up my body, my brain, screams *but he's mine*.

"Because I'm just *such* a terrible fucking person. Okay? There. You win." I throw my hands up.

He scoffs. "You're deflecting."

His expression is all sharp determination. He's not letting me dance around this one—he knows my moves too well. Pushing off the wall, I cross to the camera, avoiding the weight of his stare as I pop the SD card out and pocket it. I don't need any more recorded evidence of the mess I'm making, and I sure as hell don't need my little brother ever having a chance to get ahold of this footage. What I need is to derail Charlie's line of questioning before I break and tell him how hard it's been without him.

Like Mr. Lindsay is on my side, the REM Pod blares across the room. I nearly leap out of my skin. That's my in.

"We're not done yet," I grit out, glancing toward the noise. "I promised we'd talk when we were done, but we're not. And I know all of this ghost investigating might not matter to you, but it matters to me." Cautiously, I tack on, "And to River."

Standing behind the camera setup like it's some semblance of a shield, I watch his shoulders fall as the anger drains from his body like water down old pipes. He palms the back of his neck, gaze dropping to the floor.

"It's not that it doesn't matter to me, Win." Regret weighs down his voice, sandpapery and low. I'm both relieved and drowning with shame that I hit my mark. "I'm sorry if I made you feel that way. I just—"

"I know." I send a deep breath through pursed lips. As I swap in a fresh SD card, I try to ignore the way he looks at me. The way he still cares enough about me to come off genuine in his apology.

He exhales. "Okay."

"Okay."

I bite my lip and glance around the room. I need space from Charlie. Just a little fresh air—as fresh as I can get in this place—not tainted with his scent, not weighed down by the shattered look in his eyes. My body's buzzing with restless energy, like ants spilling from a caved-in hill, ready to attack the intruding shoe. I unscrew the camera from the mount on the tripod and fish the stabilizer from my bag again—any excuse to keep my hand to myself. My gaze darts from one exit to the next, finally settling on a hallway out the other side of the dining hall we haven't explored yet.

"I'm going to capture some B-roll. I'll be right back. Don't scare off the ghost," I rush out, not pausing long enough to let Charlie get a word in edgewise as I swipe the camera off the mount.

Five minutes alone. That's all I need. To remind myself why I left him. To remind myself why I have to stay away. Five minutes of fresh air to forget how good his sweat smells on his skin.

Charlie calls after me but I break into a jog down the unfamiliar hallway. With the windows barred and set so high on the walls, and the cloud ceiling so low and dark in the sky, it's nearly pitch black as my breath heaves in my lungs, my pulse still elevated from our little rendezvous. I navigate solely by the light strapped to my camera.

The archway at the end yawns open into another tall, multistory cell block unit. Craning my neck, I count the stories—one, two, three. Black metal stairs overlayed on top of their landings look like giant ominous X's stacking all the way up—a warning sign that those who enter here don't often come back out. The end of the tracks. Like the other block, this one's decrepit in a way things only untouched for decades become, disintegrating under the hot, relentless breath of north Texas summers, freezing rigid and cracking in its winters.

A series of three soft plinks wrenches my neck sideways, and I pan the camera over the cell it echoed from as my stomach twists. Could it have been a bug? A heavy curl of peeling metal slipping loose from the bars, disturbing whatever grime is caked on the floor? The cell stares back at me in perfect silence. Attempting to regain control of my breathing, I take measured steps across the long corridor.

Double-checking my mic's still in place, I clear my throat and dive into the nearest distraction I can reach: the episode, which needs to be my first priority. "Black Magnolia Penitentiary was built back in the 1890s with inmate labor."

My narration's breathy and far less certain than River's normally is, but I can't bring myself to dwell on it. Crossing closer to one of the cells, I pan across its compact space, the light affixed to the top of the camera illuminating it. There's a metal bed frame chained to the wall, now sagging from it, a utilitarian sink and toilet, and a single shelf. My throat swells as the light crosses a series of clumsy tally marks etched into the stone, several hashes of five lined up and stacked in a four-by-three rectangle. Tracking months? Or years?

Running my thumb along the first set, I whisper, "These men were literally forced to live in a prison of their own making."

Sadness swells in my chest—and for *what*? For prisoners, long and gone? Murderers, rapists, arsonists, you name it? Terrible people or not, I can't fathom living in this sad, lonely squalor for the rest of my days.

"The man we're trying to contact today," I start, attempting to steel the embarrassing shake from my voice, "is now believed to have been wrongfully convicted of his crime. Not by the public. Not by the justice system. But by the surviving family of his victim."

I keep walking down the row of cells, passing barred door after barred door. I'm still not convinced the guy didn't do it—even if he *was* Edith's lover—but this is the story River's latched onto, so it's the one I'm committed to. He's desperate to find the good in people—a trait I try to encourage as much as possible, even if I can't lead by example. I would sacrifice anything to protect his hope forever.

"If you're a returning viewer, I'm sure you're familiar with our resident research aficionado, River." I sniff a laugh. "He was able to dig up old newspaper articles, around the time Mr. Dewhurst was first pinned for the crime. Locals all said he was strange. Kept to himself a lot, didn't attend church regularly. He was a black sheep, an easy scapegoat. And that's what landed him a lifetime in a place like *this*. The one person who would've fought for his innocence was gone."

I reach the end of the line and pivot.

"Our research—well, River's—said that Mr. Dewhurst died of a heart attack in prison. He had seven more years of his sentence to serve when he passed." I suck in a deep breath. "And the unfortunate reality is Edith Page Milton's killer may have been living as a free person while Mr. Dewhurst had to live with the reality that the woman he loved was dead, and he was behind bars for it."

I pause and take one last look up at the cascading stairs, the seemingly infinite cells they lead to, and huff a dry laugh.

"It's no secret that our *justice* system is often anything but. And nothing can give James Dewhurst or Edith Page Milton their lives back. But at least we can do our best to share their story. And James, if you're here and willing to talk to us, we'd love to get your side of things, too."

I hold my breath. I don't blink. I don't move. I listen for *anything* around me.

Absolutely nothing. With a sigh, I keep walking.

I'm three cells away from clearing the block and making my way back into the adjoining hallway when the room plummets into darkness as my light goes out. I gasp, stomach swooping dramatically. The camera light flickers back on, but every hair on my body stands on end, and my head swivels, instinctively in search of threats.

Warmth coats the back of my neck—soft, the tiniest bit moist, like an exhaled breath, and every molecule in me ices over as I whirl around. Nothing. From the corner of my eye . . . movement. Shadow. Slinking into a cell. On the opposite side of the ones I walked by. Shit. Is something in here? With me? Hands trembling, I back up until my shoulders meet the rusty bars of another cell, not taking my eyes from where I saw something move.

"Charlie? Is that you?" My voice quivers.

No answer.

I've never felt so terrified during an investigation before. Fucking hell, if I ever did, I'd never let River do this shit again. Trigger devices and Ovilus communication and voices caught on EVP are one thing. Shadow figures are something else entirely, if that's what this is. I've read about them online. They feed on pure terror.

Something grazes my shoulder and nausea rolls in my stomach, threatening to bring up the sandwich I scarfed down for lunch before we came here. My drumming pulse is in my throat as I clench my teeth and grind out, "You are not allowed to touch me."

My light flickers again as the energy next to me oscillates, the feeling of something corporeal shifting near me. It closes in, the air around me bloating as dread creeps up my spine. Maybe if I calm myself it'll leave me alone. I suck in a deep breath, counting up to ten, but only make it to three before my hands start to shake. I try to bolt, but I can't move. It's been years since I've stepped foot in a church, but I lift a hand to make the sign of the cross. I make it as far as tapping my forehead, then what feels like a hand closes around my throat.

I lurch back in the cell, a scream splitting from my chest. I twist and contort, curling over in the corner as I white knuckle the camera, pawing at the phantom pressure at my neck with my free hand.

It's gone. The feeling's gone. I'm okay.

"Winona?" Charlie cries, slamming footsteps growing louder.

"I'm all right," I cry back, hoarse. He appears in the doorway to the cell.

"Fuck. What happened? I heard you scream." He draws in ragged breaths and crowds my space, prying the camera from my hands. He sets it down on the metal cot attached to the wall. All the nasty, heavy feelings that were invading the room only moments ago dissipate in his presence.

"My light went out and then I—I saw a shadow. I've never been so scared on a job. I can't explain it, the thing just felt *dark*. It wasn't any old ghost. And then it . . . that fucker breathed on me— touched me. It felt like something grabbed my throat, and I—" I shake my head, turning away from him, willing my eyes not to leak. "You probably think I'm insane."

He cups my face with both hands, brows peaking as he searches my face. "I do not think you're insane," he says gently, wiping a stray tear away with his thumb. "You're sure you're all right?"

"God, yeah." I swipe the rest of the dampness away with the back of my hand. "Sorry, I don't know what happened."

"Maybe let's stick together from now on. Yeah?" He tucks a loose tendril of hair behind my ear, thumb absentmindedly stroking my cheekbone.

I nod, brows pulling together as I regain my composure. Something—I wouldn't dare call it yearning—sinks in my chest when he drops his hand from my face. Charlie swipes the camera and exits the cell. Framed in the center of its barred entrance, he pauses and looks over his shoulder, free arm twitching like he almost extended a hand to me. Peeling my clammy back off the wall, I step forward, and tingles spider-crawl over my scalp instantly. A fresh scent envelops me—warm and spicy, like clove with a spritz of lemon. I inhale deeply. It's cozy. Nostalgic. A stark contrast to what just happened to me in here.

Charlie? No. Charlie smells like bright resinous pine, smoke curling through dense leaves, freshly tanned leather drying in the sun. Yet there's something familiar about this scent. Men's cologne. But not young, modern men like Charlie. No, this one smells like the principal at my old middle school, a man pushing his seventies.

My eyes widen as my jaw goes slack and The Knowing curls up behind my ribs like a comfortable cat.

"What is it?" Charlie asks.

"I don't know . . . do you smell that?"

He sniffs. "Dust? Mold? Asbestos? Lead paint? No. I'm living in delusion."

"This cell," I mutter, looking around it. "There's something about this cell . . ." As if in response, a chill passes over me. But this one isn't heavy and foreboding, like whatever screwed with me.

Charlie inches closer, adjusting his glasses with one hand as the other lowers the camera and he sighs. "What do—" His gaze falls and he stops, brow furrowing.

"What? What is it?"

"I . . ." He frowns and squats, attention still pinned on the same spot. I follow his train of sight to a loose stone in the wall beneath the cot. Reaching forward gingerly, he wiggles the brick and it gives easily. "I don't know why I . . ." He trails off, grumbling, as he inches it forward. It springs free, chips crumbling as it loosens.

"Intuition," I mumble, squatting next to him.

He unclips the light from the camera and lowers it to peer inside the hollow left by the stone. Something flat, the same dark color of blood, reflects back to us. Wordlessly, I take the light so he can reach for whatever it is. Charlie extracts an old journal, pages yellowing, corners curling, the maroon leather binding worn and aged from who knows how many years it's been down here. He hands me the camera, freeing both hands to peel apart the pages. My heart gallops as he hums and I focus the lens on the artifact. His throat bobs with a swallow as he glances at me sideways.

"Your guy . . . what was his name again?" Charlie asks.

"James." I clear my throat, inching closer to him, our arms brushing, as I squint through the harsh light. "James Dewhurst."

"I think we just found his journal."

chapter 15

ON THE INSIDE cover of the maroon, leather-bound journal, scrawled in lazy cursive, black ink inscribes: Property of James M. Dewhurst. My jaw slackens as I stare at it, unblinking, waiting for my eyes to deceive me, to prove this isn't what I think it is.

"This can't be real," I mutter, running my fingers along the name, forearm grazing Charlie's. But under my soft touch, the shape of the letters come alive. This isn't some prank left by previous ghost hunters or true crime fans.

Charlie fans the pages. Nearly all of them are filled. "Holy shit."

"The cologne." I glance around us. "I wonder if that was James. Like he didn't want us to leave this cell just yet. It must've . . . this must be his cell."

A pang of sorrow pendulums in my stomach as I take in the space, this time with a different eye. This—the metal cots stacked two high, sink, toilet, a single shelf—was all he had. For years and years of his life.

Charlie swipes a hand over his mouth as he takes a deep breath. "This is *real*, Win."

"I know." I ignore the implication in his voice that everything else that's happened today hasn't been real. An ache builds in my hip and I brace my weight on the edge of the cot to stand and relieve the strain. Biting my lip, I ask, "We should read it, right? I mean, that's why James wanted us to find it, right?"

"Why wouldn't we?" Charlie stands too, holding his hand out for the camera and light. I pass them over.

"Is it wrong? To pry into a dead man's private thoughts?"

Charlie snorts and the light snaps back on the camera. "Wasn't that your whole point in coming here?"

"We came here to contact *ghosts*. This is different. This is . . ."

"It's evidence," Charlie says quietly, finishing my sentence.

I nod. "We could capture the most authentic ghost interaction ever seen on camera, and somewhere in the world, people like *you* would still doubt the validity of it. But a journal . . . James's own words . . . People can't argue with that. If he somehow knows the truth of what happened to Edith . . . This journal could have *real* consequences."

"Like what?"

I lean back against the grimy wall, huffing a breath as I pull my leg into passé, toes pointed and drawn to my left knee, as a barrage of possibilities swim through my mind. "Maybe he admits he did it and we crush Edith's family, who are clinging to this story that he's innocent." River, too. "Or maybe he *is* innocent, and his surviving family—if he has any—is entitled to some kind of compensation for his wrongful imprisonment. Or maybe for Edith's family, if this journal *proves* they didn't catch the real killer."

Charlie pans the camera across the journal, flipping it open to show the inscribed name. "Don't get your hopes up, Win. I'm not sure the prison-industrial complex is used to owning up to its mistakes." He must catch the way my brow tightens and my shoulders fall, because he gently tacks on, "But I think giving families answers is just as noble a cause. Even if nothing bigger comes of it." His gaze drops to the journal. "So . . . you want to do the honors?"

Today isn't turning out how I expected it to at all. I thought it would be a fun romp of an episode, filmed with my brother and his usual antics. Not a reunion with my estranged husband, culminating in a raunchy, out-of-pocket makeout session, and discovering a journal which could *actually* help us solve this decades-old crime. This is so much bigger than our web series and the extra money that trickles in from it. This is peoples' real lives potentially being impacted by whatever we're about to uncover.

River just may kill me for what I'm about to do.

But if I made the correct choice two years ago, if I've been doing right by my brother ever since, if all my sacrifices are worth it, then I think he'll forgive me.

"Cut the camera." I jut my chin toward it.

Charlie's head cants. "You're sure?"

"I'm sure." I pick up the journal. "Let's read this thing."

Entry No. 1

It has only been four weeks and I fear I am already losing myself in this place. I bartered six smokes with J.R. for this journal. Three more for three BIC Crystals from R.Z.. I hope they last me. I intend to write a few lines a day. Must keep my mind.

Entry No. 17

I cannot stop thinking about my darling Edith. How dreadful it must be to die. Every night when I lie on my cot, unable to sleep as I listen to the rats and the noisy pipes, I wish to wake up a brave enough man to tell the truth of what happened to her.

Entry No. 25

Don't think the guards like me much. They think I am strange. Too quiet. Edie always understood my quiet.

As I read out loud, skipping around entries in the journal, sitting next to Charlie on the metal bed frame, he clears his throat to interrupt. "So they *were* lovers?"

I set my thumb on the page to hold my place in the mess of sloppy cursive, each line split in half in an attempt to save space. "Edith saved their letters. James wrote she understood him. It's seeming more plausible."

Charlie removes his glasses to clean them with the hem of his T-shirt, nodding toward the journal in my hands. "Keep going."

Entry No. 35
A stronger man would not have run from the love of a woman like Edith Page. Perhaps I deserve to rot in a place like this. If not for a crime I didn't commit, for the cowardice I let cloud my judgement.

Entry No. 38
One day A.P. will get what is coming to him, by the grace of God.

Entry No. 49
I picked up a Bible to pass time today and was reminded of Exodus 20:14—Thou shalt not commit adultery. It is sinful to have intimate relations outside of the holy covenant of marriage. Perhaps that is why I am locked up here—to atone.
What I felt for Edie never felt like sin. Though perhaps Eve would say the same about the apple.

My confidence in James's guilt waffles. I bite my lip and turn to Charlie. "Do you think Edith's husband caught her with James? Was *he* the one who did this?"

His brows lift. "It's always the husband, isn't it?"

Something akin to humor passes between us, an awkward acknowledgment of what he still is to me. I turn away, pinching the bridge of my nose. "It *is* always the husband. So you think they would have investigated him. And yet they still ended up pinning James for the crime."

Charlie grimaces. "What are the odds you think James ever

woke up 'a brave enough man to tell the truth' of what happened?"

I sigh deeply. "Considering he never got out of this place, pretty damn low."

I flip through a few more pages, studying the sheer amount of words this man wrote during his time here. Most of it is meaningless drivel—the terrible quality of the food, falling ill, conflict with inmates he denotes by initials only. It would take hours to comb through every single entry. With the weight of impossibility, my shoulders slump. Moving my hand to close the journal, Charlie pauses my wrist, fingers curling around to my pulse point.

"Wait. Just a few more pages. I just—" He shakes his head like a dog freeing itself of water after a swim, trying to shake out whatever thought is bothering him. "I think you should keep going."

I turn down the corners of my smirk. "Another intuitive feeling, Charlie?"

He scoffs. "Whatever you call it. Just keep going."

When I glance down at the journal, I feel it too—a sure warmth spreading through my chest, expanding inside me, a quiet encouragement stroking against my ribs. We found this artifact for a reason. The Knowing, deep inside me, has never steered me wrong. I pry the pages back open, right where we left off.

My heart stops at what I read.

Entry No. 54

Perhaps it was the fever, or the slow loss of my mind in this place, but last night I wrote a letter. I detailed everything about what happened the night my sweet Edie met God. It is a risk, as bold as I may ever take, but I have asked to speak with the warden. I plan to pass along this confession, this detailed account of the truth, and ask for true justice to be served. I only hope my family forgives me.

The shock rises in me like a cresting wave, crashing and

breaking against all my doubts. River's hope was well-placed after all.

"Charlie," I say slowly. "I think . . . I think he may really be innocent."

Entry No. 55

Warden Rhymes filed my letter away in one of his many cabinets. Said he would "consider" what I shared. I fear some men are so flawed, they lose interest in the truth.

Blood raging through my arteries, I flip through the next few pages in search of a follow-up—anything to denote the warden at least *attempted* to reach out to the proper authorities about James's letter. But there's nothing. My lip curls back as I flip through more pages. It's useless, anyway. We both know how James's story ends.

"I don't get it," I mutter. "He shared the story of what happened and . . . what? The warden did nothing?"

"Are you really so surprised?" Charlie asks flatly. He taps the page. "James says so right there. *Not all men are interested in the truth.*"

My torso twists, facing his. "Do you think . . . is it completely unhinged of me to wonder if maybe . . . *maybe* some evidence of James's confession is still around here somewhere? Like maybe that letter got left behind in the move, or . . ."

Pity loops around the edges of his smile, downturning it as he looks at me. "Unhinged? No. Recklessly optimistic? Maybe." He shrugs. "But what do we have to lose by checking?"

"Your storm?"

He pulls out his phone, checks his radar. "Still at least an hour away."

"You're in this now," I deduce, cocking my head.

He stands, one eye squinting as his mouth lifts unevenly. "I've been in it since I offered to help. But yeah, I guess I do better with more . . . tangible things."

"I'll take it." His large hand turns over, extending itself to me. I grin at it and grip it, letting him help me up. Sharp, hot lightning radiates from my hip as I put weight on it, the pain swirling down my leg, and I wince.

"You okay?"

"Fine," I grit out. "Bad hip."

His lips part. For some reason, his surprise—or maybe his remembrance—sends a flare down my spine.

"Still?"

"Mhmm." I massage the pain away as I tuck the journal to my side and attempt a subject change. "You think we can hunt down the warden's office in a place this big in under two hours?"

His eyes narrow, irises sweeping upward, as he digs through whatever's circulating his head. "I think it's across the yard. I found a blueprint of this place online a few days ago. Should've saved it, but the watch tower seemed simple enough."

Laughter peels from my chest as my head tips backward. "Oh my god. How did I *know* you had a map to this place?"

Like it's a contagious disease, a laugh leaks from his chest too as he watches me keenly, like he's trying to commit this sound to memory—the way my lips curl with the movement. His voice drops, tipping on the edge of far too intimate, as he says, "Maybe because I've never been a mystery to you, Win."

Our eyes lock and the size of the compact cell shrinks even tighter, stealing every last molecule of oxygen from the air around me. A breath snags in my throat, my lower lip falling open against my will, as the ice beneath his heavy lids shoots right down my spine, freezing me in place. He's right—he's never been a mystery to me. Generously, he never held anything back when it came to me. I wish I could say the same.

His gaze falls to my mouth and my heart cinches, laced tight like a pointe shoe tied around an ankle, as my core tightens. For as hasty as it was, kissing him in the dining hall satiated a deep-seated need inside me that had gone untouched since I packed my bag and left. Every inch of my skin charges, reacting to his proximity, like we're opposing ends of two magnets, helplessly drawn to each other, and without thinking, I lean a little closer.

Mangled and low, my stomach growls. The noise slices right through our spell, and my cheeks flame.

"Adrenaline always makes me hungry," I mumble, looking down at his shoes.

"I know," he murmurs. "I have some granola bars in my backpack." Charlie waves me out of the cell. "C'mon. I'll share."

chapter 16

OF COURSE CHARLIE brought my favorite crumbly, messy Nature Valley bars. I used to hoard them in my dorm like a squirrel packing nuts away for winter. Our pantry at home was always stocked with a Costco-sized box of them.

We sit across from each other at one of the tables in the dining hall, crunching into our respective granola bars. I keep my knees positioned to the side of the seat to avoid any accidental touches between us.

"The warden's office is on the other side of the yard," he says after a swallow. "There might be an exit on this side of the prison, but we *know* the other cell block has an exit. For time's sake, I think we should head back that way."

I nod slowly as I crunch. "Yeah. That makes sense. The warden's office is a separate building?"

"Uh-huh." He swallows. "I think the warden used to live on the premises. There's a whole residential unit at the back of the yard, per the blueprint."

I chew the inside of my cheek, staring down at my granola bar. "What if we can't get inside?"

Charlie shrugs. "Then we can't get inside. Look, Win"—he

levels with me, eye to eye—"I'll be completely honest with you. I'm not sure we're gonna find anything at all. It's been *decades*, not to mention this place closed down. You'd think they'd clean out all the records."

"But—"

"*But*"—he tilts his chin down, looking at me through his thick lashes—"I think it's strange as hell we found that journal, so who knows what else we might find? I can't promise it'll work out, but we can try."

As I pop the last bite of granola bar in my mouth, crumpling the plastic wrapper, Charlie slides another across the table and holds his hand out for my trash. I pass it over and smile in quiet thanks before tearing into the next.

"Hey, Charlie?" I swallow my bite.

"Yeah?"

"Why'd you really leave the forecasting office?" Dropping my voice, I add, "You loved that job."

The question has been stuck in the back of my head all day. It's one detail I can't seem to reconcile. From the first time we grabbed lunch together on campus, I've known working as a forecaster had been his dream since he was a kid. It doesn't compute why he'd give up something he fought so hard for.

"I wanted to help people." He shrugs, looking down at the wrapper in his hands as he starts to fold it into a neat rectangle. "Don't get me wrong, I loved all the data analysis, but all I could do is tell people 'Hey, this area *might* see something scary on this day.'"

"How does chasing help, though? Isn't it about data gathering too?"

"It is. But our crew live streams our chases, and our footage is syndicated with other chasers through this bigger network we're in. We reach thousands and thousands of people in real time. Sometimes our viewers will have friends or family in the risk areas, and something'll touch down, and they'll text them, only to find out that person had no idea there was even a risk of severe weather that day." He takes a bite, chews, swallows. "A lot of the time, chasers are the first people to confirm a tornado on the ground. We're able to warn communities even faster than local networks sometimes. We see them with our own eyes. We can let viewers know if it's rain wrapped, or a huge wedge, or exactly what street it's heading toward. We're the first on scene to help clean up in the aftermath."

I've tried not to watch very many of the Saddle Up Storm Chasers videos. I really have. I can count on two hands the number of streams I've watched (okay, maybe three hands). He's right. There's always dozens of comments in the stream chat thanking them for what they do. Someone even mentioned they texted their parents, who lived in the warning zone, telling them to get to shelter. One moment on a stream that popped up on my home feed a few months ago stands out in stunning clarity, after hearing this reasoning. Their team just missed a passing storm in a small town in southeast Dallas. But even as the dark sky dissipated, the guys drove around a damaged neighborhood, handing out pallets of water bottles, and asking if anyone needed help clearing debris.

The wrapper in Charlie's hands is a smooth, flat bar now. "I don't think I ever told you, but my mom lost her best friend in a tornado. I was in sixth grade, and all I remember is that it was rainy. My dad was in Chicago for some architecture conference, and Mom threw me and my brothers into the backseat of the van. Didn't even bother buckling us before she took off. I'll never forget the sight of it. Whole houses, reduced to toothpicks. Her friend, Liz, didn't make it."

"I'm so sorry." Sympathy for Katherine pangs in my chest as I resist the urge to reach out and touch him. Growing up in Kansas, the blare of a tornado siren was something you came to expect in the spring. Most people didn't pay them much mind. It was more of a nuisance than anything. "I guess it's easy to forget how dangerous they can really be when most of the ones back home were EF1s at worst."

Charlie growls. "The Enhanced Fujita scale is so flawed. It's damage-ranked, and doesn't take into account wind speeds or anything. So you could have a giant EF5 wedge that would decimate a neighborhood rip through a corn field and it'll be documented as an EF2. We should be implementing radar-based wind speed measurements *alongside* damage assessments to categorize storm strength. As we overbuild, and what were once rural areas develop, we're going to see more and more damaging storms, simply because we have more people in the *way* of them."

I always knew Charlie loved weather—good, bad, rare. And maybe we just fell into routine when we were still together, but I never saw much of this side of him: intensely passionate to the point of frustration. Was severe storms the interest he poured himself into as distraction in my absence?

"Anyway, after what happened to my mom's friend, I was obsessed with wondering *why* it happened. How could I help prevent that from happening to someone else? Kinda kick-started the whole weather thing for me. But yeah, it's the helping people I really want to do. It's easier being the boots on the ground."

My heart squeezes. It's another tally mark in the seemingly-infinite column of REASONS CHARLES ROSENHOTH IS A GOOD PERSON. He does what he does so he can help prevent what happened to his family from happening to another, as best he can.

"That's why you were so bitter about today," I mutter, without thinking. Not because he takes issue with Garrett's leadership. Because he likes being ready to assist.

He looks at me like I whipped out a sonnet in perfect Spanish. "You picked up on that?"

I let a tentative smile spread. "Like you said, you've never been a mystery to me, Flower Boy."

He snorts, running a hand through his hair, and it's hard to tell in the dim light, but I swear a blush kisses the peaks of his cheekbones, creeping back toward his ears. Maybe that old nickname was a dangerous play. "Yeah. Well. The fact I've had enough free time to run around talking to ghosts with you all afternoon is enough evidence for how boring this shit is. And Garrett's been extra picky about it, too. Which, I get—it's been a tough season for us. The grant money from the storm photography competition would keep us afloat well into next year. But yeah, I get antsy."

Like his words manifesting to life, he stands and stretches his arms over his head, his shirt lifting just enough to show off the light, creamy skin of his stomach. He pivots and picks up the audio recorder on the table behind us.

"What got you into all of"—he shimmies the recorder in the air—"this?" He sets the recorder by my backpack then crosses the room to grab the other.

"River did, actually." My gaze drops and softens on the recorder, everything at its edges fuzzing, as I'm drawn back, two years into the past.

When I drove back north that fall, leaving my life here behind, the promise of the paranormal was the one thing that would get my brother out of bed. River and I spent our nights chasing ghosts, running from the ones that haunted us at home.

He'd cling to his audio recorder like a rosary as we tumbled over the fence of the house around the block where Mr. Jenkins passed away when we were kids. Or as we broke into the abandoned sugar factory on the edge of town and sat back to back in the room where a manager had been murdered by a disgruntled ex-employee. And as we crouched against the bumper of my car on creepy Gallagher Road, jumping every time something rustled in the claustrophobic tree line.

On the drive home, he'd play the tapes back over, and over, and over until we deciphered meaning from the noise.

"You hear that? It said DANGER!" He shook the recorder like it was the arm of the winning prize fighter as we were headed home from another visit to the sugar factory.

"Danger? Play it back." He did; I still didn't hear it. "You ever stop to think you're hearing what you want to hear, Riv? I mean, it's like an audial Rorschach test."

He scoffed. "Whatever, Win. I'll prove it to you. Just watch."

It took him a few weeks, but he kept his word. He proved it to me.

It was a Tuesday night; I was up late job hunting. Mom was on the phone with Patrick, arguing about how much commissary money he needed, as *Ghost* droned on the TV in the background, playing for the third time that day. River knocked on my door and I knew what he needed. He needed what I'd needed when I was fifteen and trapped in that house: to get away from it all.

We wound up back at the sugar factory. I was mindlessly drilling opening positions with my feet, watching dust motes float in a beam of light streaming through the window from the setting sun while River scattered our recorders around the room. Something clanged and the hairs on my arms stood on end. Footsteps crunched against the dirty, gravelly floors, then an exhaled breath hit my shoulder, its heat building as it rushed faster, then dissipated. I scoffed and rolled my eyes.

"Okay, Riv, you're—"

But when I turned around he wasn't behind me. I was alone down there. At least, that's what I thought.

"I actually had a moment not unlike what happened outside of James's cell. Wasn't nearly as scary, though." I clear my throat and stand to help Charlie gather the various devices strewn across the room. "Like a breath on the back of my neck. Something so visceral, so unexplainable, I couldn't help but believe it." I snort as I flick off the music box from behind, avoiding setting it off. "You'd actually be really amused to know *before* that, I was a skeptical debunker who shit on this stuff, just like you."

"I'm not shitting." He brings a hand to his chest in mock-offense. "I'm questioning. It's good to question."

Tucking the music box under my arm, I lift the Spirit Candle and point it at him. "But questioning means you're actually *open* to being wrong. Not something you're great at, darlin'." The snarky pet name slips on accident, right into the deep end of *Far Too Intimate.*

But Charlie doesn't miss a beat.

"You know, some indigenous tribes in the plains region believe those smaller, less dangerous tornados are wandering spirits." Charlie huffs a laugh through his nose as he picks up the REM Pod and cuts it off, mid-squeal. "So maybe I've been chasing ghosts all these years, too."

He meets me back at my backpack, hands it to me, and I smile. "See, I knew I'd make a believer of you yet."

The distance between us is negligible. It feels like we stripped bare in front of each other, but we're both fully clothed. It's been so long since we've had such a frank, open conversation; I forgot how seamless it's always been between us. The throbbing vein in my neck loves the way his gaze slowly drops to my mouth. My chest expands with a strangled breath as I swear he leans in closer.

A twinkle lopes through his eye as he searches my face, the timbre of his voice low and earnest as he says, "I think there's a lot of things you could make me believe in."

chapter 17

THERE'S a new energy humming between us as we move through the prison—reignited with a new, tangible purpose.

True crime has never been my thing. It makes my skin crawl, the way it profits off of talking about the worst days of peoples' lives, the way internet sleuths take things too far, prying into families' messy personal lives in the name of seeking "justice." no matter the cost. The Edith Page Milton case being decades old was the only reason I agreed to this episode at all—and, okay, maybe my soft spot for River's insistence. It's hard to say no to the things that light him up, even when they bug the shit out of me, like when he took up card magic but only had me to practice tricks on.

But there's something about James and Edith's story that compels me to get to the bottom of it, like I am personally responsible for clearing his name, for figuring out the truth behind who killed her. Which is silly. We're just searching the prison for more hard evidence; from there, it's law enforcement's problem. This case has nothing to do with me.

As we pass through the front atrium again, Charlie lingers at the towering windows, drawn to the low slung gray clouds like the tides are drawn to the shore, over and over and over again. The rain's pulled back some, reducing itself to a thin mist again.

"I almost forgot how much you love these kinds of storms," I say. It's so much more than scientific curiosity for him.

The soft curve of my mouth betrays me. I miss seeing him like this: consumed by his own adoration. He's always been a heart-wide-open kind of guy.

"Love isn't the right word." Charlie adjusts his glasses and starts to walk again. I keep pace. "I respect them. I'm in *awe* of them. They're beautiful and terrifying."

I can't resist; he set me up for the joke perfectly. "Wow. Guess you have a type."

"Guess I do." He chuckles.

"That why you can't resist chasing them?"

I want to capture the sound of his laugh on one of my audio recorders and let it haunt me for the rest of my life—it's my third favorite sound of all time. The first is the way he says my name. The second is how he groans when I touch him exactly how he likes.

The levity fades and he clears his throat, an intensity settling in his tone. "Chasing storms gives me a sense of control over them. Understanding why they form. Where they are. How strong they can get. Instead of looking at them and seeing a force of destruction, I see updrafts. Rear flank downdrafts. Wall clouds. Observable, measurable phenomena."

"Keep your enemies close," I mutter.

He nods. "Can you imagine how terrifying it must've been hundreds of years ago to look up and see the sky coming down to touch the earth?"

"Hopefully they had their very own Charlie to talk them down from the panic." I bump his shoulder. "That look on your face you get when you look up at the clouds makes me feel like I'm third wheeling. Like, do you two need some time alone together?"

He sucks his teeth and rubs the back of his neck, like his bashfulness is hiding in the soft tendrils of cinnamon hair and he's trying to keep it under wraps. "Actually, yeah. Would you mind?" His face splits with a grin, and despite the roll of my eyes, my expression matches his.

The soft sound of rain guides our way. We round the corner of the first cell block we explored, a line of light falling across the cracked tile floor from where the exit is still propped open, and the text I sent River telling him about our rigged-up entry flashes in my mind. I pull my phone out and turn off Airplane Mode, my pace stuttering as I divert my attention. Nothing from River comes through, the last message still stating once he drops Payton off, he's heading back to Black Magnolia, so I take the initiative.

ME

> Update, please? Did you ever get Payton home? ETA?

The three bubbles start jiggling on the screen almost instantly —he must have his phone on vibrate instead of silent like usual. Or he's actively texting and driving—god, I hope not.

RIVER

> yeah. heading that way soon.

He already *got her home* and yet he's leaving *soon*? It doesn't take a genius to figure out they're most likely taking advantage of her parents 'staycation' and the empty house left in their wake. I fight the visceral full-body ick that lurches up my spine at the thought. Having far too much awareness of my little brother's love life was an unexpected side effect of everything.

When he started dating Payton, I thought I did the right thing by buying a small box of condoms and discreetly slipping them on his shelf in the bathroom cabinet. But when the box finally cracked open six months later, I wanted to hurl. I was equal parts proud he was being safe, disgusted that I knew my *baby brother* was potentially using them, and simultaneously hurt he hadn't come to talk to me about it first.

The lines of our relationship have blurred so much since I brought him back to Dallas with me, and it doesn't matter how much I Google or how many Reddit threads I peruse, I never feel like I actually know what I'm doing with him. Like I'm one bad call away from ruining him.

It doesn't help that growing up, my parents instilled very different standards in me, a girl, than they did Patrick, and I've been trying to tease out the good from the bad in everything I internalized. At seventeen, I'd been terrified to be labeled a 'slut'— and still ended up with the moniker after Sam Wheeler's glorious fuck up—so it's hard for me to accept that River and Payton potentially getting more physical isn't a terrible, awful thing, as long as it's safe and consensual.

"Is seventeen too young to be having sex?" I blurt, without thinking. I've always valued Charlie's opinion on things, and he was once a teenage boy. Maybe he'll have more insight than me. "Weren't you in college when you—?"

His brows jerk up in surprise. "I was eighteen, but I was still in high school."

"Right." I swallow. "Allissa Lindale. How could I forget."

Charlie clears his throat at the mention of his high school sweetheart, his first everything, the girl his parents wanted him to marry, the girl he thought he would, for a time. "Seventeen doesn't seem *too* young, but it depends on the person—the age of the person on the other end of the equation. The context of the situation. You're asking because of River?"

I chew my lip and nod as I shove my phone away and pick up speed toward the exit. River's responsible. Payton's seventeen as well. They've been in a committed relationship for eight months now. They tell each other "I love you" as if it's the most obvious truth in the universe. Maybe he's okay. Maybe this is nothing to worry about, not a sign of a reckless spiral, an emotional outburst

—not the sort of mess I would've found myself in at his age. Maybe it's just two kids convinced they see forever in each other's eyes. What's the harm in that?

"Huh. I guess I thought he was older." Charlie ruffles his hair then grips the handle on the door to the yard. "You two have really gotten close. And he lives here now?"

"Yeah," I ease out. The heavy metal door gives way and a heavy drape of rain coming down greets us, pulling us from the conversation. My eyes widen. "That's a little more than a light drizzle."

Charlie points to a building dozens of yards away, shrouded by the mist suspended in the air. "There. I'm pretty sure that's the warden's office." He turns to me, a wily grin depressing the dimples in his cheeks as one brow arches. "Great day to ditch my rain gear in the truck. I didn't think I'd need it, posted up in here all day. Guess we should make a run for it?"

I let out a strangled snort, my cheeks bunching up at the playful twinkle winking back at me from his eyes. "I mean, I guess we—"

Before I finish, he takes off, hollering over his shoulder, "C'mon!"

"But—" I shake my head, full-bellied laughter spilling from me as I take off after him.

Wet and sharp, droplets whip against my face as I jog across the barren, overgrown field; tall, damp grass tickling my ankles. My sneakers squelch on soggy ground as I push hard, trying to catch up to him, my sides stitching as I heave another guffaw at how silly this is. The weight of all my gear pounds against my back with each lope, my hip joint grinding in its socket as my leg wrenches. *Keep it together, dammit.* Let me have one good moment.

Ahead of me, Charlie looks over his shoulder, slowing when he sees how far behind I am, grin stretched as wide as the sweeping tree line on the other side of the prison fence. "You're getting drenched!" he yells over the din of rain.

There's a dirty joke buried in there somewhere, but as an ache builds in my hip, I'm too singularly-focused to dig it up. I push harder, straining to catch up. "So what!"

He laughs and throws his arm out, hand flexing in invitation. I take the olive branch, and for this one rain-soaked moment, let the complexities of the messy history between us melt away. The heat of his palm is a balm on my chilled, damp skin as he tugs me alongside him. Thunder vibrates somewhere in the distance as we race across the grass, fingers tangled, and knife's edge tingles shoot down my leg as the pain catches with a *pop* in my hip. Only a few more yards.

The old stone building grows as we near it and finally skitter to a muddy stop at the base of the short staircase leading to the porch. I slip my hand from Charlie's grip as he leaps up the steps and I do my best to disguise how I hobble up behind him, favoring my left side, and duck beneath the covering of the awning.

"You used to wipe the floor with me when we ran together." He runs both hands through his damp hair, only half slicking back the thick mop on his head which refuses to bend to his will, his back still to me.

"Out of practice, I guess," I pant. What's the point of staying in perfect shape if I can't even dance anymore?

Charlie pivots to face me and his lopsided, easy smile cuts itself short. His gaze darkens as it lowers. Heat clings to my cheeks, much like the soaked-through, thin, cotton Halbach Hunts shirt now clings to my body, leaving not a single line of my curves to the imagination. I've put on a little weight since we saw each other last, filled out all the sharp corners once kept trim for the stage, and judging by the tortured roll in his throat, the way he jerks his attention away, dragging a hand across his jaw, I'd guess Charlie has clocked the difference.

Clearing his throat, he reaches for the door handle. "Let's hope this one opens."

With a squeal and a groan, he pries it back to reveal the waiting darkness inside. We exchange a glance as we peer inside.

"Warden's quarters?" I ask, brow furrowing on the dark stone hallway stretching in front of us. Only a single small window sits at the very end, a pithy halo of light dusting the mildewing bricks beneath.

"I thought so," he mutters. "You've got a little—" With a touch so gentle it has no right to send so many sparks ricocheting down my spine, Charlie brushes a stray raindrop from my cheek. Catching himself, he tacks on, "Sorry."

"All good."

But what I really mean to say is it astounds me how this is where we are, apologizing for any innocent touch. I've given Charlie free roam of my body in ways no other man has ever had. Touch was our state of being. He'd always been hungry for my skin: a thumb arcing my knuckles, tugging my collar aside to kiss my bare collarbone, hands slipping under the hem of my shirt to graze my lower back, fluttering fingertips across my hip when we passed into each other's space at home. On slow Sunday mornings, we used to lie in bed for hours wearing nothing but each other.

But now we say "Sorry."

"After you." I sweep a hand toward the darkness as I attempt to dislodge myself from my own memories.

Things really were so good.

chapter 18

CHARLIE'S broad shoulders blot out what little light infiltrates the space and I keep close to his heels, arms tightening over my chest. Something feels . . . off.

Darting my gaze left and right, my brow furrows. This doesn't look like how I imagined the warden's office to look. No desk. No cabinetry. There isn't even enough open space to *fit* a desk, if one had ever been here. It's cramped and damp and chills crawl up my spine the longer we stay here. Heaviness settles in my chest unlike anything I've ever felt before—not the usual heaviness of a restless spirit, and not as menacing as what attacked me in the cell block. This weight is desperate. Pained. A rotted board goes flying when Charlie stumbles over it and I nearly leap from my skin.

"Charlie . . . are you *sure* this is right?" My teeth worry my bottom lip.

"The map *said* . . ." A narrow hallway branches off to our right and Charlie pivots but stops short, sucking in a long breath.

"What? What is it?"

Wordlessly, he inches to the side, making space between his frame and the stone walls large enough for me to peek around. There are four metal doors, bright red paint chipping off in rolled sheets. The hinges holding them to the wall are as long as my forearm—massive bolts pinning them in place. There are no bars on these doors, only a square pattern of holes, which remind me of when I was a girl and used to catch frogs after a heavy rain. I plopped them in a shoebox; Patrick told me I had to poke holes in it so they could breathe. When I woke up the next morning, they were dead anyway. My stomach churns as the realization washes over me.

This is a cell block.

I can't bring myself to go further than the doorway as bile creeps up the back of my throat. The reaction is too intense. I do not trust this room.

"Charlie . . ." I whisper.

Ghastly shadows distort the filthy walls, bounce from all four corners, as he crosses to the first holding pen. Like a scream from beyond, the metal hinge whines as he opens it more fully and peers inside.

In the shadowy darkness, his throat rolls as his mouth parts. "It's so small. There's not even a window. Must be the solitary confinement unit."

My eyes flutter closed as I swallow back the saliva pooling beneath my tongue and stagger backward. The darkness tucked in the corner suddenly looks infinite, the air thicker than lead as I fight to suck in a breath. Sharp pain twists in my chest.

I know the hollow ache of feeling like you're nothing, feeling like you're all alone in this world. But this cell block? This damp, dark place without even a drop of sunlight? This is the physical manifestation of that reality.

Was James Dewhurst ever confined in these cells, caged like a wild animal? For a crime he didn't even commit? In his journal he wrote of not wanting to lose himself, but a place like this would destroy even the strongest of people.

It's obvious now—this isn't the warden's office. But something brought us here. Call it coincidence, human error on Charlie's part, or something else entirely. But maybe it was James. His spirit. He wrote in his journal about how the warden, the guards, thought him strange—didn't like him. Is that why they locked him in here? Maybe he wanted us to see this place. To see how they tortured him and so many others. He suffered here. All alone.

Dark, dirt-slicked walls twirl around me as I sway. Charlie appears at my side, steadying me with a hand at the small of my back.

"Winnie. You okay?" His voice is so soft, so soothing. It doesn't fit here. In this vile place.

"I need to get out."

I don't wait for his reply and bolt for the exit. As if it weighs nothing, I throw the door back open. My heart rattles the bars of my ribcage, hammering itself in my chest, as I finally find solid ground again on the front porch and come to a panting stop, a fresh ache budding in my hip. Folding at the waist, I brace my hands on my knees and wait for my head to stop spinning.

"Hey, hey. What's wrong? What happened in there?" Soothing pressure moves along my spine as Charlie rubs my back, no "sorry" hanging off the tip of his tongue.

"Couldn't be in there." I wick the sweat off my forehead as I straighten. "That energy was . . . Do you *know* what they did to people in there?"

"Sure, Win, I—"

"And he was *innocent*!" I cry as I pace away from him, fat raindrops plonking on the metal awning above us. "He didn't do anything wrong. And they—they *tortured* him, Charlie. That's what that is." I point to the door. "Psychological *torture*."

"I know, it's—"

"I can't even let myself *think* about it." I tighten my arms around my body. "I—I just, I don't—"

How does an innocent man find himself in a place like this? Because no one was looking out for him, that's how. No one fought hard enough for him. Someone let him down. Left him here to suffer, to die—alone.

Alone. Alone. Alone. Like River had been alone, for all those years. Without me. No one looked out for him. Every damn person in his life let him down. That place was a prison for him. If only I hadn't left him there—

"Winona." It's solid and strong and even and the stability of those three syllables in his low, assuring voice cuts through the panic rising in my chest. "Breathe. Okay? Breathe."

Warmth washes over me as he wraps his arms around me from behind. I let out a shaky breath and turn around, burying my face in his chest as he holds me.

In for four. Hold for four. Out for four.

"Just like that," he murmurs to the top of my head as he strokes my hair. "Just like that, Winnie."

It feels like erosion, the way a river cuts its banks into the jagged earth over a millennia, thinking about what James Dewhurst and so many others suffered inside this place—the fear, the rage, the missing of partners and babies and mothers, the endless yearning to taste free air again knowing you never will. To think about human suffering in general—how vast it is. How wide it stretches. How deep it sinks its claws. To think about how River suffered for years—all alone. The weight of every stone I've placed around my heart doesn't stand a chance against the sheer force of it all. Even *my* carefully-curated strength crumbles in the face of something so heavy. But it's been so long since I let Charlie hold my broken pieces.

He pushes a lock of hair behind my ear as he asks, "You still have panic attacks?"

And it's so tender, so *knowing*, it almost sends me back into a spiral. Because I'm not sure how long I'll get to hold onto this from him, and I know how much I'll miss it when it's gone.

"Sometimes." I swallow back the metallic twang in my throat

and take a steeling breath. "I'm sorry. I don't know what happened up there. It was just . . . too much. I don't know why I—"

He shakes his head, one corner of his mouth ticking up infinitesimally. "You *care*, Winnie. You always have. Big hearts are heavy to carry sometimes."

I stare at him like he's talking in code. *Me?* A big heart? He's got the wrong girl. Right? I'm not warm. Not easy to talk to. Too *private*. I swallow back the thick knot of questions building in my throat.

"I'm going to take a wild guess this isn't the warden's office," I huff as I extricate myself from his arms.

"No," he agrees, running his hands down the front of his pants as he looks around. "But I think I saw another building behind this one through the window inside." He jogs to the end of the porch, leans his weight on the railing to look back behind the solitary confinement building, and shoots a thumbs up back at me. "Yup. Definitely another one back there. Bet that's it."

His long legs seemingly lope two steps to close the distance between us again and his gaze steadies on me, brows pulling taut. "Are you all right? After—"

"Fine. I'm fine." I pop my first knuckle with my thumb.

His mouth presses into a line. "You're *sure*?"

"Yes, Charlie. I'm sure. I promise. I'm okay. Just got a little shaken up. But, uhm—thanks. For, you know, giving a shit."

A small smile tips up. "Sure. Of course."

His wrist twitches and the intuitive knowing in my gut must be fraying at the wires because it swears he's trying to hold my hand. It makes me ache to consider that he's been missing me as much as I've been missing him.

Facing the way I broke his heart would be easier if he hated me.

I jut my chin in the direction of the other building. "Second time's the charm?"

His eyes flick down. "Let's hope so."

chapter 19

THE SECOND we push open the door to the other building, relief floods my veins. It's an atrium, the remains of an office space visible through the windowed dividing wall—a sprawling wooden desk, a toppled over chair, floor-to-ceiling cabinets framing a window that looks over the woods. The energy here is neutral. Empty. It's only Charlie and I in here. Shelves line the walls, mostly empty save for a few stray filing boxes and some papers strewn across the floor. Long forgotten, but they strike the flame of tiny hope in me. They didn't take everything. Maybe they left behind some long-forgotten confession from James Dewhurst. The final piece to this puzzle.

"I'll check the cabinets if you want to start with these filing boxes," Charlie says, crossing to the desk.

There's only half a dozen to search—shouldn't be hard. I strip off my backpack and jerk the first one off the shelf. Even if the paranormal investigation has gone off the rails, a renewed sense of purpose sets my jaw in determination and I feather through brittle, yellowing papers. Something beyond the veil has been pulling our strings, directing our every move like we're marionette puppets. There's a reason it brought us here.

Squinting in the dim room, I rifle through document after abandoned document, until a hazy glow filters through the glass window separating the rooms and I look up.

"You have light in there?" I call, confused.

"Huh?" Charlie pops up, and with him, the source of the light.

I grimace. "Oh my god, what are you *wearing*?"

He taps the plastic lens of the headlamp strapped to his forehead, tufts of hair scrunched beneath it. "Oh, this? Sorry, did you need it?"

I resist the urge to ball up one of these old documents and throw it at him as a grin spreads. "Absolutely not. Do you know how dorky you look?"

As if he's really sending the point home, he adjusts his glasses higher on his nose, a slow smirk flashing back at me. "You jealous, Win? Sure looks dark in there."

All the self control leaves my body. I bunch up the first sheet of paper I touch and hurl it at him. With a *tap*, it bounces off the glass and falls to the floor as I laugh. "You're a utilitarian icon."

He grabs the light and it clicks as he angles it up then back down, like demonstrating its power will sell me on the thing. One eyebrow arches. "What? This isn't doing it for you?"

Wrinkling my nose, I frown. "Unfortunately, it kind of is."

He clicks his tongue, then disappears again, voice echoing through the half-empty space as he calls, "Stay on task, Nancy Drew."

I shake off his obnoxious charm. And I do.

I dig through box after box after box of junk while kneeling on the dusty floor and find not a single trace of James Dewhurst. It's a lot of administrative bullshit I'd have no idea how to begin to decipher, but don't even see so much as a name or initials that jump out from the journal entries. In the other room, it sounds like Charlie's experiencing much of the same, wrestling open cabinet door after cabinet door and coming up short. My knuckles whiten around the lip of the last filing box as I curse under my breath.

I knew it was a long shot. I *knew* that.

And yet it still feels like paramount failure.

"Anything?" I call.

Charlie sighs. "No. Nothing. Just paperwork."

I swing my legs out from under me and pivot, slumping back against the cool metal shelf. Charlie rounds the dividing wall, boots crunching on god knows what beneath his feet, and leans in the archway, arms crossed over his chest as he looks at me. I shirk away from his pity, focusing instead on my peeling cuticles as I pull my knees to my chest.

"I'm sorry, Win—"

"Don't. It's not a big deal."

He says nothing. Simply closes the distance between us and sits down next to me, legs stretched out in front of him. His head rests against one of the vertical boards on the shelf and he lolls it sideways to look at me, still saying nothing as he folds his hands in his lap. Waiting.

I can't help it. I huff a laugh. "Dammit. You still do this?"

He snorts. "It still works?"

I scrunch my nose, quietly admitting *yeah, maybe*. He learned very early on in our relationship—possibly before we even kissed for the first time—that the more he prodded me to talk about something, the more I clammed up. Instead, he'd get quiet. He wouldn't nag or pester or even assuage me of my worries. He'd just . . . wait. Give me the space I needed to figure out what was even going on in my head, while still letting me know he was *there* when I was ready. His patience was like my own personal truth serum; I couldn't help but talk to him when he did it, much to my initial chagrin—and his amusement.

Worked damn near every time. Almost.

He rakes a hand through his tousled hair and murmurs, "You're like a jar."

"Oh, great. Very sexy," I deadpan.

He barks a laugh, bumping his shoulder against mine. "No, I mean . . . sometimes you need to be loosened up before you'll open." Quieter, he adds, "But that doesn't mean you don't want someone to try."

An inhale lofts from low in my belly as our eyes connect. Who on earth handed Charlie the instruction manual for me, and how the hell can I get my hands on it too? It took months of therapy this past year to finally open my own eyes to the impulse, the desire I have for someone to *want* to muddle through the hard stuff to dig up all my good. Someone patient enough, someone who wants *me* enough, to stay while I work through it. And somehow he's known this all along.

I'm not good at peeling back the layers. In fact, I hate it. But Charlie never minded the work.

I rest my forehead on my knees, both hiding my face from him and hiding his from me. "I know it doesn't make sense but I feel like . . . like I'm supposed to figure this out. Finding the journal was amazing, but it feels like such a tease." My groan muffles between my legs. "And now I've totally derailed this episode for no reason. We found nothing."

"Can't you come back another day? Try again?"

"The historical society who owns this place only gave us permission for today. And it's being torn down next month."

"Wait—you asked *permission*?"

His confusion coaxes a laugh from me and I picture Garrett with his crowbar when the guys rolled up to this place. "Crazy, I know."

Charlie straightens. "You still have today."

I turn my dejected scowl on him. "C'mon. This job's a bust."

The fight's fizzled out of me in the face of everything that's gone wrong. So what, we captured some disjointed footage? We didn't make contact with James Dewhurst, not in the way River hoped. We found the journal, but no confession. I'm tired, my hip aches, and I'm pissed at how these ghosts keep toying with me.

The last thing I expect Charlie to say is, "It's not."

I glare up at a dangling light, its wires clenched between the teeth of the crumbling ceiling. "Charlie—"

"Don't quit on me now, Win. You still haven't made a believer out of me. You got one more shot."

"But your storm—"

He lifts his hand and curls his fingers in a hand-it-over motion. "Give me that ghost walkie talkie."

I snort. "The *Ovilus*?"

"Yeah. That. The one that algorithmically spits out words the human brain convinces itself make sense in context." He winks and my stomach spins—at the wink, not the dig at my tool. Because he's completely wrong about how it works.

I tip forward on my knees and reach for my backpack, tugging it closer until I can reach in the small pocket and fish it out. Returning to my spot, I hand it to him. "Charm away."

He cups it in his palm and turns it on.

Charlie looks around the dim room, his headlamp bouncing off the walls like a rave. He blows out a breath and squeezes the back of his neck with his free hand, juicing out the last of his skepticism before he calls out, "Is anyone here?"

I roll my grin between my teeth. *Of course* I believe in this stuff. But coming from *Charlie*? It does seem a little ludicrous. His nonbeliever-ism seeps even into his tone of voice, whether he notices it or not, and suddenly this feels like a middle school sleepover, where you pull out a Ouija board and fight about who moved the planchette. But he's trying. I'll give him that.

He frowns down at the Ovilus, like he's angrily willing it to "algorithmically spit out words."

It stays silent.

"I'm Charlie. This is Winona. We just have a few things to say." He glances at me, like a student looking to the professor to see if they got the answer right. I give a small nod. "We're . . . uhm, we might have some questions to ask too, I think."

It isn't fair how endearing he is, all these years later. How willing he is to entertain something he doesn't believe in simply to help someone. To help me.

"We're looking to talk to someone specific here. His name is—"

"JAMES," the Ovilus reads out.

Blood turns to ice in my veins.

Charlie's wide eyes meet mine and for the first time today he looks unnerved. I'm right there with him. My hackles are raised and my senses are dialed up to one-hundred. It doesn't matter how many jobs I work like this, how many responses I get, there's always something about the eerily intelligent replies that make me uneasy. My former inner skeptic squirming in her boots, maybe.

But my heart's thumping a victorious rhythm. Maybe this isn't a bust after all.

Charlie sucks in a breath, his torso lurching back. "It's—did it just get cold? Did you feel that?"

I ignore him, bracing to listen for the tiniest disturbances, not even daring to breathe. "James? Are you here with us?"

A line carves into Charlie's cheek as his mouth scrunches to one side, his determined gaze focused on the Ovilus, and I wonder if this is what he looks like when he's coming up on the chaotic swirl of a tornado.

I stand. "Could you—" A clatter echos from the other side of the diving wall and my stomach lurches as I press my palm to my racing heart. "Come on." I hold a hand out to Charlie and help him up, dragging him toward the sound.

"The fuck was that," Charlie murmurs, voice tightened by the chokehold of nerves consuming his twitchy body.

"*Ghost*," I hiss, never missing an opportunity to be petty. Then, louder, I ask, "James? Is that you? If that's you, can you come through this device in Charlie's hand and say something? I have a few questions for you."

Thin light streams through the window and slashes over the wide surface of the desk. Past the glass, the simmering charcoal sky is an annoying reminder we're on a timeline here. His storm's closing in. My ghost's playing hard to get. I close my eyes, roll my neck, think of the next prompt to get whoever this is to talk.

I open my mouth, but the Ovilus speaks first.

And all it says is, "ASK."

chapter 20

CHARLIE SHOVES the Ovilus in my direction like it's a bomb about to detonate. I take it, gladly. I'm ready for answers.

"If you're really James Dewhurst, what were you locked up here for?"

Charlie winces and leans into my ear. "You sure you want to ask him that? Don't think it's a sore subject?"

"I'm ready to cut to the chase," I growl.

Except the Ovilus is silent. It doesn't even spit out an irrelevant word.

But maybe the silence *is* James's answer, he was wrongfully locked up here after all.

"Were you a guilty man?" I ask.

"MAYBE."

Charlie casts me a worried look, but I pay him no mind as the corner of my mouth lifts in a smirk. "I guess we're all guilty of something, aren't we?" I was born to parlay with a morally gray ghost.

"ABOVE."

I frown at the word on the screen, trying to make sense of it.

"What's above?" Charlie asks before I can.

The warmth of premature delight that he's coming around to all this spreads on my cheeks, but before I can rib him about it, the Ovilus replies, "STORM."

Charlie and I gape at each other, and my brows pitch, laughter spilling from me like a deluge. I send my elbow into his side in response to the arrogant grin he's wearing, because *of course* he had an ulterior motive with that question. But I can't even be mad; I'm overwhelmed with the level of activity we're getting, with how *intelligent* the responses are. I can't believe it.

Then it hits me: no one else will believe it either. Because I'm not recording. Dammit.

I shove the Ovilus back toward Charlie and scramble to my backpack for the camera. With clumsy hands, I affix it to the stabilizer and race back to the desk as I flick it on and hit record.

"James? Can you talk to us again, please?" I ask, eyes trained on the viewfinder.

Silence.

"You were convicted of murder, but I have reason to believe you were innocent. Is that true?"

More silence. I swallow my frustrated scream.

"Look, James. I'm really trying hard here to clear your name. I can't do that if you won't help us." A big old fuck-you-and-your-camera silence, and I start to wonder if James Dewhurst was actually a raging misogynist. "What? You'll talk to Charlie but not me?"

"Guess I'm your good luck charm," Charlie quips.

"Everyone's always loved you. Even the *dead* prefer you to me."

Sliding his hands in his pockets, he rounds the desk, gazing out the window. "You were always so fixated on everyone liking me," he starts, low enough the camera probably isn't picking him up, "but never the fact that your's was the only opinion I cared about."

Not only does his sudden raw honesty catch me off guard, but I never even knew he felt that way. I stumble over a response as I twist the lens in his direction and he turns, the light from his head-lamp glaring in the viewfinder. "Do you think you could—" Transferring the camera to my left hand, I circle the desk to him. I tug the dorky thing off.

The headlamp dangles between us and I notice how close we're standing. He holds his hand palm up, and I drop it. His fingers curl around it, gaze still on me, but neither of us move back. Neither of us says anything either. And, god help me, I can't stop myself from looking at his mouth, the way it's so deliciously crafted. Like whoever sculpted him pinched a heart on its edges, stretching, stretching, stretching, until it was just wide enough. Worked their thumb over his cupid's bow until it formed a smooth curve. And then, because no one can be *too* perfect, edged the left side up a little higher than the right.

"LICK," the Ovilus spits out.

A grin cracks on my face as my nose scrunches. "Truth or Dare's over, James."

Charlie's smirk twists into something risky. "Guess we dodged a bullet considering that wasn't the dare earlier."

As my skin heats, I twist, feigning like I'm panning a shot around the room. "Because you would've embarrassed yourself when you backed down?"

"Sure. Let's go with that." He laughs, running a hand through his hair, as he backs up, clearly feeling the same need for space as I am. "Look at us. Getting along. Remember how *excited* you were to run into me a few hours ago?"

"What can I say, you're not as bad as I remember," I deadpan, winning a chuckle in response. I zoom the camera in on the Ovilus, willing it to say something.

"You know, I—" Charlie pauses mid sentence and I turn to look at him.

"What?"

He points to the desk. "That cabinet. I didn't notice it earlier. I didn't check that one."

My pulse races. Is that why that noise lured us in here? Was something trying to tell us we didn't search every last inch of this place? I scoot sideways out of his way as he kneels in front of it and jerks it open.

I set the camera down and lean over, trying to peer in around him. "Anything?"

He lets out a low whistle and eases a bulky turntable from the cabinet. "Look at this." Settling it on his thighs, he reaches back in the cabinet. "There's some vinyls in here too."

I squat down next to him. He hands me the handful of paper sleeves and I fan them out between us. Hank Williams, Johnny Cash, Elvis, Patsy Cline, Merle Haggard, Buddy Holly. They've been tucked away in that stubborn drawer for who knows how long, and they're in pristine condition. The wide smile on Charlie's face is tinged with nostalgia as he taps Patsy Cline.

"I grew up on this stuff. My grandparents used to have this one." He shifts backward, lifting the turntable as he glances over his shoulder. "What do you think the chances are that this place still has power?"

"Slim to none."

He sets the record player down next to an outlet behind us, and fishes the power cable until he grips the pronged end. "How about this? If ghosts *are* real, this thing will work. If they're not, it won't."

I laugh and twist to face him. "You're ridiculous."

"*Or*," he stresses as he plugs it in, "I'm lucky."

He flips the power switch, and sure enough, the small screen flares a dull blue. It works. He flashes me the kind of grin that demands bragging rights.

"You're kidding me." I gape.

"I'm absolutely not kidding you." He flaps his hand at me, requesting a vinyl. I pass him Patsy.

His large hands handle the vinyl with care, and I visually trace the veins running along the backs of them as he lines it up just so and places the stylus on the outer groove. Static crackles in the stale air, then leads into the soft, feminine vocalizations of *That Wonderful Someone*. He scoots back and leans against the desk next to me, our legs grazing.

For a moment, we sit and listen. It's an ethereal moment. Thunder rolls somewhere in the distance as I tune back into the soft patter of raindrops on the roof of the decrepit prison. Patsy's rich, deep resonant vocals, the dreamy, harmonious backup layering behind her, the twang of a steel guitar, sends me straight to an era long-past as I close my eyes and soak it in.

"I see that hasn't changed." I hear the smile in Charlie's voice and open my eyes as the song transitions.

"Hm?"

He juts his chin toward my hand on my thigh, where my thumb rhythmically taps to the beat, tracking the counts of the song. *Six, two, three, four, five, six, seven, eight.*

"I don't think it's possible for me to break the habit at this point." I still my hand, curling it into a loose fist. "Even if I stopped dancing altogether."

The hours I spend testing choreography for my students, the brief moments I steal for myself when I'm alone in the studio—it's nothing compared to what I used to be able to do, but at least it's something.

"I can't picture that. I can't imagine a universe where you don't dance." He lolls his head sideways to me, his mouth made even more uneven by the pull of a half-smile. "You remember the first day we met?"

"Of course I do." We speak in soft, hushed tones, like we're nervous to wake the sleeping ghosts of our past.

"I used to love watching you."

"I know you did."

His brow furrows. "You really think you'd stop?"

"If the pain got bad enough," I mutter, rubbing my joint absentmindedly.

"It still bothers you? I thought the doctor said it would heal?"

"I pushed too hard on it," I say simply.

He clicks his tongue, a mix of disappointed-yet-not-surprised. But it's not a disappointment *in* me—a disappointment for me. "Win," he scolds. "The doctor told you rest was key. Easing back in. *Slow.*"

"Yeah. Well. I didn't listen."

"Right. Of course not." A shadow of amusement tugs at the corner of his mouth as he nudges his hand sideways, grazing the bare skin of my thigh beneath my shorts with the back of his knuckles.

This moment's so tender, yielding like an overripe peach when you sink a thumb in on accident. And I plunge in right behind it.

"It was a lot," I choke out. "Being back there. In Kansas. With my family." Charlie freezes—I swear he even stops breathing—and his eyes go a little wide, like he's amazed at what he's seeing and terrified to spook me. "Dance was the only way I knew how to cope with it when I was younger. So I just . . . I just couldn't stay away when I went back."

The pain in my still-healing cartilage had been nothing compared to the way I felt in that little Kansas rambler with the gravel driveway. The helplessness. The hopelessness. The rage. How small and caged—like I reverted back to who I'd been before I'd left. It all faded away to counts of eight as I watched my body move in the mirrors of the same rickety studio where I grew up trading janitorial work for class hours.

"You never told me that," he says softly. Sadly. It whittles out a chunk of my heart, how much he cares. *Still* cares.

"I never told you a lot of things."

"I know." His knuckles meet my legs again, but this time he doesn't pull them away. He arcs them back and forth across the hairs so thin I never bother shaving them. A silent message I hear loud and clear: *I'm here for you.* "You like teaching, at least?"

I nod. "More than I thought I would."

"Bet you scare the shit out of the kids." He chuckles.

I suck my smile back. "I—*well*. Scare is . . . a strong word."

"Right. I bet you convince yourself they just *really* respect you."

"They do!"

His laughter crescendos, and the sound is so warm and smooth, I can't resist joining in. It balms every single scab he unknowingly picked at.

"I'm a better choreographer than I am dancer, actually, so teaching's worked out great."

He scoffs. "C'mon. Don't play like that, Winnie. You were good. Fuck, you were more than good. You were incredible."

"You just didn't know what you were looking for—"

"Bullshit. I told you earlier I believe in the things I see hard evidence for. And that? That's something I've never questioned."

It's not often I feel bashful. Normally, it's easy to convince myself someone's just bullshitting me, but that's not who Charlie is. I try to scrub the unfamiliar feeling from my cheeks. "I really wasn't—"

He squeezes my thigh above my knee. "C'mon. Prove me wrong then. Show me how *bad* you are, Winona."

"I don't—"

He laughs and doesn't draw his hand back. "Don't make me run all the way back to the dining hall to grab the moonshine. Because I *will* make you drink on that."

"You're embarrassing me in front of my friends," I whine, waving a hand vaguely around us as I try and fail to swallow my grin.

He drops his voice into a ridiculously deep, growly register, the perfect parody of a grumpy dad. "I never liked the company you kept. Seemed a little dead in the eyes."

That's when I burst, folding in half with shaking laughter, and he does too. I curl sideways, leaning my weight on him, and his arm instinctively wraps around my waist, tightening around me as

I clutch at the front of his T-shirt. Gripping my hips, he attempts to push me to my feet, both of us struggling to breathe. Even still, that possessive hold on my body does embarrassing things to me, specifically the spot between my legs, shocking my awareness like a bolt of energy. It's the only reason I get it together, gasping for air as my side stitches and I extricate myself from him.

"Okay, okay! Fine." I stand. "But only so you'll stop harassing me."

chapter 21

I FLICK the camera off as I melt back into the music, listening for its pulse. Patsy's singing one I don't recognize, something about cigarettes in an ashtray, and the more I track the lyrics, the more I try to tune them out. Too on the nose. Flipping through the random strings of choreography that live in my head, I settle on something that fits the slow, crooning tempo, a combination I taught my freshmen last fall. As the song ends, I move the needle back to replay it. Charlie stands, leaning against the desk, arms crossed over his chest and a cocky smile looking far too comfortable on his face.

Letting a deep breath fill every space between my ribs, on the next twang of the steel guitar, I move. Slow at first, teasing into the song, this last minute thrown-together performance. My shoulders roll back as I settle into my center and sweep my feet together, arms arching above me as the melody lifts. My leg extends, spine curving as I throw my head back. My foot comes back to the ground, graceful as I can be in my bulky sneakers, and my left foot glides forward, kissing my heel. Rounding my arms, I push up off the grimy cement, claiming Charlie's blue eyes as my spot. My right leg lifts and I spin, whipping my head around.

Sharp as the blade of a knife, agony shoots through my hip and down my thigh. It sucks the breath from my lungs as I wince and fall out of my stance, losing my footing from the shock of it. I gasp, clutching my failed joint as I stumble forward, and two long arms wrap around me.

"I got you," Charlie murmurs. "Are you okay?"

I clench my fist in his shirt, like I can channel that sting out of myself and into the fabric. "Fine," I grit out as the tip of my face burns with the self-pity my eyes refuse to leak. "Stupid injury."

"You're okay." His lips crush against my hair. "You're okay. I got you."

The stabbing dulls into a throb as I catch my breath in Charlie's arms, crumpled against his chest. I want to scream. I want to break something. Fuck my hip. Fuck my broken body. Fuck this labral tear that still haunts me, refusing to heal. Fuck the resting, the not resting, the physical therapy, the aqua therapy, the steroids, the acupuncture, the red light therapy that didn't do shit. Fuck all the money I've wasted trying to fix my broken body.

"That's why I can't dance anymore. Not really." My voice breaks alongside the rest of me, and I burrow into him, losing myself in his woodsy scent. I should've known this would happen—my hip has been aching since we ran across the soaked grass. I'm too goddamn stubborn for my own good.

Charlie squeezes me tighter, and his voice is rough when he says, "Good thing I still can." One of his arms wraps around my waist, the other sliding down the side of my body, and he lifts me, positioning my feet on top of his. "Can't promise I'm as good as you, though."

In perfect timing with the music, he shuffles us twice on a right angle, once on a left, then backward, turns, then repeats it again, moving us around the room with ease.

"This okay?" he murmurs. "Doesn't hurt?"

"No," I answer. "It's good. I thought you didn't know how to dance."

Recognition flickers in his eyes as he positions us in a relaxed waltz stance. The night I kissed him. "Not like *that*. And I never took you as the two-step kind of girl."

"I was a dance-with-my-husband kind of girl," I whisper.

That softens him. "I guess I always felt a little intimidated. Dance is your thing. I never thought I'd be a good enough partner for you."

It's a simple admission, but it sinks like a hundred-ton rusting anchor in my gut.

"I get that," I say, more honest than he even realizes. My knees weaken under the weight of the complex swamp of emotions I'm wading through: frustration and affection and despair, and so much regret it makes me dizzy.

I lean my cheek against his chest. "I wouldn't have expected you to be perfect. As long as you were on the floor with me."

The vinyl transitions into *Walkin' After Midnight* as he takes us in another circle of the small space and reality crashes into me like a meteor—fiery, hot, destructive. A year of biweekly therapy and I can't *not* recognize the hypocrisy in my own words, promising Charlie he didn't need to be perfect as long as his mess was with *me*, when two years ago I never would have believed that about myself. Even now, I find the idea hard to chew on. Someone like him deserves grace. I'm not sure I do.

Especially not after how I handled everything. I was thrown into the deep end, no flotation device, no lifeboat, just me and my own knack for survival. And like a feral animal might chew its own leg off to escape a trap, I severed the one connection that meant everything to me because it seemed like the only way out. So many of my sessions with Christine revolve around what happened two Thanksgivings ago—the way I handled it, the way I bungled it, the way I regretted everything, the way I didn't know how to or believe I was ready to fix any of it. Not to mention the emotional fallout of everything back in Kansas.

Would Charlie understand if I told him the truth? If I told him I left because I was protecting him?

"Hey, Winnie?" Charlie interrupts my emotional reverie, voice smooth as silk as it vibrates from his chest beneath my cheek. I hum in response because I don't trust my raw throat. "That stuff you said about going home—about being back in Kansas? I wish . . . I'm sorry if you thought you couldn't tell me that kind of stuff. You could have. I wish you did."

Charles Anthony Rosenhoth is the antithesis of everything I'd been taught up until the day I met him. He's so earnest, so open, so willing to tackle the hard shit.

"I'm not sure you would've understood," I admit, pulling back to meet his eyes. "You come from such a normal family."

He squints at me like it bothers him I said that, and I recognize the impulse. That bone-deep feeling that no one *actually* knows what you've been through, and how dare they assume. I'm sure he has plenty of stories I've never heard, but I've filed away enough evidence from the stories he's told me, the numerous family dinners I attended, and every holiday at his parents' house. We come from different worlds, whether he can admit that or not.

He ditches the pattern we've been tracing across the floor and sways us in a lazy circle as he studies my face. "Have you ever thought maybe that's exactly what you need?"

His question takes me aback. I expected a tongue-in-cheek quip about the things I don't know. Brain glitching, all I echo back is, "What?"

"Fresh perspective. From someone who did grow up differently than you. Someone who could look you in the eyes and honestly say what happened wasn't normal. And that you deserved better."

You deserved better. Five syllables—a chisel straight to my heart, splitting it in two. A lump swells at the base of my throat as I search his face for an answer of where that came from.

He's so eerily close to grasping the right straw, I have to stop myself from asking what he knows—if he's been secretly emailing with Christine on the side, breaking all kinds of HIPPA laws to extract information on me. My family is the one thing I never really talked about with him.

My hands slide from his chest to wrap around the back of his neck, brushing against the hair at his nape. "So, you think if I'd talked to you about it, it would've been easier for me?"

"Can't say for sure." His forehead tips forward to rest against mine. "But I do know hard things feel a lot easier when you have someone in your corner looking out for you."

"You would've looked out for me, Charlie?" It comes out breathy and soft and more vulnerable than I intended. His hold on my hips draws me closer.

"If you'd let me, yeah." His whisper is laced with what's left of the moonshine we drank hours ago, and I breathe it in, stealing a taste. "There's a lot I would've done if you'd let me."

A lump swells impossibly large in my throat. "I have a lot of bruises."

"I could've kissed them better."

I'm all pulse and self-reproach as he looks at me so intensely it's as if he can see the wave of nostalgic memories playing in my head, set to our soundtrack of Patsy Cline. What might've been different if I'd let him try?

His face tilts, nose grazing mine. My lips part on a wispy exhale. Slowly—so slowly—his hand smooths up my back, and I study the way his throat bobs, the way his mouth mirrors mine. I'm drowning in this tension that's been pulling us together for hours.

His chin inches forward. Hesitant. A quivering breath fans over my chin as my fingers delve deeper in his hair. Pressing up on my toes, I inch forward too, our top lips brushing and his hand flies to cradle my neck. Does this count as a kiss if we stay here forever, suspended in time? If we promise not to move, at least until Patsy croons her last verse? If neither of us closes this infinitesimal gap, can we ever consider it a mistake?

Would it be one? A mistake?

There are no more excuses. No moonshine or meddling ghosts for us to blame. This ravenous want—no, *need*—I have for him, is all me. All us. And Charlie knows it. Because he's pulling me in too.

chapter 22

A FIRE LIGHTS in my veins, the unavoidable byproduct of our ever-bubbling chemistry, as his mouth catches mine with a fury. He's the oxygen to my gasoline and that sweltering heat between our lips is the spark that sends it all into a blaze. It's just me and Charlie and every single kiss we've missed out on in the last two years.

"You haven't grown out of me by now?" I pant as his mouth drops to my throat, his tongue slipping against my charged skin.

"I don't think I could ever grow out of you." He sears his words like a promise in a line across my collarbone.

His hands slide to my ass and he hoists me up. The room twirls beneath my heavy lids as he sucks on my pulse point and the backs of my sneakers bump the desk cabinet door with a soft thud as he sets me on its surface. The heavy wood doesn't even groan beneath my weight.

Body curled over me, he growls, right to my heart, "Put me out of my misery, sweetheart." His hands track up my thighs as his anguished mouth buries against my neck beneath my ear. "If you're done with this, done with me, serve me the papers. Because every day since you told me you weren't coming back, I've asked myself why you haven't ended this." My head tips back as his teeth snag my earlobe and I kick off my shoes. "If maybe there's a small part of you who still wants this."

"Charlie, I don't—" The words catch in my throat as tears bead in the corners of my eyes and my hand tangles in his hair, pulling him closer.

"Don't say it. Please. Not right now." Sliding up the sides of my waist, his hands loosen my tucked-in shirt. "Can we at least have this?"

"Yes," I pant.

"You want this?"

"Yes."

He pulls back enough to meet my eyes, the darkness and want swirling in his making my stomach flip. His lips find mine again, kissing me so gently it aches like torture. I don't deserve his gentle. I deserve his rage.

Thighs locking around his waist, I mutter, "Don't go easy on me."

His mouth pulls into a smile against mine. "I remember what you like."

His palm splays on the side of my neck, inching up and back as we kiss. With a careful tug, he loosens my hair tie, letting all that wild dark fall. His fingers tangle in my roots, clenching enough to make me whimper as my lips part, inviting him in deeper.

I sneak beneath his shirt to feel skin, raking the tips of my nails down his back. He groans and I can't fight my smirk. Guess I remember what he likes too. His Adam's apple bobs up, then down and I trace the line with my tongue, reveling in the way it makes him shudder. He sucks on the sensitive skin where my shoulder meets my neck, the spot that feels like it's been weathered for centuries into a shape just for him.

It's so different from what happened in the cafeteria. Hotter. More needy. Neither of us holding back. Nothing can stop this momentum we've been building toward all day.

I take off his glasses, fold them, and set them aside, uncovering the Charlie only I get to see. He's beautiful like this, his features so heavy with want and nothing obstructing me from studying every inch. I cup the side of his face, thumb brushing his cheek bone, and he intercepts me, placing open-mouth kisses on the inside of my wrist.

"I want to see you." Another kiss, his tongue dragging over the heel of my palm, warm and delicious. "Strip for me."

He edges me off the desk with his free hand then plants both on either side of my hips, caging me in. We're standing so close I can't stop my elbows from grazing against him as I pull my shirt off. My hands shake as I drop it on the desk off to the side, and Charlie drinks up every new inch of exposed skin. Without dance keeping me strict, my body's grown softer in all the ways my heart has not. What if he doesn't like it? As I reach for the clasp of my bra, his impatient hands reach for the button on my shorts. The subtle graze of his knuckles, low across my belly, has my legs turning to jelly beneath me.

When I'm down to my underwear, Charlie brushes a stray tendril of hair over my shoulder. My heart pounds. His palm spreads at the base of my throat, heavy eyes meeting mine. "My beautiful fucking wife," he growls. Then his mouth crashes against mine.

I melt against him and his thumb sweeps across my tightened nipple, pinches it, rolls it between his fingers. His hot mouth moves lower, leaving a searing trail in its wake as he sucks on my peaked flesh. A flick of his tongue, a gentle swirl, enough teeth to make my toes curl. I lace my fingers in his hair, pulling his head down as I arch my back at the pleasure. I capture a whimper with my teeth as he teases the band hugging my hips.

Cradling my waist like he's scared to let me go too far, he shrugs out of his button-up, and uses one hand to spread it over the wooden desk top behind us. With a frantic jerk, he sets me on top of it, hands lingering on my hips as he rests his forehead against mine.

Looping his thumbs around my underwear, he rasps, "I'm so fucking hungry, Winona."

My insides swoop, so sharp it makes me dizzy. I suck in a breath, chin lifting, as he kneels between my legs. He presses a soft kiss to my bad hip, then bands an arm across me to hold me in place. Warm breath soaks through the thin cotton separating us and I moan as my weight falls back on both hands.

"Hips up," he instructs, and I obey, as he tugs my underwear off.

The first time his mouth meets my bare center, electricity shoots through me in waves. It's so intense, and I'm so sensitive, I have to bite back a breathy laugh as I squirm. It's been so long. Languid and indulgent, he reacquaints me with his tongue and I rock my hips against him. Each slow glide feels more incredible than the last and, *god*, I can't help but think he's somehow even better at this. A combination of the two years of pent up want and the thick drench of his pure desire sweating between us. One quick flick of his tongue and I cry out in a whimper. He groans against me and holds me tighter.

I arch up, getting the angle just so. His lips close around my sensitive clit and as he gently sucks it, his tongue brushing against the ache, I pant out more desperate noises. A low chuckle vibrates against me, shooting tingles up my spine like falling stars, and I clench his hair in my fist.

"Enjoying yourself, Rosenhoth?" I manage to grit out.

An *mhmmm* hums against me, laced with arrogant amusement that only turns me on more. Pressure builds low in my stomach; I can't hold off much longer. I don't want to.

We move together like the waves kiss a shoreline, rolling back and forth in perfect, powerful timing, and the tide crawls higher, and higher, and higher. My sounds grow shorter, sharper, and my thighs clench tighter around his head as my stomach hollows out with each gasping breath. Choked and cut-off, my cries echo around the empty room as every good feeling in the world washes over me at once. Charlie tastes me all the way to the end, his motions slowing and easing up as I shudder from the overwhelming stimulation.

My breath eases, body turning soft and gooey. I slide my fingers through his hair as I softly request, "Come here."

He wraps his arms around me, cocooning me in our sweaty warmth, and presses his damp mouth to mine. This is my favorite thing, how we swing from sexy and playful to sweet and gentle without missing a beat. Somehow he always knows exactly which I need in the moment. And *god*, I've missed the way he holds me.

We kiss like we're college kids again—unhurried, with all the time in the world outside of our class schedules. We melt together with each gentle caress we exchange, and I'm overcome with a desire to never, ever let him go again. It pinches, right behind my sternum, and then I'm swallowed by the swell of all my regrets. I kiss him harder, trying to chase that hurt away.

I need him closer.

I reach for his belt, bute stops me. "I don't have a condom."

"Jesus," I huff. "Me either. You think I'd bring one here?" I tuck a kiss beneath his sharp chin. "I still cycle track. I'm good today."

His jaw feathers beneath my lips and he lets me get in a few more kisses before muttering, "There's other risks."

I still as it hits me what he's quietly asking.

Have I been with another man?

Fresh tears bead at my eyes and I blink them away. I can't bring myself to look at him, too ashamed that this is what I've turned my marriage into. That he has to ask this question at all.

"Charlie," I whisper. His hands clench around my hips as my throat goes raw. "I—I haven't been with anyone since you."

He sucks in a long, sharp breath, but says nothing. Makes no move to proceed. And a new fear blossoms in my chest.

"It's fine if you . . ." I scramble to save face. To hide how much that would shock me. How much it would wound me to hear—I have no right to that, do I? "I mean, if *you've* been with . . ."

He cradles the back of my skull, angling his head down so his mouth presses to my forehead. I squeeze my eyes shut so hard a twinge of pain builds between them as I fight not to cry. I don't deserve to. *I don't deserve to.*

"Sweetheart, I'm a married man"—his voice roughs around the edges—"and I meant every word I said to you in our vows. I'm not doing this with anyone else. The only woman I want crying out my name is my wife."

A single hot tear springs free as I overflow with relief, regret, guilt, need. I can't thank him. I can't apologize. I can't come clean and explain everything. I can't speak at all. All I can do is take his face in my hands and pull him in for a devastating kiss, so wanting, so full of yearning, it makes my own breath catch in my throat.

My hands dip to the hem of his shirt and he sucks in a breath as I inch the fabric up, reveling in the feel of his hot skin. I drink up the scenic route across his body: the cut of his hips peeking out from his low-slung jeans, the defined stomach, the broad chest, the —my mouth falls open as I tug his tee all the way off.

Dangling from the thin gold chain that's been hiding beneath his collar all day is a solitary gold ring. His half of the matching set we bought in our last-minute scramble to throw together an elopement.

His wedding ring. All this time.

He still wears it.

I clench my left hand, like I can hide the fact my fourth finger's naked as I stare. His gaze drops to his chest, like he forgot it was there. Instantly, his hand goes to it, thumb and forefinger linking with the precious metal in a gesture so smooth I can't help but wonder if it's one he does often. Another tear must've fallen, because he drops his hand and swipes one away with his thumb.

"Why do you still wear it?" I rasp, not pulling my eyes from it.

He sighs, a sound so tortured it makes me wince. "Why do you think, Winnie?"

His implication cracks right through my heart, all of its guarded walls. His hands fall to the tops of my bare thighs and I can't stop myself from reaching out. Tracing the perfect, infinite 'O.' Even in the dull light feeding in through the window, his eyes look red and glassy. He places his hand over mine, halts my obsessive tracing, and in his piercing gaze I see the rink we used to skate near campus; the cheap blue neons that scattered on the walls the first night I kissed him; the cloudless spring sky the afternoon we promised each other forever.

I can't fool myself any longer.

I love this man. With every inch of my being, every last drop of my rotten soul. I love him.

Sliding my hand low enough to feel his pounding heart, I whimper, "I need you, Charlie."

I mean it in multiple senses of the word, but the one he latches onto darkens his gaze on me instantly.

"I need you too." His fist tightens in my hair as I work on his belt and jeans. "It feels like I only half-exist without you, Winnie."

I'm but a puddle wrapped around his hips as he helps work the rest of his clothes off. He doesn't bother to neatly set them on the desk, just kicks them to the side, not taking his hungry gaze off me for more than a second. As I wrap my hand around the hard length of him, he heaves a sigh, and a soft shade of color on his thigh catches my eye. When we were together, I explored every inch of him thoroughly—that is new. A tattoo?

One hand still cupping my face, he grabs my hip and slides me closer to the edge of the desk, widening my thighs as they spread around his. Behind him, my ankles lock together. He twines his fingers with mine as he lines himself up and eases inside me. I greet the sensation with a gasp, and he traces the bottom curve of my mouth with his thumb, like he's trying to remember the shape of how much I enjoy him.

"Fuck. You're so wet." He groans as we move slowly, getting used to each other again. "You have no idea how much I've missed you."

For a long time, I tried convincing myself I'd move on from Charlie one day. My decision to leave was for the best for him, and the shatter lines in my heart would fuse back together if I gave it enough time. Every wound, no matter how deep, heals eventually. I could survive a scar.

But as he holds me with gentle reverence and his mouth finds that favorite spot on my neck and I feel the exact same as I did before I broke us, I realize I'd been so incredibly wrong.

Charlie was never a blade to my fragile body. He is the spreading ink of a tattoo, etched onto me forever. A ghost I can never exorcise. A constant in a sea of variables. Even if I never come back, I will never be free of him. I don't think I want to be.

Sweat pills on my skin as the clip of our rhythm races ahead and I arch my back at the pleasure we're careening toward and all the building intensity I feel for him. His drawn-out moan as I drag my nails down his back sends a thrill through me. His eyes darken on me, catching my mouth in a deep, bruising kiss, as I do it again. As his bite sinks into my bottom lip, I moan right back at him.

Charlie's teeth swipe against my earlobe as he murmurs, "Lie back." My shoulder blades meet the soft cotton of his shirt as he drags his hand down my stomach, gaze roving over my curves. "Look how pretty you are like this."

I melt under his praise and he crawls over me, my ankles locking behind him as our bodies close in on each other until my oxygen is his and his is mine, our noses grazing. His hands crown my head, his thumb brushing my sweaty hair from my forehead as our eyes meet and I pull in a choked breath as we join again. My nails dig into his biceps and I revel in the low noise it pulls from him. On top of me, his pace mellows and I feel every single inch of movement as I writhe beneath him, desperate for more.

"Faster," I pant.

But he shakes his head. "You said don't go easy on you. I've been waiting for this for so long, baby. I wouldn't rush it if you begged me."

Like the world's most luscious punishment, his hips roll against me so frustratingly slow, building pressure in all the right spots, I can't help but whimper. His front teeth sink down on his bottom lip as he watches the effect he has on me, looking far too satisfied. But it doesn't matter how hard I try to take control, bowing up to meet him, he doesn't give an ounce of it over.

I drag my nails everywhere I can reach—his corded arms, his muscled back, his neck, the curve of his ass. With enough pressure to make him moan, I bite down on his shoulder. The smell of us, the taste of him, his heated skin burning against mine, it threatens to send me over the edge again. As another wave of pleasure crashes over me, the satisfaction on his face carves into pure awe as I cry out and tighten around him, my trembling release cascading over me.

With his moans in my ear, Charlie crests too, one hand cradling the back of my head as we fall together.

Too bad there's nothing to catch us at the bottom.

chapter 23

A FEMININE HAND with vermillion red stiletto tips twines its fingers through a lush, vibrant bluebonnet bouquet, the colors of it so rich and intense even the thin shroud of Charlie's leg hair doesn't dull it. It's unexpectedly sexy, seeing something so beautiful and delicate spanning his muscular thigh.

They're the flowers I clutched when I promised him forever. Coincidence, maybe. They're also an iconic symbol of Texas, the state he was born and raised in. I trace the art up and down, my cheek pressed to the steady rhythm of his heartbeat as we lie tangled up on the desk. I want to stay in this glass bubble moment as long as I can.

His palm glides up my naked back. "That was . . ."

"I know," I mutter. I suppress a giggle against his sternum. "You still eat pussy like it's your job."

He laughs too, squeezing my ribs. "I'd probably be paid better if it was."

I round another lap of the blue blooms and swallow. "What's the story with this, Flower Boy?"

"Reckless decision." Amusement lilts in his voice and he presses his mouth to the top of my head. "Garrett talked me into it. Thigh seemed like an easier place to hide for work purposes. But it's grown on me."

"I never pegged you as the tattoo type."

"What? You never did something dumb after someone broke your heart?" He means it to come off lighthearted, teasing. But after being so thoroughly turned inside out, I'm too raw to take it that way.

Shame descends on my body like the flu, churning in my stomach, heating my skin by a dozen degrees. I don't know how to begin to reconcile the situation with River, with my mom, but I also don't know how I'm going to walk away from my husband for a second time. I push up on one arm, creating space between us.

But, god, looking at him like this is a mistake.

He's bruised with all my want.

"I left a few marks," I rasp, brushing the shapes I dented in his skin with my teeth, the pink beginnings of a hickey on his chest. "Sorry."

He rubs the side of his neck. "Don't be. They're souvenirs." Softer, he adds, "Something I get to keep."

There it is.

He doesn't see this happening again.

And why would it? The moment we shared together was pure bliss, but rekindling our relationship is something else entirely. I've fought so hard to compartmentalize my world into parts—my life before Charlie, and my life with him. But now that the lines are blurred, I don't know how to make sense of it all, can't figure out how to marry it all into one.

I'm just not sure how to walk away again.

I can't decide if the glimmer in his eyes is sadness or hurt or disdain, and I'm not really sure I want the answer. His name is thick in my throat as I choke it out, "Charlie—"

"It's okay," he says gently, bringing my hand to his mouth to punctuate his defeated words with a kiss on the inside of my palm. "At least I get a real goodbye this time."

The granola bars in my stomach lurch. Is that what this was for him? One last time? The thought makes me ill, my guilt over what I've done burrowing even deeper in my bones.

"No," I choke out, tears blurring my vision as I shake my head. The words spill out quicker than I can think through them. "I'm not—I don't . . . Dammit, Charlie. I miss you. I miss *us*. I'm so sorry. Being with you today was so . . . I mean, god, it was like no time's passed. Right? We're *good* together." My feverish gaze bounces like a ping pong ball across his face as I sniffle, desperate to find the right words. "I don't know if I want to say goodbye again, I—"

"Don't do this," he says stoically.

I freeze. The warden's office spins around me.

On a heavy sigh, his hands claw back in his hair, pausing to clench at the crown of his skull. As he releases a slow, controlled breath through pursed lips, more tears build along my lashes. He swallows.

"You don't get to leave without warning, lead me on for months about if you're coming home or not, only to tell me you're not, conveniently *never* send the divorce papers and leave me wondering what the fuck you want, only to run into me here, sleep with me, and think it gets to be this easy." A muscle in his jaw ticks. "You don't get to spring this on me after only a few hours together and pretend like saying you're *sorry* fixes everything."

I angle my neck up, attempting to stave off tears as my lip wobbles, all my usual defenses blown to pieces. "Is that—is that what you *want*? The papers?"

There's a reason I haven't sent them. The thought of losing him—really losing him—makes me feel like I'm ripping apart at the seams.

His eyes flare, so dark and stormy they're more gunmetal than ice, piercing me with ease as he wrenches up on his elbow. "You think I would've made love to you like that if that's what I wanted?" He closes his fist around his wedding band sitting beneath his collar bones, eyes narrowing. "You think I'd still be wearing this if *that* is what I wanted?"

I chew the inside of my cheek until I taste blood. "I'm sorry—"

"I don't want your apology right now. I need to know where your head is at. If you want this or not. Not that you miss me. Not that you think we were good together. Not that you want to sleep with me. I need to know if you want to be married to me."

My clammy skin unsticks from his as I sit fully and turn, sweeping my legs over the edge of the desk. Shaking hands slip my bra over my shoulders, clasp it behind me, as I try to untangle the threads of racing thoughts in my head. If I was the sort of person who got to live a charmed life, I'd be his wife until I took my last breath. Of course I want to be married to him.

But should *he* want to be married to *me*?

With all my baggage and the awful cloth I've been cut from and all the secrets I've kept about it all? With all the freedom he'd have to give up to be with me now? For years, with him, I thought I could be someone new. But it doesn't matter how hard I push; I cannot outrun the place I came from. Two years ago, I made this choice for him. Not for me.

"It's not that simple." My whisper splits down the middle and I jerk my shirt over my head.

Charlie is silent. I snatch my underwear and don't dare look back at him as I slide off the desk.

"Do you know," he grates, voice low with subdued anger, "how hard it's been to watch you blindly believe in these ghosts, when you couldn't find a way to believe in us?"

I rub at the tears sliding down my cheeks with one hand and jerk my shorts up with the other hand. The little button, the silver zipper, are the only things holding me together.

"You left me via *voicemail*."

I armor my arms across my chest and pinch my eyes shut, wilting under the pain flecking his hoarse voice.

"I don't know what I did wrong, Winnie." His voice breaks on my name, the one he helped me reclaim.

A whimper cracking off in my throat, I whirl to face him. "You didn't do—"

A shrill ring projects from his crumpled pants on the floor and we both glance at it. "I need to get that," he mutters.

Still stark naked and unabashed, Charlie swings his legs off the desk, grabs his glasses, and secures them back on his face. Not meeting my eyes, he bends and fishes his phone from his pocket, resting a hand on his hip as he answers, the harsh light of his screen cutting through all the gray. "Hey."

As if in response, the sky grumbles overhead as thunder echoes somewhere in the distance. Phone still pinned to his ear, Charlie gathers his clothes, tosses them on the desk, and sifts through them as his brows furrow.

"Yeah, yeah. Got it. I will. Uh-huh. For sure. Yup, I did that first thing. Yeah. See you later." Setting his phone down, he bends over to pull on his boxers, ass muscles shifting with the movement. "That was the guys," he says flatly. "Nothing on the ground yet, but storm's looking really good. It's been dropping tornados all across northwest Texas—heading this way. It's picking up speed like crazy."

I'm hollowed, a fetid core of an apple scooped out with a jagged knife and I don't know what my next move is. Of course I want him. But leaving him was for his own good. He deserves better than being roped into my mess.

But I can't let him go either.

As he buttons his pants, he swipes across his phone screen, then stills, fingers resting against his zipper. "Damn," he breathes. "That is one tight velocity couplet. Nasty storm."

I have no idea what that means, but the awe lifting his voice tells me enough: this storm's going to be very good for his crew's goal. Which means not so good for everyone on the ground.

"We need to get up to the guard tower." He yanks his T-shirt over his head, ruffling his hair as he carefully pulls the collar past his glasses.

I nod, grateful to have an out from our conversation.

"And Winona—you owe me a hell of a lot more than an apology. You can start with the truth." He pulls on his boots, avoiding my gaze. "Because I know this didn't all come from something stupid my mom said. I'm not sure our marriage will ever work if you can't be honest with me about why you really left."

Setting my jaw, I slip my sneakers back on. "We both know I was never good enough for you."

"Do we? Do we both know that, Winona?" He grumbles, "Bull-fucking-shit." The room lights as lightning flashes, casting his face in dark shadow as he snatches his button-up from the desk, then his backpack, shoving the soiled shirt inside it. "I've fought like hell for you from the very first time we met. It was always me. Asking you out. Asking you for more. Asking you to marry me."

"Just because you wanted me doesn't mean you didn't deserve better." I grab my camera and follow him toward the exit.

"And who said you get to decide that? All on your own? Without even *talking* to me?" He stops short and pivots; I brace so I don't run into him. The rage I wanted earlier, the rage I know I deserve, slants down at me in his eyes. "No. You don't leave a happy marriage because you suddenly don't feel worthy. That's a fucking cop out and you know it."

I look away. What do I even say? Where do I even begin? He has no idea the extent of it. Stiffly, I grab my backpack and swing it over my shoulder, wishing I could disappear into myself, turn back time, undo everything. If I'd never asked for his number that day in the dressing room at Colby, if I'd never believed the fallacy I could become someone new and soft with him, none of this would've happened. I never would have hurt him so deeply.

"Sleeping together was a mistake," I bite out. Eyes downcast, he swipes his hand over his bruised neck painted with the shape of my teeth. "It was selfish and self indulgent and stupid of me. I shouldn't have done that. It clearly gave you the wrong idea."

We stare at each other haggard, deflated, equally wrecked.

"I love you, Winona. I couldn't stop if I wanted to." He swallows. "But there is a lot more I need from you if we're ever going to fix this. And right now, I'm not sure if you'll ever give it to me."

The knife twists even deeper, and so many ugly feelings bubble up in my chest. I wish I'd never run into him today. It would've been easier to mourn him forever than to face this. The walls he skillfully tore down today, stone by stone, slot back into their rightful place and I close the gates on all this pain.

"Maybe I should just stay down here. Record some more." Lifting my chin defiantly, my expression neutralizes alongside my tone. Perfectly bored. Entirely unaffected. "Wouldn't want to get in your way."

His head cants in a half-shake. "We're not splitting up. I'm not taking any chances."

"I'll go to one of the cell blocks. You think this giant stone prison isn't safe?" I spread my arms wide. "I'll be fine."

He rubs at his chest—the spot where I now know his ring hides beneath the fabric. "Things can shift in an instant. I'm not taking risks like that just because you want to run from how hard all this is."

My jaw flexes and I lie through my teeth. "I'm not trying to run."

"Sure." He scoffs. Palm swallowing the door handle, he opens it to the hammering storm. He looks at me over his shoulder, the hard lines of his expression softer. "Please. Come with me."

It feels like it was ages ago he caught me when I fell out of my turn and whispered *I got you* like a promise, lips crushed to the top of my head. The same instinct flares in his pupils now—that want to keep me safe. Another kindness I'm not worthy of. But I won't deny him this one.

"Fine." I brush past him and walk right into the rain.

chapter 24

THE SKY IS CHARCOAL. The air electric. Smooth clouds spread like moldable smoke, smudging darker on the horizon.

Ferocious wind whips my soaked hair around me like tentacles as I climb the rickety metal stairs to the guard tower one slick step at a time. The persistent drone of rain dulls the nervous worries in the back of my head. *Don't slip. Don't slip.* I avoid the hole that nearly took me out earlier, and on an exhale, my shoulders loosen. Almost to the top.

Behind me, Charlie is dead quiet. His anticipation buzzes in place of the words we don't speak, attention pinned to the storm at our west.

I clear the last step to the platform and yank open the door to the observation post, rushing in to escape the rain. Charlie paces to the DSLR on the tripod tasked with recording timelapse footage and I prop myself against the wall, shoulders sagging as I catch my breath. He assesses the camera setup, simultaneously swiping open the iPad on the table which splashes a cool glow over him in the dim tower. The violent reds, yellows, and greens of the radar come alive beneath his touch as he flicks through layers and different views—all of which mean nothing to me.

This is not the easygoing Charlie who breezily explains why he thinks lightning, and therefore chemistry, is sexy. He's methodical and exacting as he analyzes this language I don't speak like it's second nature to him. A bolt of lightning splits the sky, followed by a crack, and I flinch. Charlie only briefly glances up, completely absorbed in whatever he's doing.

So am I.

The way his brows stitch together, how he sucks his bottom lip between his teeth, how he moves with so much surety. He mutters words under his breath that may as well be French to me—*updraft, couplet, wind shear, mesocyclone*—but he makes it sound like poetry all the same.

"You're staring, Win," he murmurs, sliding his phone from his pocket without looking away from the screen.

"Just lost in thought." Flushing, I swing my backpack off my shoulder, attempting to busy myself. I feign like I'm digging for something.

"Chad texted. This system spit a tornado out about twenty miles east-northeast of here that him and Garrett are chasing right now. Narrowly missed a new neighborhood development, thankfully."

He tucks his phone back in his pocket, and retrieves a second camera from his backpack, affixing a hefty lens to it. A breeze kicks up through the window open in front of him, playing with his hair as he brings the viewfinder to his eye. *Click.*

I move to his side, curious to see the storm how he sees it, and my brows lift as I truly take in the view. We're up high enough I can see past the thick tree line to the expanse of fields that run for miles beneath the tortured sky. To my untrained eye, it's a swirling gradient moving from ash to gray, the impressive stacked shape of it like a toppled-over wedding cake.

Charlie captures a few more shots then lowers the camera, admiring the sight without obstruction. Wonder sparks behind his lenses. "Absolutely gorgeous," he mutters. "Been a while since I've seen a storm this clean. Bet the timelapse is insane."

"What's so special about this one?"

"The structure's incredible." He shakes his head, awed. "Those sculpted striations mean this meso has some deep, powerful rotation. Makes it look like a stack of plates, or an alien spaceship."

"You and your spaceship clouds," I quip.

He doesn't laugh but he cracks a smile. I'll take it. "You can't deny how striking it looks." Adjusting his glasses, he draws his outstretched finger in a line. "That's the inflow tail into the updraft. And there"—his finger sweeps left—"that clear slot in the clouds, that's the RFD. Rear flank downdraft. If the inflow keeps doing its thing, we should see a wall cloud tighten up eventually. From there, if we're lucky, a tornado. Although this supercell on its own might be enough to win us that grant money. It's textbook."

Gratification flows beneath all his words, and I'm happy for him. I am. But envy stitches my ribs together. He got what he came here for and I didn't. Charlie raises the camera again and I take my cue to give him space to work.

Slumping back against the wall near my backpack, I cross my arms. The journal was a dead end, with no confession letter to prove anything of substance, and every time we coaxed a spirit to intelligently communicate with us it ended in . . . it ended in me and Charlie kissing. Lindsay in the cafeteria, James in the warden's office. Strange coincidence, now that I think about it.

I scoff silently. *Or is it?* Have these ghosts been playing some kind of twisted joke on me all afternoon? Meddling in my failed marriage?

I didn't come here to have my nose rubbed in all my mistakes and shortcomings. I came here to *help*. To provide closure, to prove a dead man's innocence. And that dead man had the nerve to fuck with me? Very classy, James. The afterlife must be boring.

But I can't shake the feeling I'm not done here.

A cool draft passes over me, setting my hair on end as goose-bumps rise on my arms. My stomach hollows out, a flare lighting in my gut. Charlie's hair is perfectly still. That wasn't a breeze.

There's something up here besides the two of us.

Maybe James isn't done either.

But I'm craving more than the one-word answers of the Ovilus. Squatting to unzip my backpack, I ask, "Hey, Charlie? How long do you think this'll take?"

"Wall cloud's still trying to form, so probably at least a solid twenty before anything more interesting than this happens." Excellent. I only need fifteen. "Why?"

"I need help with something." I fish out my headphones, then the Spirit Box. No blindfold—I must've forgotten to pack it—but I can shut my eyes. "An Estes session. I need a second person. I . . . I know you don't owe me anything, especially after what just—"

He sighs wearily, pushing his windblown hair back from his face. "Yes, Win. I'll help. I told you I would, didn't I?"

He's probably counting down the seconds until this storm passes over and his inner Boy Scout can confidently let me out of his sight. He must be sick of me. "Don't worry," I say flatly. "This is the last thing I'll bother you—"

"I didn't mean it like—"

"These are noise-canceling headphones. I won't be able to hear you when they're on." I loop them around my neck and plug them into the spirit box. "I'll close my eyes too. Sensory deprivation. I'll plug into this Spirit Box, which scans radio frequencies to pick up on EVP, and I'll call out anything I hear. Your role is asking the questions. It's like a blind study—I can't tailor my interpretations of what I hear if I don't know what you're asking in the first place."

A brow lifts as the corners of his mouth tip down. Seems I've finally intrigued the scientist. "What do I ask?"

"River usually starts conversationally, talking about what we're doing here before launching into any questions—build rapport.

You're good at that. Stay curious, nonjudgmental. Polite." I grab the leather journal and hug it to my chest. A good luck charm. "And let's see if we can find out what James really knows about who killed Edith Page Milton."

"I'll give it my best shot."

Lightning tears into the horizon line, trailed by growling thunder, and adrenaline dumps in my veins like gasoline goading a fire. *How could I forget?* All this bleeding electricity creeping closer with the storm—it's a feeding frenzy for the dead. Far better energy to feast on than my meager phone battery.

This is going to work.

I don't realize my hands are shaking until I slide on the headphones and the world goes quiet. I close my eyes. I flash Charlie a thumbs-up, turn on the Spirit Box, and I'm thrust into fractured static.

White noise splices with fragmented radio clips, disembodied voices, leaking chaos from the circulating radio frequencies. My heart pounds as I singularly focus on what I hear.

Sticky air flows around me, bringing with it the tangy iron petrichor so thick I taste it in the back of my throat as I breathe. A shudder rolls through me, the thunder overhead muffled to a purr that's more sensation than sound.

Something comes through. I strain to make it out. "*Who are you?*"

Everything distorts again.

I take three deep breaths. Listening. "I think I hear . . . *apple?*"

My lips pinch. I should've set up the recording equipment for this session. I was so caught up by the burst of The Knowing, I didn't slow down to think. This one will have to be just for me.

Navel to sternum, I suck in a breath. That voice was clear as day. "It's a—a male voice. Sounded like he said *lovers*, or *loved her*, maybe."

Here we go. My nails saw into the hem of my shorts, fidgeting out the restless energy buzzing through my skin. I'm as charged as the atmosphere. Tempted as I am to peek at Charlie and get a read on how this is going from his perspective, I can't risk the distraction right now.

The same voice breaks through the din. I repeat, "*Not me.*"

I feel stupid for it, but I smile. That's right, James. It wasn't you.

Somewhere along the way, as Charlie and I unraveled James's fractured story across this prison, I ended up tangled in the threads. Only hours ago, I'd been dubious at best about his alleged innocence, and now there's a relentless tether pulling me toward figuring out how to prove it that I can't trace the origin of.

My brow furrows as I parse the distortion in my ears. "*Brother,* I think."

I understand the draw this investigation had for *my* brother. The life he's rebuilt for himself is seated in the foundation of his idealism. River *needs* people to be good. For better or for worse, he will scrub the mess until he finds something that shines. Something hopeful. We are opposing sides of the same coin.

But what about this mystery has crawled so deeply under *my* skin?

Another breeze, this one stronger, sends loose strands of hair flying in my face as the ghastly voice crackles in my headphones. "*The river.*"

As in *water*, which the Ovilus spit out in the cafeteria. My pulse quickens. The repetition can't be coincidence; this must be an important clue. Is that how Edith was killed?

Almost immediately, I pick out something else from the garbled noise. "Sounds like . . . *bad.*" Even in the fractured voice, I sense a deep sorrow.

It wasn't just the townspeople who believed James was bad. He believed that about himself too. His self-condemnation was scribbled on every page of his journal, whittling down his life solely to his shortcomings.

But he sacrificed his freedom over a crime he didn't commit—

was dealt a punishment he didn't deserve. I'm certain he was more courageous than he ever let himself believe. Who was he protecting? No one destroys their life like that without a damn good reason.

I should know.

I had a very good reason for ruining mine.

Only what I did wasn't brave. Was it? It was survival. It shredded my soul. Even if I did it to protect my brother, protect Charlie from drowning in the mess. Brave isn't the word I'd use for the way I shattered my marriage. Cowardly, maybe. Every day since, I've been serving a sentence of my own, punishing myself for not being stronger.

A lump swells in my throat as the humming static overpowers all my senses and my hair whips into a frenzy.

But . . . if James's decision to wreck his life came from a desire to shield someone else, is it really all that different from what I did?

Something touches my shoulder and I jump, ripping off the headphones as my eyes fly open and oscillating static is replaced with droning rain. It's only Charlie.

"Sorry, didn't mean to scare you." His eyes are wide with excitement as they slide between me and view out the window. "Things are picking up out there."

It's a shock to my system—reorienting to the world around me. The thick air, the rushing wind, the wash of green in the sky. Charlie's already moving to the open window, camera at the ready, as I clutch James's journal to my chest. So much for my good luck charm.

"How'd the session go on your end?" I ask.

"It was good!" For a skeptic, he's far too chipper, already humming from the thrill of the churning sky. He doesn't elaborate.

We'll have to debrief later. He did his part and the storm he's been waiting all day for is finally rolling right for us. His head's in the charcoal clouds. I set the journal down on the table with the Spirit Box and pull off my headphones. Pressing a palm to my warm head, I take a deep breath.

Two truths wage war in my mind. One: the session went well, solely going off of the quantity of what came through the audio jack compared to the norm. Two: it still doesn't feel like enough. It gave me something, but I'm greedy for more. I *need* more.

I have so many lingering questions about why James kept quiet about the truth for so long, and unfortunately, even the most methodical Estes session would leave non-believers doubting everything, no matter how convinced I am of his innocence. A few vague journal entries prove nothing.

I want the damn letter he wrote the warden.

Rolling my shoulders, I stretch out my frustration. No point wanting something I'll never get.

Peering out the open window next to Charlie, I frown. "I don't see any tornadoes."

Charlie snorts, clicking the shutter on the camera. "No, but we've got a persistently rotating wall cloud now. See there? Where the clouds look like they're dropping down?"

I squint, but it's all thunderstorm to me. "Uh-huh."

"That's where we'll get formation, if we get it. North of the RFD. But—"

I gasp, pointing. "There!" A sinewy tendril of gray sinks from the cloud mass, a rough-hewn funnel.

But Charlie's unperturbed. "Just a scud cloud." He snaps another photo. "Harmless."

I rest my hand on my hip, head tilting. "You said not all storms spit out tornadoes, right?"

"I did. But this one's going to give us something. I have a good feeling about it." He lowers the camera, flicking through his shots on the digital screen. Dropping his voice into a lower register, like he's more focused on what he's looking at than what he's saying, he mutters, "Intuitive spark, I guess."

I say nothing, unsure if the extent to which he listens to me and catalogs what I say makes me happy or sad or some twisted compound of both. Just beyond the prison walls, the atmosphere is boiling, the storm rotating with ripping fury. With each passing second, more sunlight dims into shades of gray.

Charlie sucks in a sharp breath and my gaze flings to him. Silly, because the spectacle is brewing right in front of us.

It takes me a second longer than him, but then I see it. A dimple, protruding from the base of the wall cloud. *Click, click, click*—Charlie captures photos in succession, then ducks to check his timelapse setup. The sharp excitement pulsing around him like a forcefield pins his grin into place. "Look at that!"

Like otherworldly demon fingers, the soot gray clouds descend. I'm not sure how I mistook the earlier cloud formation for a funnel because this—*this* is the real deal. This is the swirling birth of a tornado I remember catching on the local news every spring as a girl. But, dear god, it's so much more mesmerizing up close.

Charlie's camera clicks wildly, but all I can do is stare in awe.

The jagged tendrils reach further and further and further, dust kicking up all around. Until finally, the atmosphere kisses the earth.

There's a tornado on the ground.

chapter 25

IT STARTS AS A SNAGGED THREAD, ripped from the heavens. An opaque cord of spinning cloud.

"You got your tornado, Charlie!" I cry. "There it is!"

But Charlie's absorbed. He holds the camera at his chest as he stares intently, muttering, "C'mon. Give me a little more."

He must've photographed hundreds of tornados like this before. This one's better than nothing, but it won't be winning any grant money. My leg bounces, teeth worrying my bottom lip, willing the storm to kick things into gear. This is the make-or-break moment.

The narrow thread bends and bows as it winds clumsily across the horizon, unsettled and searching.

"Don't rope out on me, dammit," Charlie grits.

But the storm regains its footing. The clouds build again. Low hanging tatters tighten around the core, and it's clear to me now how this system feeds into the whirling column, as if the tornado itself is breathing it in. Feeding off of it as it grows.

Like a burst of writhing smoke, the crown of the storm gathers, widening at the cloud base. Then all at once, the structure fills out and fattens. A solid mass of twisting sky descending to swallow the world.

Charlie lets out a sharp, electrified laugh, punctuating it with a whoop. "Holy shit! It's stunning! Look at that thing!"

His exhilaration is contagious, and a shrill laugh bubbles in my chest too as he snaps a flurry of photos. "It's incredible!"

Lightning arcs above, a rippling staccato through the thunderhead like radioactive veins, and casts an unsettling green glow. Thunder cracks right behind it. This storm is showing off.

But then another funnel starts to dip from the seething sky, stretching all the way to the ground. My brows pull taut as I gape, utterly amazed.

"You're kidding me!" Charlie hollers.

"There's *two*?" I cry.

"No! It's multi-vortex! Like a tornado made up of smaller tornados! Jesus, that's one violent circulation!"

It's like watching a dance as the funnels orbit each other, sweeping through an open field and stirring up more debris—a twisting, whipping fouetté. A chill races down my spine.

For the space of a heartbeat, it looks like the heavens are striding across the earth, a looming titan walking among us. A blood-curdling eldritch horror, a humanoid monster made of soil and storm.

"Did you see that?" I cry, pointing just as the twisters collide, coiling into one.

"We call that a Dead Man Walking!" Charlie shouts over the howling wind.

I laugh in disbelief and swat his shoulder. "The dead man came out to play with the ghost hunter? You're making that up!"

"I'm serious!" His grin is all-consuming, pupils blown wide. "I can't believe I caught that on video! That was crazy! Garrett's going to lose his mind!"

My giggles overflow, the thrill spilling out of me. I'm high off my own adrenaline, mind reeling at the sheer scale of nature's power.

But Charlie's grin slips, brow pulling low over his eyes as he stares out ahead. His levity burns off, cooling into tension. Fist bracing on the desk, he zooms in on the iPad, flicking rapidly through different radar layers.

"What's—" I start to ask.

But I turn back to the sky and—I stop breathing. The ferocious mass of swirling air is seemingly stationary on the horizon.

I grew up in Kansas. I know what that means.

The tornado is headed right for us.

"Charlie?" My pitch leaps and I clutch his arm, digging my fingers into muscle.

"I know." A muscle in his jaw feathers and he slides the iPad into his backpack, already moving to break down the tripod. "Wind shear shifted. Doesn't happen often, but neither does a Dead Man Walking."

The name sounds more like a foreboding omen than a tease this time.

"You have all your stuff?" he asks.

"Yeah, I—"

Outside, the winds pick up, howling as the trees sway and my heart lodges in my throat. I grab the headphones and the Spirit Box off the table, before rushing to my backpack slumped on the floor.

"We're going to head back toward the atrium." Charlie's voice is calm and controlled, but it's erring too far in the opposite direction. Beneath this collected facade, he's nervous. "There's an interior cell block on the east side of the building I scoped out earlier when we were looking for the cafeteria. That's where we'll go. Find a cell with a bunk still attached. Keep your head covered."

A burst of air forces through the open window, rushing around us. *Crack.* Something hits a window, busting through the aging glass. I shriek, lurching forward, as my shaking hands try to make space for the equipment in my bag. Stupid things won't fit.

The door to the tower springs loose from its jamb, clapping open and closed.

"Let's go!" Charlie cries, tugging on my shoulder. He pulls me to my feet.

I pivot to snatch my bag, but something flickers in my peripheral. *James's journal*. The wild wind sends its pages wheeling open on the table. I scramble to grab it, but something goes flying. A square. A folded piece of paper, spinning upwards. I hurtle forward, snatching it. As I rush to tuck it back in the binding, I catch a few scrawled words. My mouth falls open.

Warden Rhymes, you have the wrong man.

My body numbs out, tingling with shock. *Oh my god*. This is it! This is James's confession! This will prove his innocence beyond a shadow of doubt, giving me the answers I crave. I unfold it, desperate for more.

"Winona!"

The Page name was a good name. The Milton name was a good name. The Dewhurst name was not.

God dammit—I just need to know! Why did he do it? *Why?* I skim faster.

The wind roars. "WE HAVE TO GO!"

—if I ever said a word, he would see to it my sister met the same fate as Edith. If I kept quiet, he would make sure she was provided for until her death.

Hot tears bead in my eyes.

There it is. That's it. That's why he did it. He did it for his sister—someone he was desperate to protect.

This was the love James destroyed himself for.

The person who mattered more to him than his freedom. The proof he wasn't the villain everyone made him out to be. Nor the villain he believed *himself* to be.

James was innocent.

And if he wasn't the bad guy in his story, maybe I'm not the bad guy in mine. Another burst of air ripples the letter in my hand. I clutch the yellowing paper to my chest, protecting it. James deserves his retribution.

Maybe I do too.

Charlie grabs my wrist, jerking me backward. "Come on!"

"This is it!" My voice breaks, snapping in half around the growing lump in my throat. "This is his letter!"

But he's dragging me toward the exit, not even registering what I said. I peek over my shoulder and my stomach plummets. Storm, sky, it's all one. The tornado is closing in. Fast.

Green light flashes somewhere in the distance, then as far as the eye can see, the world falls into darkness. Another burst of lightning cracks overhead. Outside, the platform is slick with rain, and Charlie's pulling me so fast, I feel like I can't find traction. Nausea roils in my gut. God, we're so high up.

"Hang on!" I cry, clamping the railing and resisting his tug. "Slow down! I—I'm slipping!"

Charlie whips around, threading his arm around my waist without a second's hesitation, and reels me to him. "You're okay. We have to go."

"But I—" My whimper cracks in two.

"I'm right here, baby." He crushes his arm around my ribs, grip solid as steel, and tucks me against his body. "I've got you. I won't let you get hurt."

I shove the letter in my pocket and knot both arms around his waist, clinging to him with every quivering muscle in my body. I have to trust him.

We descend the wet metal stairs so fast it feels like flying, my heart suspended in my throat as the wind surges and slams against us. He won't let me fall.

"Wait!" I stiffen, slowing our momentum. "My backpack! It's still up there!"

His head shakes as he keeps us moving. "Leave it."

"But there's hundreds of dollars of equipment in there! And—" My mouth pops with a gasp. "The journal!" I cry, wrenching backward. "I left it! Charlie, we have to go back—"

"We don't—"

"But I—"

He heaves me forward, coolheaded composure finally wavering as he bellows, "Forget it, Winona!"

Rattled, I squeeze him tighter and nod. "I'm scared."

"It's okay. You're going to be okay," he soothes, echoing like a mantra. "We're almost there."

A piercing screech cuts through the air, and we both whip our heads in the direction it came from. The electrical fence at the far perimeter is folding under the force of the wind, bowing in surrender.

Time stops.

The commotion dials down to nothing.

My ears ring.

The rusted red paint.

Everything else fades away except my shitty old car barreling toward the prison, only a few hundred yards from the toppled fence.

And my little brother behind the wheel.

"What kind of idiot—"

"River!" I cry, ripping away from Charlie.

It's almost supernatural, the way my fear dissipates. It leaves behind only a deep, carnal instinct: I have to protect him.

The tree line is so thick, what if he doesn't even see the tornado? Thinks this is just a nasty thunderstorm? Is he driving with the music too loud? Ignoring emergency alerts on his phone, like I do? I have to warn him.

I tear down the stairs; they don't intimidate me anymore. But Charlie catches my wrist, and I stumble.

"Wait! I need to get you somewhere safe!"

I twist out of his grip and run. "I have to get to him!"

Charlie follows. "It's too dangerous!"

"I'm not leaving him!"

I clear the last flight and Charlie's right on my heels as I charge through the door, taking off down the corridor to the atrium. My hip joint grinds into itself with every pump of my legs, but it no longer hurts.

"The door's still jammed! Winnie, please!" Desperation tweaks his voice. "You're out of your fucking mind if you think I'm letting you out of my sight!"

"And you're out of yours if you think I'm not going after him!"

The prison moans and shivers as the wind howls louder and the last leak of light filtering through the cathedral windows dims to nothing.

"You won't get to him in time!" Charlie's words peal like a gunshot, ricochet off the stone walls.

It's the same stuck tape that played in my head over and over as I raced down the interstate back to Kansas two Thanksgivings ago. I left my husband then, and I have to leave him now.

I know I should take cover and save myself. I know it'll be impossible to outrun this storm. I know that, with every fiber of my being.

But I *have* to fight for my brother.

A guttural rumble, like the ground itself has come alive, stops my heart. The shrieking wind is deafening. My ears pop, like I'm sinking beneath the surface of the ocean. I clap my hands over the ache as glass shatters somewhere behind me.

"Winona!"

The rush of wind swallows Charlie's cry as it swarms the building, flexing it, like the prison has a pulse of its own. More windows pop. Bare light floods the corridor and I look up. Horror strangles my scream. The roof's gone.

Something solid crashes into my back, knocking the breath out of me. I slam down on my knees and catch myself with my hands. Charlie's arms knot around my stomach, shielding my body with his own.

I scream his name but nothing comes out against the relentless roar of the world turning inside out. Squeezing my eyes shut, I clutch my hands behind my head and tuck as low to the ground as possible. My skin stings with the burn of a thousand tiny cuts as the surging wind blasts dirt and debris all around us. My bones are quaking. The merciless atmosphere keeps churning.

A gasp snaps in my throat, my stomach dropping. For an infinite, sickening second, I'm weightless.

Then the arms around my stomach are gone.

chapter 26

MY EARS ARE RINGING.

The wind still roars, but it's more distant now.

I let out a hacking cough as I breathe in the cloud of dust. My heart is smashing my ribs. My whole body is shaking.

It's over.

I'm alive.

But where's River?

And where's Charlie?

chapter 27

I'M on my hands and knees. My neck aches as I look up. The prison's unrecognizable. Like a bomb's detonated. Insulation falls like snow over the rubble, the strong walls reduced to crumbled brick, as raw sky lords over the destruction.

My lungs burn with filth as I shriek. "River! Charlie!"

The only response is more ringing. Rough edges cut into my knees as I scramble over the debris, nails scraping raw as I dig. Even as the tips of my fingers bleed, nothing hurts.

Where are they?

I swim through the dust-drenched air, heart thundering, breathing ragged. I have to find them. I have to get to my brother. Charlie was right. I'm too late.

"Winona!"

It's a tiny, muffled sound—takes me a second to recognize it's my name.

I turn. A body crashes into me, kneeling in the rubble and wrapping me in a hug. Charlie? *No.* My own eyes, clouded with pure terror, reflect back at me.

"River!" I sob.

He's okay. He's here. He's alive.

I wasn't too late.

Gripping his collar, I tuck my face against his neck. "Oh my god. You're okay!"

Curling into me, he sniffles. "Yeah, yeah. I'm fine. I saw a bunch of shit flying and ran the car off into the trees. I might've dented it—"

I choke out a phlegmy laugh. "It's fine."

He pushes me back and takes me in. "Are *you* okay?"

Nodding, I insist, "Yeah, I'm good."

A tear slips down River's cheek, lancing me through the heart. "I tried to call you, to warn you about the storm. I got the alert. You were still on Airplane Mode." He rasps, "You didn't pick up the fucking phone, Win."

My expression crumples as I fight not to cry again. "You shouldn't have come back. It wasn't safe."

"I wouldn't leave you," he says fiercely, brow furrowing. "You didn't leave me."

"But I did." I cup the back of his neck and pull him in again. "I did and I'm so fucking sorry."

"But you came back." His tear-stricken words muffle against the damp fabric of my shirt and I hold him tighter. It's the most direct we've talked about that night since it happened.

"I'm always going to put you first, okay?" I lean back, meeting his eyes, our broken expressions matching. "You hear that? Always."

River nods, throat bobbing.

He so deeply deserves to be loved selflessly. To have someone in his corner who will give up everything if it means doing what's best for him. I will choose him before myself. Before our parents. Before my job. Before my marriage.

My marriage.

Charlie.

Bile crawls up my throat. "Oh god—"

"The car's over—"

"Where is he?" A sob racks through me as I stand, bracing against River's shoulder. "Please be okay. Please be okay."

I swivel frantically, looking for any sign of him.

River stands. "Where's who?"

"CHARLIE!" My vocal cords are shot, sandpapered down as I trip over piles of fallen stone.

River's talking but I can't hear him over my own shrieking, the name I plead with everything I've got. I scramble aimlessly. Searching for any signs of him. *Please let him be okay.*

I should've fought him off. Should've sent him away to take cover. He was protecting *me* when the roof blew off. He was holding *me*. Then he wasn't. This is my fault.

"Charlie. Please," I whimper, but it feels like nothing is listening.

"You were with someone?"

Oh, god. I never got to tell him the truth about why I left. About River. There was so much I never told him. So many pieces of myself I kept hidden. And for what? What good did it do us? I thought I was doing what was best for him but what does any of that matter if I lose him for good? If he dies still believing he did something wrong?

I didn't even get to tell him I love him.

If Charlie dies, a piece of me dies with him.

"Help me find him. Please." I tug River's hand.

"Who—okay, yeah. Sure."

Frustration and desperation and terror boil up in me and I whip my head over my shoulder, left, right, back. God dammit. Where *is* he? I cry out his name again.

"ATTIC."

I drop River's hand and jerk toward the mangled, robotic sound of the Ovilus. A slash of red is wedged between two stones, the antenna snapped off, next to the standing remains of a wall. I stumble to it and snatch it, holding it to my chest like a rosary. I pray he's okay. All I want is for Charlie to be okay. To tell me I was an idiot for not listening to him. To tell me he thinks ghosts are stupid and not real. To tell me he hates me. To tell me he loves me. To tell me anything at all.

"FRENCH."

"Stupid thing," I sob, shaking it.

"Uh, Winona?" River points.

I spin.

Through the thick cloud of wet dust in the air, there's a slope of shoulders under a twisted piece of metal. A flash of cinnamon hair. My heart pounds with a desperate hope: *Let. Him. Be. Alive.*

"CHARLIE!"

River and I clamber over the hills of rubble to where he's sprawled on his back. Filth coats his skin, blood weeps from the corner of his forehead caking in his hair. His glasses are nowhere to be found, but his eyes flutter open. Every muscle in my body goes slack as I fall to my knees and a breathy, wild laugh bursts from me as tears stream down my cheeks.

He's alive.

I clap a hand to my mouth as I reach out, hovering my trembling fingers over the trail of blood seeping from a gash through his eyebrow. "You're alive."

His eyes are foggy as he takes in the sight of us. "Winona?"

"Yeah. It's me, baby." I cradle his head in my lap.

"You're okay," he says, awed.

I nod, more tears falling. "Yeah. Yeah, I'm okay."

"Oh, fuck," River blurts. "I'll call nine-one-one!" He pulls out his phone, lofting it high like he's searching for a signal.

Charlie shifts his weight on one arm, wincing as he weakly says, "No, I'm okay." He coughs a laugh, wincing again. "I don't have great insurance."

My brows knit together. "But—"

"I'm fine. I just need to get this shit off me." He attempts to push the twisted metal sheet up, but it doesn't budge.

"Let me help." I gently shift his head out of my lap and stand.

"Winnie, no. Not by yourself—" His light eyes flick toward the direction River prowled off. But River's too far away and I need this thing off of Charlie right now.

"I got it," I insist, squatting to grip the edge.

"But your hip—"

"Is *fine*!" It's not a lie; I'm still numb with adrenaline. "Now are you going to put your goddamn hands under it to help push, or do you want me to do this alone, Charlie?"

He puts his goddamn hands under it.

"One. Two. Three." Taking a deep breath, I brace my core and lift as Charlie pushes. "*Fuck*," I pant. Heavier than it looks. It's up a few inches but not enough.

"Try getting underneath it. Your shoulder . . ." Charlie strains, a muscle popping in his neck.

Nodding, I sink lower and twist my body, nudging it beneath the sheet. Jagged metal cuts into my skin as I grit my teeth. My thighs burn as I grunt and lift the weight again with a strength I didn't know I had. When it's high enough, I push it over. Scraping the stones beneath, it topples, freeing Charlie.

Except his shirt clings to his abdomen, soaked through with fresh, bright blood as he sits up, his backpack crushed beneath him. My fear ratchets back up and I sink to my knees next to him.

"Oh my god, Winnie." Charlie clutches me to his chest, hand cradling the back of my head as he kisses my hair. "You're okay. I thought—I thought I lost you. You took off and everything went black."

The smell of iron turns my stomach as I nestle in the crook of his neck, sobbing. God, it feels so good to be in his arms. To feel his thundering pulse beneath my cheek. He's alive. "I know. I'm so sorry. I never should've—"

"Sh, shh." He strokes my hair. "It's okay. You're okay."

"You're bleeding." I press my hand to the wound hiding beneath his shirt.

But he ignores me, tipping my chin up so I'm looking at him. His eyes are wet but a tender smile curls on his mouth. "That's River?"

My heart bursts, more tears falling. What a first meeting. I nod as I brush at the blood crusting by his eye, trickling from a jagged cut near his hairline. "I think you need stitches."

He snorts a phlegmy laugh, passing his thumb over my cheek. "I see the resemblance."

I cup the back of his neck, tipping my forehead against his. "Oh god, Charlie. He was the reason. It wasn't you—it was never you. I needed to protect him. And then my mom—god, my mom. But it was never you. Okay? I promise it was never you. I was trying to keep you from getting mixed up in it all."

He shakes his head slowly. "I don't understand—"

"I'll explain. Everything, okay? All of it." I swallow. "But let me take care of you first."

He tenses, hissing as I peel up the hem of his shirt. His stomach heaves with his tortured breathing. The usual taut muscle is puffy and swollen, pink with inflammation. But it darkens into a mottle of purple and blue, heavy bruising spreading across his torso. Blood smears across the colors, spilling from a nasty gash across his ribs.

I blink back tears as I trace the wound without touching. "Charlie—"

"Don't worry about me," he grits. His hand sweeps over my bad hip. "Are you hurt?"

"How many times do I have to tell you I'm fine? *You're* not. I need to do something about this bleeding."

He's losing blood, and I have no idea if the amount soaking his clothes is dangerous or not, but I can't get caught up in a panic. Staunching the flow is the first priority. I yank my shirt, trying to rip off something I can use to apply pressure, but it doesn't give. Groaning in frustration, I tear the stupid thing over my head and bunch the fabric in my fist. He sucks in a breath as I straddle his lap, and gasps in pain as I press it to his wound with force.

"I'm sorry it hurts," I mutter, damp tendrils of hair falling around me as I lean forward, putting my weight into it.

"Itssokay," he slurs, eyes pinching shut.

He clenches my waist as I press harder. And god, his touch feels so good. A bubble swells low in my throat as it hits me, the reality of what just happened. "Charlie, I—I was so scared I lost you."

His forehead drops to my shoulder, breathing labored. "Me too. You were all I could think about."

The tears I've been fighting spill over my lash line. "All I could think about was how I wished I'd told you I love you."

Charlie lifts his head. "You love me?"

The sight of him utterly wrecks me. The amazement, the affection, the splintered hope, the wet eyes. I huff a snotty laugh and cup his face. "Yeah. I do."

His smile stretches with wonder, the relief washing over him all at once as his hands move to my hips. "Say it again," he murmurs, stunned.

"I love you so much, Charlie." And then I kiss him.

The first kiss we shared today was heat-of-the-moment greed, a need for one more taste. The second kiss was laced with raw desire. But this one, tainted with sweat and the acrid scent of blood and wet insulation, is a homecoming. How did I ever think I could live without him?

When we part, I peel back the compress. "Bleeding's mostly stopped."

Charlie chuckles. "Can't imagine how you managed that when you've got my heart pumping so hard."

I flick a hand out sideways. "Something, something, power of true love."

His dazed expression is so soft and happy that an ache pinches behind my sternum. I made him suffer for so damn long.

Clearing my throat, I climb off of him and shake out my crimson stained shirt, pull it back on, and stand. Then I offer a hand to my husband. "Let's get out of here."

My hip protests as I sink my weight into it and help Charlie stand, then again when I pry his backpack from the rubble. Nothing I can't push through.

I start to walk. "River said the car's—"

But Charlie snares me back, drawing me to his chest and holding me so close I don't know where I end and he begins. I don't want to find out, either. As his kiss crushes against my forehead with ferocious intensity, I loop a finger through the gold ring at his chest hanging outside his collar for once.

"Uh—Win?" River clears his throat.

But it doesn't deter Charlie. No, my husband only takes his mouth off of me when he decides he's done.

River's shoulders sag, the corners of his mouth downturning as he looks between the two of us, completely unimpressed. "So, uh, no disrespect or anything, and I'm glad you're alive dude, but . . . who the fuck are you?"

I choke on a cackle. I should get onto him for talking to complete strangers like that, but after everything that's happened today, delirious laughter is the only reaction that makes sense to me.

We survived. Everything else is gravy.

Charlie snorts and mutters in my ear, "Definitely related to you." He clears his throat and says at a volume River can hear, "Your brother-in-law, actually. Charlie. It's nice to finally meet you."

River's brows pull down in confusion, then spring right back up as realization hits. "Oh, shit. You're *that* Charlie."

"Is there another Charlie I should know about?" my Charlie stage-whispers to me, making me giggle.

But my little brother looks pissed.

"You guys almost died. And you're laughing right now?" River's glare sharpens as he sizes Charlie up, then flicks to me. "And . . . you're still married? I thought . . ."

"It's a long story." I sigh. "I'll fill you in later."

River's jaw sets in the same way it does every time I tell him something he doesn't want to hear, and my stomach sinks. It took months to get him somewhere stable, longer to help him adjust to life down here in Texas, away from our parents and everything he'd ever known. What if Charlie's too big of a wrench to throw into everything? What if—

I take a deep breath, squeezing Charlie's hand at my side.

We'll figure it out—the three of us.

I look between the two most important men in my life, warm, tingling gratitude washing over me. "C'mon. Save the pissing contest for later, Riv."

"Whatever," he grumbles. "Couldn't get ahold of nine-one-one either—no signal. Which I guess is fine, considering you guys felt fine enough to give each other hickeys and shit while I was trying to call for help."

There *is* a hickey on Charlie's throat, but River has the timing all wrong, and now isn't the time to unpack any of this shit anyway. "Hey, we weren't—"

"Bro, I know what a hickey looks like." River scowls and turns on his heel, stalking toward the tree line. "You get onto me for them all the time. Don't tell me the tornado took aim at his *neck*."

"Will you ple—" I lift my leg to scale the pile of crumbled stone and follow him, but my hip grinds and sears with pain. It flares down my thigh like the smoke stream sinking beneath a firework. I groan, hand flying to my joint, and River whirls.

Charlie grips my waist. "You okay?"

"*Peachy*," I growl, leaning into him.

"Here." River's at my other side, taking Charlie's backpack

from me. He swings it on his shoulder then ducks under my arm, sandwiching me between them.

I squirm against their support. "I'm fine. Charlie's more hurt—"

Charlie huffs a laugh, pain instantly carving into his expression. "We're both messed up here, Winnie. I'll lean on you. You lean on me. Okay? Let me help."

I look up at him, eyes welling all over again, and nod. Without a lick of grace, the three of us hobble toward the car parked in the trees.

I wish I'd let Charlie help sooner. I wish I'd let him tend to my wounds instead of hiding them from him like a coward. *This* is what he would've done for me—I know it, deep in my soul. He would've asked me where it hurt. He would've kissed it better.

Instead, I ran. Because I didn't understand the language of feelings or how to acknowledge anything that wasn't: *I'm fine, it's fine, nothing's wrong*. All I knew was the turmoil that knotted inside me, that slept in the cracks of the foundation of my parents' rambler back in Kansas, that no one in my family ever spoke of. All the things we swept under the rug, despite the fact it was thin and flimsy and we *all* knew exactly what was under there.

But loving someone means letting them in.

Charlie's the reason I know this. His love was the model my parents never gave me. Growing up, their twisted version of it fit like a shoe half a size too small—it slides on your foot but rubs it raw with blisters, toughening the skin with callouses over enough time. Charlie was the first person who taught me vulnerability didn't mean weakness, and letting someone see how your scars formed didn't mean you were opening yourself to be hurt.

If I'd never allowed myself to be changed by his love, I'm not sure I would've been strong enough to make the call to take River away with me at all.

I just wish I'd let Charlie see everything. I wish I'd laid bare with all my mess—let him see this fractured kaleidoscope of who I am, and trust that he'd love me through it. Two years ago when everything fell apart in the space of a breath, I was pulled so deep underwater I couldn't kick my way back to the light.

But we're here now. The sun is shining, speckling through the clouds, and I'm going to show him all my tattered pieces.

He deserves the truth.

The only question is if he'll still want me once he knows.

chapter 28

TWO THANKSGIVINGS AGO

I COULD ALWAYS TELL Katherine Rosenhoth wished her golden boy had married Allissa Lindale instead of me—all her underhanded remarks made it abundantly clear. But now that I've met Allissa for myself, I can see exactly why.

As I set elegant gold-trimmed porcelain bowls on each matching plate, I linger at the dining table, a voyeur studying Charlie and his former high school sweetheart talking in the other room. She's obnoxiously tiny next to him, with a chic auburn bob, French-manicured hands, and a dainty pearl necklace that's probably a family heirloom. Her career in medical sales is *far* more practical than my pipe dream of dancing, she goes antiquing for fun on the weekends, and I wouldn't be surprised if she has a standing volunteer date at a local animal shelter or hospital for sick kids.

She would've been the perfect trophy wife to match his perfect trophy life. I duck my head to hide my smirk. Too bad my husband has a thing for girls who bite.

Katherine glides in from the kitchen with *yet another* stack of matching dinnerware—bread plates. Placing one just so, she clicks her tongue. "Winona, I've been meaning to ask you, how's dance? Charlie mentioned you had an injury?"

"Yes, labral tear. I landed wrong last month." I force a polite smile, knowing it's what she wants from me. "Doctor said it should heal up fine with a few weeks rest and PT."

"What a shame." She sets down the last plate then tweaks a dahlia stem in her stunning fall-toned centerpiece arrangement. "You were beautiful on stage. But if you're being forced to take a break anyways, it might not be a bad time to work on grandchildren, hm?"

I'm shocked she waited so long to broach the subject. Inviting the Lindales to Thanksgiving at the last minute after their travel plans were thwarted must've thrown her off. But before I can answer with one of my rotating responses, Charlie swoops in, arm sliding around my waist.

"Kids? Already?" He sips his wine, eyes rolling.

"It's nearly been four years since you got *married*," Katherine says. Even all these years later, Katherine still scowls at the word. She'll never forgive me for stealing her eldest's wedding day right out from under her—and her chance to do the florals.

"Is it a crime to want to remind myself what it feels like to *breathe* now that grad school's over?" His fingertips arc a path over my hip. "And Win's still job searching. We've got plenty of time, Mom."

Katherine's smile is pure plastic. "Right, of course. Sometimes I forget how young you both are. The wedding just happened so *fast*." She throws a breezy chuckle over her shoulder as she slinks back into the kitchen.

My hands tighten into fists at my side as I mutter, "She hates me."

Charlie kisses my forehead. "She just doesn't know you like I do. Ignore her." He sets his glass on the table and cups my jaw, thumb stroking my cheek. "You graduated. I finally got my masters—my dream job. We bought a *house*!" He laughs. "Life is really damn good, Winnie. Wouldn't change it for a thing, no matter what my mom says."

I bite back the reminder that his parents helped us with the downpayment for said house, and Katherine referred to it as "the money we'd set aside for a wedding" at least four separate times during the closing process. Charlie's right. Life is really damn good.

Thanksgiving dinner is merely survivable.

Much to my dismay, Allissa earns a few genuine laughs from me, but Charlie's dad remarks how *interesting* my sweet potato casserole is after he takes a bite, and when I cut a slice of cherry pie Katherine reminds me that *without dance to keep me trim it'll catch up quicker than I realize.*

The group shifts to the living room, crowding around the football game on TV, as Charlie's younger brothers clear the table. Charlie disappears for a refill on his wine, and when he doesn't return right away, I get up to see what's distracting him. I offer to take the last stack of dirty dishes for Max and Luke, but as I stride into the kitchen, I don't see Charlie. But I hear him, muffled and tense from behind the half-closed door of the laundry room. Katherine's voice bleeds through next. I freeze.

"—so *private*. Closed off. I just never pictured you with someone like Winona." My chest pinches as I freeze in the middle of the kitchen. "I thought you'd find someone gentler. Like Allissa."

I pull my bottom lip between my teeth, waiting for Charlie to speak. To defend me. To say anything at all.

"It's not that I don't like her," Katherine continues, "she's just very—"

"That's my wife you're talking about," Charlie warns, low and growly. My shoulders sag with relief.

"We don't even know her family," Katherine hisses. "She never talks about them. Don't you think that's strange? You've never even met her parents, have you?"

"I don't see why that matters—"

"Family is everything, Charlie. Where we come from dictates where we go."

It's the thing I've feared since I was old enough to see the moth-eaten holes in the cloth I'd been cut from. My family name is a stain I'll never wash out. I flex my fingers wide, the thin gold band on my ring finger reflecting the light back to me—the thread that ties Charlie to a life living with all my baggage. Even his mom sees the burden and she doesn't even know me.

I set the dishes in the sink as quietly as possible and dash out of the kitchen. But the world tilts sideways when a rare text from my mother comes through.

MOM

River took too many pills. Maybe on purpose. Ambulance here. Thought u should know

Time stills. My stomach hollows as I read it over and over.
Maybe on purpose? My baby brother?
My hands are shaking but all my thoughts funnel into a singular, steady vision: River.

I'm well into Oklahoma by the time Charlie gets home from his parents' house and doesn't find me laid up in bed with a migraine like I told him I would be and instead finds the note I left.
Family emergency. Headed to Kansas.
I send all his calls to voicemail and keep my foot on the gas.
Keep begging whoever will listen that I'm not too late.

It's 1:52 in the morning when I pull up the gravel driveway I haven't seen in years. An hour ago, Mom texted me a single word:

Home. Dad's truck is gone; Patrick's beloved Tacoma is blanketed in leaves. They still leave the front door unlocked.

I walk right into a time capsule. The same knock-off oriental rug Mom bought at a garage sale; same framed retro movie posters hung haphazardly on the wood paneled wall; same glut of house-plants, magazines, DVDs. And of course, my mother, still curled beneath her favorite quilt on the worn buffalo check couch with an empty wine glass on the coffee table, as if she hasn't moved since I left.

She stares at me like I'm a ghost. "What're you doing here?"

"Where's River?"

"Sleeping. He's fine. You didn't have to drive all the way out here." She waves me off. "Although, it's nice of you to show your face finally. Nice to know it's not *me* you're willing to come visit, but your brother."

Years ago, I would've said anything to placate her. Now, I fight the urge to scream. To dare her to care about someone besides herself for once.

"He took *pills*, Mom."

"You know, we named him after this one." Avoiding my scrutiny, she turns up the TV and I recognize the music instantly. It's River Phoenix in *Running On Empty*, the Juilliard audition scene. "Can you believe he actually learned to play for this role?"

I shrink to nothing under her indifference. Exactly how she likes me. Invisible. A shadow who will bend to her will.

"If you're going to stand there doing nothing, at least make yourself useful. The floors need mopping in the kitchen, Winnie Jean."

The name I hated as a girl because I wished I could be someone else. The name my husband helped me reclaim as something good. It sounds vile on her tongue. Revulsion curls my lip and I snap.

"You really think he's *fine*? You called an ambulance, Mom!"

"He was trying to get high! It was an accident!" She jerks up on the couch. "That's what he said. Stole my Ambien. Took too much—"

"How much?"

She falters. "Well, all of it—"

"And you just accepted it when he said he didn't mean to? Didn't question it?"

Of course she didn't. I see it written all over her twisted expression: the truth is so much harder to confront than it is to convince herself everything's fine.

She shakes her head. "It's just a drug problem. Like Pat."

I bark a humorless laugh. "And you think that's *okay*? Do you even hear yourself when you talk?"

She rises, anger punching between her brows. "Who are you, assuming you know anything about what goes on here? You've been *gone*. For years."

My spine stiffens in defense. I hate how much I look like her.

"Have you heard Patrick's been in county for six months? One too many DUIs. What about how your father left me? He's living in Kansas City now. Did you know that, Winnie Jean? Did you know *any* of that?"

I stare at her, reflecting back the brick wall that she is. I refuse to let her feed off my shock, my guilt, the way it churns in my stomach. This is not what I came here for. I'm here for my brother. Wordlessly, I cross to the hallway, not giving her another crumb.

"Welcome home, Winnie Jean," she spits after me. "So *nice* to see you, darlin'."

River's bedroom door creaks as I inch it open. Everything's cast in aquamarine, bathed in the light from his lava lamp. He's curled on his side in bed, the snipped hospital bracelet on his night stand.

"Winona?" he mumbles, rubbing his eye.

"Hey." The phone calls and video chats don't do justice to how much he's grown since I last saw him, how deep his voice is now. It hurts, acknowledging how much I've missed.

"What are you doing here?"

"Missed you is all," I say thickly. "Room for one more?"

He scoots back. I curl up next to him on his twin bed, fist tucked beneath my chin.

"What did Mom tell you?" He sounds too weary for fifteen.

"I'm not sure if you've noticed yet, but Mom says a lot of out-of-pocket shit. I don't really care about what she told me. I want to hear from you."

He buries his face in his arm. I stroke his messy mop of hair, my nails snagging on a tangle which I delicately unknot for him. I swallow the lump in my throat. If he's not ready to talk, I need to be. Even if I've never been good at this.

"Riv," I start slowly, hoping the right words come to me—something insightful. Something beautiful, impactful. Something *warm*. Instead, what I land on is, "Our family's kind of shitty, isn't it? I hated living here when I was your age."

It floors me, how reckless this honesty feels. But it's necessary. Our family has always been the perfect picture of midwestern stoicism. We simply got up and moved on with our lives instead of acknowledging the tender spots, the ones that bled. We never let anyone kiss them better.

"Explains why you left," River mutters to his elbow.

I was barely nineteen when I made that choice. I was young and caught up in my own world and wasn't thinking about anything but how much happier I was in Dallas. I never imagined leaving River here would end up like this. "I'm so sorry."

"Doesn't matter."

"Except it does," I say quietly, still brushing through his hair. My pulse drums in my ears and I muster up the courage to ask, "Was it really an accident?"

He looks up at me, one skeptical eye peering past his forearm. For six raging heartbeats he's silent. Then his gaze lowers, his brows pinch, and he shakes his head.

And I break.

I crumple over him, tears sliding down my cheeks as I tuck his head beneath my chin and squeeze him in my arms. It doesn't add up in my brain, the goofy little boy I remember being swallowed by so much darkness.

"I wish you had told me." I sob. "Told me what you were going through, told me you needed someone. I would've started driving immediately. I would've stayed on the line with you the whole five hours. I would've done anything, Riv."

I suck in a quivering breath.

"You matter. So fucking much. Not just to me—to everyone. To people you haven't even *met* yet. I know things feel shitty right now, but I promise you they can get better. I'm proof of that. I'll remind you every single day if I have to. I never should've left"— my voice breaks— "I'm sorry. I'm so sorry. But I'm here now, okay? And I'm not going anywhere."

Muffled against my shirt, he sounds so young and fragile as he asks, "You'll really stay? Here?"

It carves out a chunk of my heart. I don't hesitate for a second before answering, "For as long as you need."

I have no idea how to tell Charlie I'm not who he thinks I am.

I'd been so hungry for a fresh start, not tainted by all my baggage. I didn't want to be someone he felt sorry for, didn't want to offer up my family to be judged by someone who would never understand where I came from. I didn't lie to him, but I wasn't fully honest either.

And to explain to him why I have to stay here for River, I have to explain everything else too.

Ever since our first kiss, he's always felt a little too good to be true. Over time, I stopped waiting so fiercely for the other shoe to drop, but the impulse remains, simmering underneath.

What if this is what ruins his image of me? What if this is what breaks us?

A steaming mug of stale black coffee sits next to me on the back porch as the line trills and my foot bounces in the grass. I don't know what I'm going to say, but I have to tell him something.

Charlie picks up on the second ring. "Hey. You finally called." My pinched shoulders soothe; it's so good to hear his voice. "What happened last night? Is everything okay? You're back in Kansas?"

I visor my hand over my eyes as late morning sun cuts across the field. "Yeah, I am. Sorry I didn't get to say goodbye. It happened so fast."

"What did?"

My stomach seizes and I falter. "I—uh. Just some family stuff. We're fine."

"What stuff? What's going on, Winnie? I'm losing it over here. I've been worried sick about you."

It feels like a needle is stitching between my ribs, sewing me up tight. All the work I've done to open up to him, reversed, just like that. This is still too raw to share. My animal instinct kicks in, telling me to run.

"Just family stuff," I snap. "I'm taking care of it. It's fine."

"Will you not just talk to me?"

"Maybe you'd be happier with someone less *private*," I sneer, echoing his mother's words.

"You heard that?"

"Yeah." I sniffle. "And you barely fucking defended me."

It's a red herring, nothing more.

But it works.

"It wasn't like that, I—"

"I don't have time for this."

"What is going *on*? This isn't like you. We never fight like this. I don't get—"

"Will you just give me some space?"

"Space. As in . . . you packed a bag in the middle of the night and drove across state lines without even telling me, and the only reason you'll give is *family stuff*? That kind of space?"

"Yeah. That kind of space."

"Win—"

"I gotta go. I'll talk to you later." I hang up the phone and drop it in my lap.

I split my life in two when I left Kansas for good that Christmas—a clean demarcation between who I was here and who I was becoming in Texas. But now, the boundaries are fuzzing and everything's blurry, and as I sit, watching the sun rise in a place I swore I'd never return, I don't know how to fix it.

But what I do know is River needs someone in his life who won't shrink him. And it's not going to be our mother.

It's the dead that finally brings my baby brother back to life.

I've been back in Kansas for weeks trying to support River however I can, but I finally see the spark reignite in his eyes when he asks if I believe in ghosts and I say no. He insists he can prove they do if I drive him to the abandoned sugar factory at the edge of town. It's the first time I get him to leave the house for something other than school.

When he asks if we can go back again the next night, of course I say yes. It's the best I can do since our mother refuses to take him to therapy, insisting he's *fine*.

He can't talk to our mother about anything real, which is exactly why I have to stay. I have no idea what I'm doing, or if I'm even really helping, but being here for him is better than not.

Even if I hate this place. Even if I miss my husband—the life I left behind. Even if the only way I can stay sane when River's at school is by pushing through the pain at my old dance studio, and picking up hours at the local grocery store to pocket some cash.

My brother is worth the cost of staying.

Except everything changes in late January when an email comes through—a response to an interview I went to months ago for an assistant dance teacher position at Winslow High School. They offer me the job.

Back in Dallas.

I'm accepting the job. I'm moving back. I'm taking River with me, come hell or high water.

But what on earth do I do about my husband?

I pace the backyard, wearing a path across the cold, dead earth, ready to chew my own ankle off to find a way out of this mess. All the texts Charlie has sent me that I haven't responded to haunt me.

Can we please talk?

It's been weeks.

Any news?

Everything okay?

I love you. I'm here for you. We can work through whatever is going on together. Please call.

Can we work through this though?

If all goes according to plan, I will be leaving Kansas with legal custody of my little brother.

It's not that I don't trust him. It's not that I don't think he can handle it. It's that he deserves so much more than being tangled up in my family drama.

A weight's been lifted off of him since he finished grad school. He's made it clear he doesn't want to even think about having kids for several more years. Committing to raising a teenager is a massive responsibility to take on overnight. He wants to enjoy his newfound freedom; I won't ask him to sacrifice it over a decision I made.

Because I know if I did, he would. He'd give it all up. For me. But I could never live with myself if I let him.

It's simple: I love him too much to put him through this.

I dial his number. It goes to voicemail.

I'm taking the coward's way out, and I'm disgusted at my own relief.

"Hey, Charlie. It's me—Winona. You must be working. I—" I swallow back the knot in my throat. "I know you deserve to hear this in person, but I don't know when I can make that happen. But I . . . I can't do this anymore, Charlie. I'm so sorry. You deserve so much better than I can ever give you. I love you. Please take care of yourself."

I end the call. I sit in the dead grass where a patch of wildflowers always grows in the spring, curl my knees to my forehead, and cry.

I pull myself together, go inside, and wash my face.

I knock on River's door and tell him the good news: I'm bringing him home with me. No matter what.

I wait for one of Mom's good days and come prepared to fight; I'm not taking no for an answer. After being back here for months, I've seen the way this house has become my brother's prison, and our mother's unpredictable moods the warden locking him in. No way in hell am I leaving him here again.

After dropping River off at school, I find my mother in the kitchen, brewing a pot of coffee. I take a deep breath, steeling myself as I cross to her. She starts to say good morning but pauses when I slide the manila folder on the counter.

"I was offered a job," I say casually.

Smiling, she pours herself a mug. "That's exciting. Doing what?"

For a brief moment, guilt hitches in my ribcage. On her good days, my resentment feels cruel, but the calm never lasts for long.

"Teaching dance. At a high school back in Dallas."

Her curiosity piques. "You're moving back?"

"I am. And I want to take River with me." I push the folder toward her as her body goes rigid. She doesn't look at me as she picks it up and opens it.

"You want me to"—she squints—"*relinquish my parental rights*?" Scoffing, she sets it back down. "I'm not signing that, darlin'."

"I'll take you to court, then." I knew this wouldn't be so easy.

"You'll lose." She barks a laugh. "What judge in their right mind would think a twenty-three year old is fit to be a parent? Over *me*?"

All seven family law attorneys I called said as much. I don't have a case—it's too hard to prove the insidious impact of my mother's parenting. Which is why I desperately need her to agree to this.

"I'm more than happy to drag you through the system if you want to test that theory." My molars clench. "I'm not leaving him here."

She weighs her stoney gaze on me, and in an instant the good day is gone. "You can't have him."

"He'll be happier with me. I can take care of him. I can put him in therapy—"

"I don't want anyone digging in his head," she bites, jerking the filter basket from the coffee machine. "You know who they always blame? *The mother*."

All the pain and hurt she left me with comes bubbling up my chest in the name of my brother.

"He *hurt* himself, Mom," I growl.

She slams the filter basket on the counter, damp grounds flying out. "You think I don't think about hurting myself? I think about hurting myself, and no one gives a single shit about me! About what I go through! For you! For all of you! I don't get so much as a thank you! And you—*you*. You left. You *left* me! My little girl *left me*. Here! All alone! With your father. He never loved me. That's where you get it from—your cold, rotten heart."

Like the orb weaver spider on the backyard gate spins its same web between the eaves day in and day out, my mom spews the same shit I've heard my whole life. Accusations and threats and twisted truths that used to cut so deep, I stored them in my marrow—let them rewire the code of who I thought I could be.

From the day I was born, she built the walls of my world, and for years, I couldn't see the sunlight beyond the mildewing stone towering the perimeter. She never taught me to trust, to open myself up. She taught me to run. To fight, fight, fight. It's all she's ever known. The difference is now I've seen enough of the world beyond to know she's wrong. About all of it.

Since meeting Charlie, I know how it feels to be loved. Truly loved.

I tune her out, letting her shrill voice dull into static as I focus on the sound of my breathing and just take it. When she realizes I'm not feeding her rage, it fizzles like the stray coffee dripping on the burner.

"What will it take for you to sign this?" My tone is unnervingly calm, juxtaposed with hers.

She shakes her head and sweeps the mess she made into her palm. "I'm not signing away my rights."

"I'm not leaving until you do. I already found us an apartment. The enrollment secretary at the school I'll be working at said they have a spot for him."

She tosses the grounds in the trash, rinsing her hands at the sink.

"He needs more, Mom." My voice cracks. "He's too scared to ask for it, but he does. I can help him. It doesn't mean you'll never see him again. He *wants* to come with me, Mom. Please."

Her obstinate resolve dissolves. Turning back to me, she drops her face in her hands. "I don't know where it all went wrong. I only ever tried to be good to you kids. "

"I know," I say gently, even though I don't fully agree. "You love him. I know you do. Which is why you should let me take custody—it's just simpler that way. *You* will always be his mom."

She crumples and I know I hit my mark. My nostrils flare as I lift my chin and hold steady, resisting my lifelong urge to pick up her broken pieces.

"I can't do it, Winnie Jean," she blubbers. "I can't."

My anger at her curdles into pity. She lives in a prison of her own making, too. But she's caving perfectly to my plan. I shot for the stars, knowing she'd never agree to my first offer.

"So just let me take him then. Work with me. Help me enroll him in school, find him a doctor. We can keep this between us. Does that sound better?" I don't breathe as I wait for her response.

She blows out a slow, defeated sigh. "Fine. I'll do it."

Relief washes over me so ferociously my eyes water. I pinch them shut and whisper, "Thank you."

"But I'll need support."

Money. My mother wants *money*.

"Support," I echo stiffly, disgust churning like a storm in my stomach.

"You know I can't work—"

"Fine," I grit. It's not worth fighting her on this.

She tips her head back, blotting her damp cheeks with the heels of her hands and asks dryly, "What's your husband think about this?"

Her question slices like a blade through my chest. If I wasn't positive she hadn't overheard the voicemail I left Charlie a few days ago, I'd swear she did it on purpose. It still hasn't sunk in—what I said, what I did, what I had to do. I've been too caught up building this new life for River and me to let myself feel the ache. I tuck it back behind my sternum so I can keep myself together.

Because even more worrisome is the scheming glint in her eye. My mother's always been good at getting exactly what she wants.

Her gaze pins me. "What's it like living such a well-to-do life out there, anyway? His family's pretty comfortable, aren't they?"

There it is—what she's getting at.

With him or without him, I'm not letting her come after Charlie. His family. I won't let her hustle him for money just because he made the mistake of falling in love with someone like me.

"Why do you think I came up here alone? I left him," I say, feigning boredom, hoping she doesn't hear the shake in my voice. "It didn't work out."

"I guess we're both unlucky in love." My mother turns her bitter smile on me which might be pretty if it weren't so hollow.

This. This is where I come from.

But I don't care what Katherine Rosenhoth believes, this is *not* where I will go.

I can't change the past, but I can influence the future. I can be for River what I never had growing up: a safe space to land.

chapter 29

THE HAZY GOLDEN glow emanating from the front porch cuts through damp night to greet us as River pulls into the driveway of a house I never thought he'd see. The strangeness, the wonder of it all, clenches my heart between its teeth. I fell in love with the compact craftsman the first time we toured it, but only had a few months here before I left. Charlie's let the flower beds go a little wild, but the lush rose bushes flanking the front two tapered columns are in vivid crimson bloom. My palms sweat as I grab the pizza box off the dash and get out of the car.

"Here." I hand the box off to River and duck to offer Charlie assistance in the back seat.

"I'm good." He waves me off, wincing as he stands. His sore body probably feels even worse after the hour-long drive back from the prison.

"Two broken ribs, one fractured, and eighteen stitches across two areas of your body doesn't sound like *good* to me." I loop myself under his arm and help anyways.

"I broke *ribs* not my leg. Besides, your hip—"

"Is fine. Whatever overpriced ibuprofen they gave me worked like a charm."

River waits at the door with the pizza, and Charlie calls out the code for the smart lock. I can read my brother's expressions so well —that little half eye-roll scowl combo means he thinks Charlie's a complete idiot for trusting him, a stranger, with such sensitive information. Or maybe he thinks the smart lock's pretentious. Or he holds it against Charlie that we lost all of our gear.

Or he simply doesn't like Charlie. Yet.

River didn't say much when I explained what happened while we were at the hospital, keeping his cards close to his chest. The most I could pick up on was that he was nervous, like he thought Charlie showing back up might upend our lives or shift our dynamic. But he didn't ask any questions.

I was grateful because I still don't have any answers.

River lets out a low whistle as he walks inside. He quirks an accusatory brow at the commanding fireplace then at me. "You lived *here*?"

I half-shrug, smiling apologetically. Leaves a lot to be desired about the dumpy apartment we share.

The house is different than I remember. Emptier. Less . . . alive. Familiar, yet strange. Charlie's taken down most of the decor. Not a single photo of us remains on the walls.

"How many bedrooms is it?" River peeks around the corner into the dining room, sneakers squeaking on the hard wood as he pivots.

"Three." Glancing up at Charlie, I clear my throat. "Speaking of that, Riv, I talked to Charlie and he said we could stay here tonight, since it's so late and we're still a half hour away from home."

River's brow furrows as he slides the pizza box on the kitchen island. "Oh. Okay. Sure. Whatever. I just need to cancel with Payton. We were supposed to do movie night tonight."

My eyes narrow, silently chastising, *You were supposed to just say "Thanks, Charlie," you little twerp*. But for as frustrating as his response is, I know he's had an unbelievably long, taxing day and a lot of wrenches thrown in to process on top of it all. He deserves some grace.

Charlie glances between us. "She can come over here? If that's cool with you, Win?"

"No offense, but you don't look like you own the kind of stuff we watch. It's not usually on streaming," River says, with so much attitude I'm struck with bonafide *I'm-so-sorry-about-my-kid* embarrassment.

"Riv!" I hiss.

But Charlie chuckles. "I have a bunch of your sister's old collection in the console cabinet."

River shoots me a pointed look, waiting for me to vouch for that.

"I know there's at least a copy of *Little Shops of Horrors*." I roll my eyes and am pleased to find the plates exactly where I remember them being. I set a stack out.

"So, she can really come over?" River parrots.

"Sure. Make yourselves at home," Charlie says. The word *home* ties itself in a delicate bow around my heart. "If it's okay with your sis—"

"Bet." River swipes open his phone. "You're cool with that, right, Win?"

He's already halfway to the living room, waiting for Payton to pick up his FaceTime when I holler, "Sure. Why the hell not."

Charlie and I exchange a glance. I sigh and amusement flickers back in his eyes. I'm not sure if it's the adrenaline wearing off or the lingering effect of whatever they gave him for the pain at the urgent care clinic, but he's been quiet ever since we left Black Magnolia. Quiet in a way that makes my stomach twist itself into knots.

Our bubble of trauma-bonded bliss, holding tight to each other in the wake of survival, is near popping. We can't avoid reality forever. Charlie's words from earlier echo in my head.

But there is a lot more I need from you if we're ever going to fix this. And right now, I'm not sure if you'll ever give it to me.

"You okay?" I ask quietly, acid churning in my gut.

He nods and rests against the counter. "Just strange."

"Strange?"

Five heartbeats pass before he speaks in slow, measured syllables. "Having you back here."

My breath hitches. "Oh."

"I imagined this scenario in a million different ways since you left," he says distantly. "This wasn't how I saw it happening."

I can't get a read on his tone and it makes me want to scratch my way out of my skin like an animal. "I—uhm . . ."

Charlie opens the junk drawer next to him, bracing his injury with one hand and digging through it with the other until he extracts a glasses case. He pulls out a thick-framed black pair that take me right back to the first year we dated.

I snort. "I don't think I realized you kept those."

"As backup." He slides them on his face.

"You wore them, what? Twice?"

"Three times." His mouth curls as he takes the lenses back off, cleaning them with the hem of his filthy shirt. "And then you said you liked my old ones better."

"And I never saw those black ones again. Until now," I say. In silence, he works a stubborn spot on the glass. I clear my throat. "Thanks for letting us stay here tonight. Saving us the drive. It's been a long day."

"Mhmm," he hums, satisfied with his work. The glasses go back on. For some reason, I'm more endeared to them now than I was in college.

"Is the guest room already made up?" I bite down on the inside of my cheek as I rub my elbow and decide to take the leap. "I might need an extra blanket. River's a cover hog."

He presses his lips into a slash and meets my eyes as he reads right between my lines. "I'd really prefer it if you could just ask me." Quieter, he adds, "What here is worth saving if we can't even talk to each other, Win? What is so wrong with us that you can't even fathom asking me if you can sleep in our bed tonight?"

My throat clogs with the sting of his words, but before I can try speaking, River glides back into the kitchen.

"Pay and I are gonna eat outside. The string lights are a vibe." River scoots between Charlie and I, oblivious to the tension he's slicing right through, and stacks two plates with pizza. "Her Uber's almost here."

"Same rules stand, okay?" I bump his shoulder with mine. "No closed doors. Same curfew."

"Uh-huh. Sure," River muffles around a mouthful of crust.

Charlie and I stand in silent stand-off until the back door shuts.

"The weirdo eats his pizza backwards." It's a lame attempt at a joke and it doesn't even work. I flit to the box River left wide open. "You want me to make you a plate?"

He stares at me, some fusing of disappointment and frustration storming behind the unfamiliar lenses. "I'm not hungry," he mutters, rubbing the back of his neck. "Think I'm going to shower."

He starts for the hallway, his gait favoring his left side. My whole body is so rigid with fear and resistance, I want to scream at myself: *TALK TO HIM*. I pinch my thigh hard as he disappears, daring myself to work up the courage. I chase ghosts for fun, dammit. Communicating with my husband shouldn't be so challenging. Lashing a groan, I follow after him into the bedroom we used to share, tired of my own bullshit.

"Charlie—"

"I'm capable of showering alone," he deadpans, pushing open the door to the en suite bathroom. Contrary to what he said, he winces as he bends to twist the faucet on the brass wall mount shower affixed to the clawfoot tub.

"Likely story, considering you look like you're about to pass out every time you reach for something."

"Win," he sighs. Turning toward the vanity sink, he takes his glasses off and pinches the bridge of his nose. "You're giving me whiplash here. You put me through hell when you left. This afternoon you couldn't wait to get away from me, and then you kiss me. You sleep with me. And now you—what? I don't even know what you want."

I catch his gaze in the mirror as steam fogs at its edges, like we're tumbling through a dream. I've hurt him so much, but I'm ready to fight and make it right. I'm ready to come home, if he'll take me.

I take his hand, still staring into his reflection. "I want to talk, Charlie." I twine our fingers together. "Earlier, I thought I lost you. And I realized that I couldn't live with myself if I never told you the truth." I exhale a shaky breath and his grip tightens. "Maybe it won't be enough for you to forgive me, and you'll want to walk away from this for good. But you deserve to know."

Charlie sits on the edge of our bed; I pace anxiously in front of him and start from the top: the text I got about River on Thanksgiving.

He listens intently as I detail the terror I felt and what I came home to. I wade into the murky waters of explaining the dynamic we grew up in—the chaos, the unpredictability, the emotional turmoil, the self-medication with alcohol.

"My dad had moved out. My older brother was in jail. And I couldn't stomach the thought of leaving River alone, so vulnerable, with someone so mentally unwell who refused to help him or herself. As soon as he told me it wasn't an accident, I knew I had to stay."

I pin my gaze to the rug, too nervous to gauge his reaction to any of this.

"When you asked me what was going on, I—I panicked. I'd tried so hard to keep it all from you, what my family was like. It was easier to deflect. To make it seem like I was pissed at you—needed some time away. I wasn't ready to answer all your questions."

"You thought I didn't know?" he asks quietly, stopping me in my tracks. "You thought I didn't pick up on how you never wanted to talk about your family? Never said I should meet them? Winnie, I always knew. But I trusted that you'd tell me when you felt ready."

It knocks the wind from me. *He knew?*

"I didn't want to be that girl anymore," I choke out.

"I still loved her. Even if you didn't."

His admission rings true—deep in my soul. Like a part of me always knew, even if I denied it. Maybe the problem was never if Charlie could love that side of me, but if *I* could.

"So . . . you left me because you didn't trust that you could tell me what was going on?" he asks, hurt tugging at each word.

I shake my head, wipe my sniffly nose, and keep tearing across the floor. "No. It's not that I didn't trust you. I did—I do. I was trying to protect you."

"From *what*, Win?" His shoulders sag with exasperation. "I'm trying to understand here."

"I—I'm not good at this. Sometimes it feels like my throat's closing up or a car's sitting on my chest, and everything in me shuts down, and I can't find the right words to open up even if I want to. But, *dammit*, you've always felt worth trying for."

"So just tell—"

"I took custody of River," I blurt. "I mean, not legally. But he's been living with me for the past two years. Somehow, I convinced my mom. She's been surprisingly cooperative, for the most part. She signs what I send her. We visit on some weekends. River talks to her on the phone. I send her a monthly check. And it—"

"Hey," Charlie soothes. I still, eyes closing as my chest heaves.

"Take a deep breath. I'm right here. I'm listening. I'm not going anywhere, okay?"

He's quiet. Waiting for my response.

I nod.

"So River lives with you," he says.

"Yes."

"And . . . that's what you were protecting me from?" he asks, confused.

I mash my fingers to my temples. I'm terrible at this: *talking*.

"I'm stubborn, Charlie—"

"I know."

His well-timed gentle tease coaxes a smile from me, loosening some of the tension pinching between my shoulder blades. "When I made up my mind to get River out of there, there was nothing in this world that would've changed it."

Swallowing, I finally turn to face him head on—his tangled hair, his blood-stained clothes, his stitched-up forehead. So torn apart and shredded. As mangled as I felt when I made the choice I thought was right two years ago.

"You'd just finished grad school," I whisper, hands wringing in front of me. "You didn't want *kids* yet, none the less an entire teenager to raise. A kid you'd never even *met*. You were just starting your career. I couldn't let her come after you for money. You had *everything* ahead of you, Charlie. And I didn't want you to give any of it up for me."

His chest rises and falls three times before he speaks, low and gritty. "You think that was your decision to make for me?"

My brows pitch and I falter, terrified I'm screwing this up. "I . . . . it was—"

"You don't get to decide what I'm willing to put up with." Charlie stands and my heart leaps into my throat, moisture beading on my lashes as he moves to me. He looks down at me beneath heavy lids. "You don't get to tell me that my wife's life is too much for me to take on." He takes my hand and a single tear slips down my face. "I know you thought you were looking out for me, but, sweetheart, I promise you I'm capable of doing that on my own."

Under his tender, ferocious gaze, I crumble. I bury my tear-stained face against his chest and he holds me tight, stroking my matted mess of hair.

"When I married you," he says, voice rough, "I married *all* of you. Not just what you deemed worthy of sharing. Not just the easy parts. I want your mess too, Winnie. Give me all the hard parts." A ragged laugh breaks in his throat. "You know I like a challenge."

I cry harder as his words turn me inside out, filling me so much I spill. It's raw and it's real and it's exactly what I crave, but the grief devouring me over all the years I never felt love like this still struggles to believe it. "But I've been so selfish, so stupid—you've always been too good for me."

"Not even close. And get me off that damn pedestal because I don't want to be there if it means you won't be standing next to me."

My lip trembles. "So you're still in this with me?"

His smile stretches wide as he blinks back tears of his own and he brushes mine away with his thumb. "We have a lot of shit to work through, Winnie. But I'm not giving up the fight if you're not."

He cups my face.

And then my husband kisses me.

chapter 30

HEAVY STEAM SETTLES in our bathroom like wispy cirrus clouds as I help Charlie undress, mindful of his injuries. Head to toe, he's covered in sweat, filth, and dried blood as I expose all of his gruesome injuries and violet bruising. My gaze falls to his thighs, the splash of color half-visible behind fabric.

"Earlier, I was wondering . . ." My teeth saw into my lip as hesitation tightens in my throat. What if I was wrong?

But he sees right through me.

He exhales a silent laugh. "Yeah, Winnie. I got a tattoo of the flowers my wife held at our wedding *after* she left me. Pathetic, I know."

I'm swallowed whole by his affection. I twist up a crooked smile. "Guess you're lucky I came back then."

The corner of his mouth twitches up. "Yeah. Guess I am."

His hands brace against the vanity sink, stomach hollowing on a sucked-in breath, as I lower his boxers so he doesn't have to disturb his broken ribs.

"Might not be a good idea for me to shower alone after all," he murmurs.

My cheeks flush, eyes flicking up at him. "You're sure?"

His brow lifts. "You sound surprised."

"I guess I just . . . didn't expect you to forgive me so easily." I pop the button on my shorts.

"I think we have a long road ahead and some marriage counseling bills ahead of us," he admits. "But that's what love is, Winnie. Forgiveness. I know your heart; I know you didn't intentionally hurt me. And if you're willing to do the work with me to fix this—then yeah, I forgive you."

I dip my chin in silent thanks. To be loved like this, so unconditionally, weighs like a boulder in my chest. Probably one of the pit stops along the long road—learning how to accept the good without hedging for the bad.

"Haven't you ever watched a movie before?" I deadpan. "You're supposed to make me stand outside your window playing Peter Gabriel or fix up an old house exactly how you dreamed to win back your love. Grand romantic gesture."

The sound he makes is more breath than laugh, probably to spare his ribs. "I don't know. *You* getting emotionally vulnerable felt pretty grand to me."

He makes no secret of watching me strip off the rest of my clothes. I hold the curtain back for him to get in first, then slot myself behind. Even the thin spray of hot water that manages to reach me past his shoulders is an instant balm for my weary body. He rinses his hair and I tell him to tip his head back as I squeeze shampoo in my palm. We're both quiet, enjoying the reprieve, as I work the soap through his dirty hair.

"How is he doing? River?" Charlie asks quietly.

I smile as I loosen a knot, careful not to pull. "He's good. Really good. Completely different from how he was when I drove up to Kansas. He still goes to weekly therapy—still on his meds. He has some great friends here, he's been dating Payton for eight months now, and I promise he's not always such a little asshole.

Between the storm and meeting you out of nowhere, I think he was thrown for a loop. He'll warm up to you."

A satisfied noise pops in Charlie's throat. "I got you to, didn't I?"

I snort. "Resident expert on feral midwesterners."

"I'm glad to hear that, though. You two seem really close."

I lather more shampoo to make sure I didn't miss any spots and chew on my lip as I scrub it behind his ears. "You're sure you're okay with that? With him?"

"Why wouldn't I be? He's your brother, Win."

"Rinse," I direct, and he bows his head under the flow. "Because my life's a lot different now that I have him. After this shower, I can't go curl up naked in bed with you. I'll have to go tell Riv to get his girlfriend home safely, he'll say *okay we're about to go*. I'll give him ten minutes before I nag him again—and I *always* have to nag him again. When he leaves, I won't be able to fall asleep until he's safely back. I'll keep an eye on my phone just in case he gets a flat, or gets pulled over and needs someone to talk him down from his panicking."

"Things will change. I hear you." Finished rinsing, Charlie squeezes past me to trade places.

Facing him, I tip my hair back in the water. "He plays his music really loud. He leaves dirty dishes in the sink, and he's really bad about turning lights off when he leaves a room. He thinks he knows *everything*, and I mean everything. I don't think I've been on time to anything but school since he moved in with me, and that's because I work there. He sits on his phone for like twenty minutes when he takes a dump—"

Charlie chuckles, a broken off strained sound. "First of all, you're forgetting I grew up with two younger brothers. And I was a teenage boy once too. I get it. Second of all, why does it feel like you're trying to talk me out of this?"

Taking a deep breath, I rake sudsy shampoo over my scalp. "Because I need you to be *sure*, Charlie. One hundred percent sure.

I can't handle the thought of you waking up one day resenting me for turning your life upside down. And I *know you*, Charlie. You'll give everything for the people you care about. But I never want to be someone who makes you sacrifice."

"Jesus, Winnie." He huffs, eyes reddening. So softly I almost miss it, he says, "I didn't know it was possible."

My head tilts. "What?"

"Falling more in love with you than I already was. I've never met someone who loves as deeply or as fiercely as you. Looking out for your brother. Looking out for me. You give every goddamn ounce of yourself to the people you care about." His arm loops behind me and he presses his hand to the small of my back, drawing me closer as his other hand glides over my cheek. "But you need to let other people love you in that way too."

The swelling in my throat is almost unbearable as I shake my head on instinct, like I'm squirming out from under his words. "I —I don't—I don't know if I can. Charlie, I—" My voice catches. "I hurt you. I screwed up. I'm not soft. Or warm. Or easy to love—"

He tips my chin up with his knuckle. "Careful. You're talking about my wife. I'll defend that woman with everything I've got."

My knees buckle at the title I've missed so much as I flatten both hands to his chest, my psyche searching for cracks, loopholes, signs of danger.

"You're the one person I'd sacrifice everything for, Winona. Gladly. You have the biggest heart of anyone I know. You're worried about me forgiving you but I think you need to forgive yourself first."

Right now, it feels impossible. But the adoration in his eyes, the sturdy way he holds me—it makes me think I can do it. With my husband by my side.

And probably a hell of a lot more therapy.

I meet his eyes and I nod, too raw and worked up to speak. As I detangle my raggedy strands of hair, I turn and face the shower head. Not because I want to hide from him, but because sometimes it's so overwhelming to be seen. And he gives me that space, running a comforting hand over my bad hip to let me know he's there, because he knows I need it.

And he knows this because he loves me, exactly as I am.

chapter 31

WE FINISH IN THE SHOWER, clearing away the layers of grime and tension in a familiar silence. A passing of soaps, a trading of spots, a trailing of fingernails here and there. We dry off, change into clean clothes, and I follow Charlie back into our bedroom.

But he stops short, turning to face me.

"I'm really glad you're home, Winnie," he murmurs.

He takes my face in both his hands and crushes his mouth against mine, so urgent and hungry it makes my head spin. I suck in a sharp breath and open to him, winding a hand around his neck as he kisses me deeply. It's the most complete I've felt in a long time. But this is the first of many hard days ahead of us, and I've never been so grateful to fight for something.

Our marriage will be different. Changed. The fissured cracks molded back together with our imperfect work. But it will be something new and beautiful on its own. It will be *ours*.

Charlie told me earlier he's fought like hell for me since we met.

But now, I'm getting in the ring with him.

Nails skimming his nape, I locate the clasp on the chain and open it, letting the gold band slide off in my hand.

Charlie pulls back. "What are—"

"Stay married to me, Charlie." My hands shake as I pinch the metal between my thumb and finger, holding it between us.

He blinks a few times as he stares at it, like his brain's still buffering. But then a smirk eases on his face, and I melt. "Married? Wait, wait. I thought we were friends?"

I widen my eyes at him in warning, holding back my amused grin. "Don't you dare tease me, Flower Boy."

"Yes, Winona," he says, so tender and gooey. "I'll stay married to you."

He holds his left hand out.

"I promise to fight for this with you," I say as I slide on the ring.

He holds me by the hips and murmurs against my temple, "We renewing our vows, Mrs. Rosnehoth?" With a breathy laugh, I nod. "I promise to support you and your brother however I can."

My breath catches as he presses a soft, warm kiss beneath my ear.

"I promise to talk to you. Even when it's hard."

"Especially when it's hard," he corrects, teeth grazing my throat. "I promise to defend you. Against my mom. Against yourself. No one talks about my wife like that."

My wife. A wild thrill races up my spine and I laugh. *Yes I am.* "I promise to stay."

"I promise to take you dancing." His tongue slides against my charged skin.

"We're going to bust your stitches," I huff.

I can hear the grin in his voice, mouth against the column of my throat, as he goads, "Is that a promise?"

"Your ribs are literally *broken*, Charlie."

"Only two of them." His kisses move to my jaw, working

toward my mouth, as he pulls my body flush against his. "I can take a little pain."

I lean sideways to drop the chain he won't be needing anymore on the nightstand by my side of the bed.

I gasp.

The ribbon. Is it still here?

Half hanging onto Charlie's waist, I yank the drawer open, relieved to see it's exactly as I left it. I dig through bobby pins, body lotion, scrunchies, expired tubes of Biofreeze, then sift through old programs from Colby Theater until I find the one for *All That Jazz: Swan Lake*. Still pressed inside of it is the baby pink ribbon tied into a bow that Charlie proposed with six years ago.

Charlie huffs a disbelieving breath. "I didn't realize you kept that."

"Of course I did." I smirk, lashes fluttering. "It's my engagement ring."

He takes it from me, brows drawn, studying it like it's the latest run of a weather model and he's making sense of the data. "Fiancé was a cheapskate, huh?"

Smiling, I curl my right hand back around his neck, hovering my left between us. "No. We were just young and in love and a little impulsive and very, very broke."

Delicately, he slides the ribbon on my ring finger. "Still fits like a glove, Mrs. Rosenhoth." So does my husband's last name, which sends a thrill up my spine. He brings my hand to his mouth and lays a kiss between the two cascading tails. Flipping it, he murmurs against my palm, "Now, where were we?"

"You were trying to justify your own bodily harm." I delve my other hand into his damp hair.

"I'm fine."

"You can't even *laugh* fully."

"Okay. *Yes*, I'm in a little pain." Glaring at me, he nips my wrist. "But you're here. You're *really* here"—his voice falters with emotion—"And even breathing hurts. So, if I'm going to be in pain no matter what, I might as well do something worth suffering for."

The deep ache that's been etched in my bones for so long finds it hard to believe—that *I* am something worth suffering for. But my husband has always been an honest man.

I level Charlie with a critical stare, smoothing over how damn infatuated I am with him. "*Little Shop of Horrors* is only an hour and a half."

"We can work fast." He flashes a shit-eating grin I don't trust for a second as his nose nudges mine and he drapes my arm over his shoulder. "You were a *very* cheap date earlier in the prison cafeteria."

I scoff, cheeks flaming, but before I can hit back with a snarky reply, he interrupts me with a kiss. Instantly—*frustratingly*—I yield to him and his warm, curious mouth without a fight. His arms wind around me, gliding slowly over every peak and valley, like he's remapping the planes of my body, revisiting all his favorite spots. He inches us toward the bed.

Pulling back, I cup his face and frown. "I don't want to hurt you."

He drags his thumb over my bottom lip, tracing the shape of it. "So be gentle, sweetheart."

My smirk curls as I tease, "Was the desk earlier not enough for—"

His thumb moves to quiet me, all his playfulness darkening on his face. "I've been trying not to say this; I don't want you to feel bad. And I know you, Winnie. I *know* you will." His other hand slides up my spine, chasing right after the breath rising in my chest. "But it has been two *very* long years." He twists my dripping hair around his fist. "This sharp pain in my chest from a few fractured bones is nothing compared to how much I fucking ached when you were gone." He angles my head back, mouth moving to my throat. "So no. What happened earlier wasn't enough." His lips skim down to my collarbone. "You have no idea how badly I need this." With a jerk against the small of my back, he crushes us together, and I draw in a sharp breath at the hard length of *exactly* how much he needs this straining through his shorts. "Need to have you without thinking it'll be the last time."

His confession leaves me breathless. He catches my chin with his fingers and rests his forehead against mine. Staring deep into my eyes, he takes my left hand and sets it on his chest, the yearning heartbeat stirring beneath.

"And all I want to do is fuck my beautiful wife while she's wearing the ring I gave her and nothing else."

My pulse careens at a dizzying pace as he kisses me with so much flourishing want. Hand tangling in my hair. Fingertips curling into the flesh at my hips. Tongue sliding against mine relentlessly as I whimper into his mouth. And god, I love it when he's bossy.

"I need to feel her nails on my skin." He catches my lower lip between his teeth and I oblige him of his request, sinking my claws into his shoulders until he groans.

"I need to smell her sweat on my skin." Framing my waist with both hands, he walks us back toward the bed. As he sits on the edge of the mattress, the only sign of the pain I know he's hiding for my sake is the knot straining between his brows.

"I need to see every fucking inch of her." His touch slips beneath the hem of my T-shirt. Just barely. It swoops around to my front as I brace one knee on the other side of his spread legs, careful not to rest any weight on his shoulders. My stomach hollows as his palm slides up, so agonizingly slow, watching me with his rapt attention.

"I need to hear her moan my name." He barely grazes my tightened nipple, but my entire body reacts, heating as a breath hitches in my chest. I exhale a whimper as he pinches it between his fingers, rolling it gently.

Desire thick in my throat, I swallow. "That's quite the list of demands."

"We have a lot of time to make up for."

I peel my shirt over my head while he tugs off my shorts. We work together, gently maneuvering fabric and limbs, as his clothes come off next. It's so deeply intimate, the way he lets me help him in such a vulnerable state—this is love, the way he trusts me. I store this memory in my mind for safekeeping.

Once I'm wearing only the ribbon tied around my finger, as requested, I rake a hand through his hair, tipping his face up to mine. "Lie down, Flower boy."

Wincing, he angles and shifts back against the pillows, legs swinging on the bed. His firm stomach, mottled with bruising and stitches, ripples with his ragged breathing. What I wouldn't do to siphon all his pain away. I'd take it myself if it meant he didn't have to suffer.

I crawl over to him and I've never felt more beautiful than right now, under his attentive gaze. The way his blown-out pupils consume every bit of me and still look hungry. Straddling him, I fold forward as he grips my hips and brace my hands on either side of him, holding up my own weight.

As our mouths collide, he jerks me closer, grinding me down against him. I empty all of me into this kiss, and as Charlie groans into my mouth, I think he might be doing that too. I give him my fear, my hope, my longing, my frustration, my self-hatred, my forgiveness. And he takes it all, dishing it right back.

This is real and raw in a way we couldn't have been earlier. When neither of us knew the ending—knew we'd fix what had split. I understand what he meant now, in saying he needed this.

His hands are so fucking greedy, rounding my curves, circling my ass, squeezing it, stroking up and down my thighs. His kisses are even worse. So persistent they're almost punishing as fingers tangle in my hair. My hips rock against him, fanning this fire burning between us. Pressing his nose against my jaw, he nudges me, and as I lift up, his lips carve a path down my chest. He catches my nipple in his mouth, swirling, sucking, and *god*—he makes me sound so fucking desperate as I dig my hand into his hair.

"I missed you so much," he murmurs to my heart.

Arcing my thumb around his ear, I look down at him and whisper, "I love you, Charlie."

His hand comes to the back of my head, cradling me as he smiles. "You've always been my favorite storm to chase."

I huff a laugh. "I think it's about time we enjoy the sunshine a little."

Charlie draws me to his mouth again and kisses me in a way I think I'll feel forever. His tongue, and teeth, and the vibration of a moan in the back of his throat—all etching into me with intensity.

His hands wrap around the backs of my thighs and he urges me forward, gaze darkening. "Come here, sweetheart. You know how I want you."

Just the way he's looking at me is enough to send me spinning. Grabbing the headboard, I pull myself up and plant my knees on either side of his head. The ache low in my belly tightens as he loops his arms beneath me and back around my hips, fingers digging into my ass. With one strong tug, he brings me down to his face.

Charlie drags his tongue across me, slow and torturous as he groans. I shiver at his exquisite warmth, rolling into the feeling. He works me, leisurely and teasing with each gentle stroke, and a soft moan pitches in my throat as I clutch the wood headboard tighter. From above, I watch him—the way his brow divots with his focus, his enjoyment. I brush my thumb next to the black-stitched split on his forehead, knot my hand in his hair.

A sharp gasp cracks in my throat as he sucks my sensitive flesh. My breathing kicks up, my mouth falling open on another whimper, my tipping hips demanding more from him. And he gives it all. Lashing against me harder, faster. One finger pushes inside of me, then another. I arch and bend and pant his name and press so fully against him I'm not even sure he can breathe anymore. But neither of us stop.

The coiled tension behind my hipbones winds itself tighter and tighter as I moan. And then—my thighs clench around his head. My fists tighten in his hair and I cry out, but he still doesn't stop. Then everything loosens—all at once. I prop an arm on the headboard, sinking my forehead against it as I try to catch my breath.

But the asshole keeps going, grazing me with featherlight pressure that's still enough to twist up pathetic little whimpers in my throat. It's so good it hurts.

"Charlie—" I whine, jerking my hips up when the sensation becomes too much.

"You can take it, Winona," he growls. "Just give me one more." And he pulls me down on his face again.

I writhe and squirm against his exquisite, merciless mouth. It's too much. It's just right. His arms around me tighten, locking me in place, forcing me to take it. Knowing it's what I need. Another wave crashes over me, sending sparks up my spine as I cry out, muffling the sound against my shoulder. My whole body goes limp, every inch of me tingling.

Charlie kisses my quivering inner thighs. "I knew you could do it."

I prowl back down his bruised body, languid as a cat that's been lying in the sun, and nip at his satisfied smirk on the way. His hooded gaze watches as I position myself across his lap, up on my knees. I reach down and wrap my hand around him and he grips my hips as I sink down, lashes fluttering at the sensation. I'm the one on top and yet he's the one controlling my every move, incrementally guiding me lower and lower as I clench around him. My mouth falls open in an "O" when we're finally fully joined.

As I set the tempo, gingerly at first to test how much this will hurt him, Charlie worships my body, hands stroking reverently over my curves, my face, my breasts, through my drying hair. He pulls me down as my hips work slowly against him and kisses me, whispers how I good I feel into my ear like a prayer. It's a special thing, being so full of him and knowing we'll both be there to catch each other when we land. No tense conversations. No hard questions. Just my sweaty body panting in his arms.

It makes it so much easier to let go. To revel in his desperate moans, the sweat shimmering on his battered skin. The striking veins on his forearms as he holds me. The way he draws me so close I can't help but settle some of my weight on him, and despite the pain, he holds me anyway. The way his relentless hips wrestle me for control, sharp sounds breaking off in his throat.

I feel every thick, pulsing inch of him, hear every rasping syllable of his low "*Fuck, Winnie.*" Smell the citrus of his shampoo. And it feels like coming home. Right here. To the person I belong to. It's not a question—Charlie carries a piece of me inside him. It's so fucking decadent, our push and pull as our bodies collide.

How rich to ache like this. How indulgent to be so in love.

I chase after the tightening bowstring in my core, riding him in fluid, sweeping movements. Winding loose tendrils of hair around his hand, Charlie tugs me to his mouth, like he's starving for my moans. It tips me to the perfect angle, sparking a delicious pleasure against my clit. One strong hand moves to the small of my back, grinding me down harder, and I choke out a cry.

I'm an unrestrained mess in his arms, kissing, licking, biting every inch of skin I can reach as he drives up into me faster. My lip catches and curls along his jawline as he murmurs encouragement and praise into my ear—*Just like that sweetheart, you're doing so well*. It's sloppy and clumsy and so fucking hot, but what makes me lose it is watching Charlie's restraint stutter and slip before he even has a chance to warn me. Like he couldn't hold on a single second longer.

He fists a handful of my hair, squeezing until it stings as his body goes rigid, every muscle pulling taught. He takes in the sharpest breath I've heard all night, hissing—I can't imagine how much it hurts, tensing like that—and as he moans on his exhale, a shiver races up my spine. My toes curl. He jerks up beneath me, giving me a piece of himself, and I shatter into stardust right behind him.

The breathless come down is the sweetest part—the way Charlie kisses me gently on the lips and wraps his tired arms around me as we stay joined. Still hovering my weight off his ribcage, I bring my hand to his chest, the delicate pink artifact of our past flowing crooked over my knuckles.

"I think we checked off everything on your list," I whisper, smiling.

"And more." He lifts my hand and kisses the ribbon ring.

I graze my fingers along his jaw. "You really think we can do this, Flower Boy?"

"I may be a skeptic about most things in life, but if there is one thing I have blind, unwavering faith in, it's us."

Before we emerge from the bedroom, I educate Charlie on my method of making enough noise to spook River and Payton into decency before entering a room where they're alone together. A failsafe for avoiding awkward moments.

There's twenty minutes left on the movie when I reheat a few slices of pizza for me and Charlie. We eat standing up at the island, and River happens to look over his shoulder right as I lean over and kiss Charlie on the cheek. My brother's face twists in disgust, as subtle as a teenager can be. Meaning: not at all.

"You ready for this life?" I ask Charlie, head tilting. "Splitting a pizza for dinner with River and his girlfriend. Sneaking away for a moment alone together. Watching him roll his eyes every time we kiss."

"I think so." He smiles softly and grabs my hand. "Feels right.

This place always seemed a little big for just the two of us"—he glances back at my brother, his arm slung around Payton's shoulders—"and he seems like a good kid."

"He is."

He's seventeen. He holds the world in the palm of his hand, and he doesn't even know it. He's here. And god, I'm so grateful for it. When he argues with me, when he insists I'm wrong about something I'm not, when we couldn't look each other in the eye for days after I walked in on him with his hand down Payton's sweats over winter break. It's all worth it because it means he's *here*.

And it feels silly to think, but when I look at him, I think maybe . . . maybe I can do this. If River can bring himself back from the precipice of the worst place on earth to sit here right now, leaning over to whisper something in Payton's ear that makes her laugh, then I can fix my marriage. All the times I've overheard him tell Payton he's sorry, or he asks her to be patient because he's had a rough day, glimmer like hopeful beacons across a shore. Like striped sunlight flooding through barred prison windows. He's not perfect, but he's *good*. And he tries every day.

I'm not perfect. I never will be.

But my husband loves me exactly as I am—flawed, vulnerable, completely his. Some of our days will be hard, some will be easy. But together, we'll wake up tomorrow and choose to keep fighting.

There's no doubt in my mind we'll win.

chapter 32

I NEVER FORGOT how good it felt to wake up next to my husband, but it's even better than I remember. The scent of his skin that's entirely Charlie. The steady rise and fall of his chest. The way even as he sleeps, his hand follows my body like a magnet, always touching somewhere. I could lie here and watch him for hours, but I woke up ravenous and I'm sure the guys will too.

Careful to avoid the old boards that creak, I sneak out the front door with my keys and pray the donut shop on the corner's gotten with the times and takes Apple Pay, considering my wallet's scattered in the remains of Black Magnolia Penitentiary with the rest of mine and River's gear.

By the time I come back with a dozen warm glazed donuts, and a bag of sausage and cheese kolaches, the house is still quiet. I find the bottle of ibuprofen in the same cabinet by the sink, balance it on top of the donut box, and grab a glass of water. I bump open the bedroom door with my hip.

Charlie's awake, his phone hovering over his face. He peeks around it, soft confusion blurring his eyes. Then he smiles. "I woke up and you were gone. For a second I thought I dreamt everything last night."

You were gone. The words sock me right in the gut as I set the water on his end table. "Sorry, I should've texted you. I didn't want to wake you."

He taps his ring with the thumb on the same hand. "This was a pretty decent reminder it was real."

"Gold suits you." I trace the shape of it on his finger, relishing in how it feels. I'm antsy to make it back to my and River's apartment later to slip mine from the stone dish on my dresser and put it on.

"I brought breakfast," I say, setting the box on the bed. Charlie moves to sit and sucks in a sharp breath, the rest coming after, short and ragged, as his face twists. I reach over him for my pillow, propping it up behind him, wishing I could do more to help. "Meds, too."

"Thanks," he half-gasps, before relaxing back against the pillows. "Hurts a lot worse today."

I level him with a deeply unimpressed look and the most violent scowl I can muster. "I wonder why." I tap out the ibuprofen and hand it to him with the glass.

"Worth it." Grinning, he tosses the pills back. "Don't act like you didn't enjoy yourself."

He slides the chunky black glasses on his face as I roll my eyes and crawl back into bed next to him, curling up on top of the blanket. It's muscle memory, the way he lifts his arm and I tuck into the crook of his shoulder. As I snuggle closer, a faint gray shadow moves toward the open door, then backs away from it. I cock my head.

"Riv?"

My brother sheepishly inches forward, still wearing the old tee and athletic shorts Charlie let him borrow, his hair a crazy mess. "Thought I smelled food."

Laughing, I wave him in. "Yeah. Here, help yourself."

He briefly glances at Charlie, who's focused back on his phone but offers a *good morning*, then shuffles across the room to perch at the foot on my side of the bed. He reaches for the kolaches in silence.

I swipe a donut for myself and tap Charlie's knee. "You seem busy this morning."

His brow pulled taut, he doesn't stop texting. "Sorry. Getting the safety lecture from Garrett." He snorts. "And I guess he and Chad swung by the prison this morning"—he flashes a look of apology at me, then River—"unfortunately, they didn't find any of your equipment. At least, not in one piece."

"So, the episode's a bust?" River asks around a mouthful of bread.

His disappointment is a knife to my gut. "I'm sorry, Riv."

He heaves a long, accepting breath, and nods. "Yeah. It's cool. Just glad you didn't, like, lose a leg. That'd really kill the channel."

I kick at his leg and he grins. "Forget your sister. God forbid anything happens to your *streaming* career."

"I'm not a *streamer*." He pouts. "I was saving up for a mobile hot spot, so we could start. But I guess I have a lot of other shit to save up for now."

"I've got a mobile hot spot you can use," Charlie says. "And, miraculously, all my camera equipment made it out without a scratch, save for one cracked lens. You're free to borrow it, until you can replace yours."

River casts him a skeptical look. "Really?"

"Sure—why not? Not like I'll get much use out of it for a few weeks." Charlie motions vaguely to his busted ribs.

River chews. Swallows. Pokes his tongue into his cheek, gaze dropping to his kolache. "Cool. Thanks."

I slip my smile between my teeth. Is this the tentative beginning of *bonding*?

"Unfortunately, I don't have one of those ghost walkie talkies. Or the candle. Or the thing that plays music. I actually might have a cat ba—"

River scoffs. "Ghost *walkie talkies*?"

My eyes widen and I jolt out from under Charlie's arm. Launching off the bed, I scramble into the bathroom and dig my soiled shorts from the hamper. I reach into the back pocket and an exhilarated laugh bubbles in my chest. The SD card I snagged before the investigation went off the rails.

And James's letter.

"You okay?" Charlie asks as I crawl back on the bed, unfolding the yellowing paper. "What's that?"

"James's letter!" I squeal.

River gapes at me, bug-eyed and a little bitter. "Wait . . . *what*? You didn't mention anything about a *letter*!"

"I forgot all about it until now." Shaking my head, I give River the short version of what happened at the prison. About the on and off communication, the creepy shadow figure that pushed me into the cell, and Charlie finding James's journal—which is now lost among the debris of the prison. "This letter is all we have left to prove any of it was real."

River groans. "And I *missed* all that?"

I flash the SD card. "I also have this. It's not much, but maybe we can piece together a blooper episode." River reaches for it but I close my fist around it. There's some indecent footage of Charlie and I that I need to delete first. "I'll get it to you later."

He rolls his eyes. "Can I at least see the letter?"

"Read it, Win," Charlie says. "Out loud. I want to hear it too."

River scoots closer until all three of our heads are bowed over the one saving grace from yesterday's investigation. I clear my throat and begin to read."

Warden Rhymes, you have the wrong man.

I did not murder Edith Page Milton, but I know who did. However, even if I am not guilty of the crime, I'm not innocent either. Allow me to explain.

The Page name was a good name. The Milton name was a good name. The Dewhurst name was not. Robert Milton, Edith's surviving husband, was heir to a dairy fortune. All I was set to receive from my father was a failing pea farm. It wasn't enough to be worthy for a Page, but it would be enough to support my sister, Martha, who took ill as a baby and lost her sight.

My sister is an important piece of the puzzle, Warden. The man guilty of this crime threatened that if I ever said a word, he would see to it my sister met the same fate as Edith. If I kept quiet, he would make sure she was provided for until her death. I was torn between the two women I loved, but the choice was easy, being that one was already gone.

Unfortunately, I recently received word from the care home in which she lived that my sister, Martha, had passed. I have no reason to keep my silence any longer.

I was smitten with Edith Page from the very first time I laid eyes on her, and by the grace of God, she took a liking to me too. We were high school sweethearts. When we finished school, she spoke of getting married.

Edith was the most swell girl I had ever met, but my family did not have the funds to offer a girl like her. Edith's father had passed a year prior, and her brother, Andrew, handled the family finances. Andrew never liked me. Thought me strange. I knew I would never receive his blessing, and I denied Edith's request to elope together. At the time, I thought I was doing what was best for my Edith, but I have come to see what that choice truly was: an act of cowardice.

Edith went on to marry Robert Milton. It was not a love match, but a financially strategic one encouraged by her brother. She had two beautiful children with Robert, but as Edie once wrote to me, Robert was not a kind nor loving man. She said this was what drew her back to writing to me—our companionship. It started innocent enough, as these things often do. Out of respect for Edith, I shall leave it there.

One evening, we arranged a meeting at the river. That night,

Andrew Page caught us. I had never seen a man so blind with rage. He spoke of the shame this would bring on the family, and chastised his sister for risking her marriage and the wealth it gave them access to. He attacked Edith. Wrapped his hands around her throat. He wouldn't let go, even as I tried to fight him off of her. That was how he left my dear, sweet Edie. Cold and alone on the banks of the river.

I was delirious with grief. I couldn't think. Hardly breathe. I wish I had gone straight to the sheriff, pounded on his door in the night. But I could not leave her side. The police arrived on scene and of course I looked to be caught in something dreadful. They arrested me even though I insisted I was innocent. They had no interest in listening. They thought I was mad when I told them Edith's own flesh did this to her.

Andrew Page, the well connected man he was, had one of the guards slip me a note. In this note, he made his threat on Martha's life and told me to plead guilty. What choice did I have? With my sister provided for, on Andrew's word, and the love of my life dead, what did I even have to fight for? I accepted the charges the next day.

I have lived with this terrible secret for all these years, and the pain it's caused. Not only the guilt of knowing a dangerous man is still walking free, or the unending sorrow over losing Edith, but also the realization that I was not the man I should've been. Perhaps, if I had believed myself worthy and accepted Edith's request to elope, she would still be here today. Perhaps, if I had been a strong enough man to resist a married woman, none of this would have happened.

I have made my peace with spending my last days in this place. Even if I were to ever get out, I would still suffer the torture of my own mind.

But I could not live with myself if I didn't share the truth of what happened to my Edie. She deserves to have her story told.

Warden Rhymes, would you kindly see to it that this information makes it into the right hands? I would like to see justice served for the man who took Edith Page Milton's life.

The color drains so thoroughly from Charlie's face, I wonder if he's having some kind of complication from his injuries. Skin sallow and expression tight, his gaze becomes unfocused as he stares somewhere distant, sitting perfectly still.

"Charlie? You okay?"

"What the fuuuuuuck," River mutters, snatching the letter.

"Yeah, I"—Charlie shakes his head, throwing off the reverie—"sorry, that's just incredibly similar to the answers I was getting during the . . . what was it called?"

"Estes session?"

"Yeah. That. I—it's uncanny . . ." His brows furrow, like he's trying to piece all the data together to figure out the forecast.

River's mouth slashes into a grumpy line as he looks at Charlie like he just said the earth is flat, then turns his accusatory look on me. "Bro. Don't tell me you married someone who doesn't believe in ghosts."

Sparkling laughter bursts from my chest. "Yeah, I did."

"Hey, I'm a healthy skeptic," Charlie says. And I love him even more for it.

I squeeze Charlie's bicep. "Guess we'll just have to convince him. Like you convinced me, Riv."

"This letter isn't proof enough?" River waves it in the air.

Charlie rubs his jaw. "Honestly, I can't explain that."

"Right," I snort. "Because it's *ghosts*."

Whatever Charlie does or doesn't believe, I know one thing to be true: James Dewhurst was an innocent man, and this letter proves it beyond the shadow of a doubt for me. And he deserves to have his story told. He deserves this retribution. Like I'm trying to believe I deserve mine.

Until his last day, James lamented not choosing Edith. Not letting *her* choose *him*. I twine my hand with my husband's. No one can alter the past, but wherever he is, I hope James Dewhurst knows what an integral part his story played in changing my future.

"What do we do with it?" River chews on his bottom lip, still scanning it, like there's a secret code stashed between its lines. "Do we . . . turn it into the police?"

I shake my head. "I doubt they'd do anything with it. Riv, can you pull up the very first email about this case? From . . . ?"

"Apple," he scoffs, pulling out his phone. "Her name was *Apple*."

He offers me the device and I scroll to the bottom, humming a satisfied noise when I prove myself right. "I *thought* I remembered there being a phone number. Look, there is. Here at the bottom. She said she's close to the family. Maybe she can get us in touch with them."

"Hello?" A feminine voice picks up the call, River's phone cradled in my hand on speakerphone. All three of us hunch together in anticipation.

"Hi," I say. "Is this Apple?"

"Excuse me?"

I frown. "Apple? This is Winona. From Halbach Hunts. You reached out to us about the Edith Page Milton case?"

"I—what? I'm . . . I'm sorry, I don't know what you're talking about." Not-Apple's voice pitches, like she's flustered. "My name's Evelyn—Evie. I'm not sure how you got my number, but I—I'm Edith Milton's granddaughter. Are you messing with me?"

"No, ma'am, not at all. I received an email about the case with this phone number attached." I glance between Charlie and River, their faces matching looks of tense intrigue.

"Case?" Evie hums wearily. "What exactly is it you do?"

I straighten my shoulders, aiming for ironclad professionalism as I say, "My co-host and I run a web series for our paranormal investigations."

"*Paranormal*?" Evie balks and I roll my eyes. *Great*. She's a skeptic. "What do *ghosts* have to do with any of this?"

"The person who reached out to us, uh, allegedly on your behalf, wanted us to publicly exonerate the spirit of James Dewhurst and try communicating with him," I say. "They claimed Edith Page Milton's family wanted that, you know, after finding the letters sewn into the quilts and assuming they were lovers."

"This must be some kind of prank, it's—*wait*. They knew about the quilts?"

"Yes, ma'am."

River's eyes flare at me, putting something together I must be missing. My excitement is deflating by the second. It must've been a gag after all.

"Strange," Evie mutters. "Only my immediate family knows about the quilts. But who would *do* this? We're very private about these matters."

"The person who reached out to us went by the name Apple, if that's any help." I sigh. Charlie rubs the small of my back in silent consolation. "Apologies for bothering you, Evie. But we did run the investigation the other day and managed to find a letter James Dewhurst had written to the warden, telling his honest account of what happened to your grandmother. I've read it myself, and I can confirm, he was innocent. If you'd like to read the story yourself, I'd be happy to share it. I have it right in front of me. I can send a photo, if you'd like?"

For all I know, Andrew Page was known in their family as a loving uncle; I'm not about to out him for his crimes and get in the middle of generational drama. Evie can find out for herself, if she so chooses. River smooths out the folded letter and positions it in front of me. I take the photo, load it up in a text to Evie's number, and hover my thumb over "Send."

"Evie? Did I lose you? Would you like to see the letter?"

"Apple, you said?" she asks quietly.

My brow furrows. "Yes. Apple."

"That's . . ." Evie gives a puzzled hum. "That's very interesting. I mean, it's—it's not possible, right?"

I lean in closer to the phone. "What's not?"

"Apple—that's what he called her. That's what James called Edith in all the letters. My Apple. *The apple of my eye*," she murmurs. "The first time I read that, somehow I just knew he didn't do it. I couldn't explain it, but I *knew*. James never would've killed his Apple."

"Your intuition," I mutter, awed as it hits me.

Instantly, chills race down my spine. The Knowing flares in my stomach. River fists his hair with both hands, mouth flying open in an "O" as his eyes focus on me, as big as saucers. Even the rigid facade of Charlie's concentrated face falls as his lips part.

Apple . . . is Edith.

"I'd like to see that letter, actually," Evie says.

I tap the screen, sending it off to her and stay on the line while she reads.

As Charlie would argue, there are plenty of reasonable explanations for someone sending that email signed with Edith's pet name. The family isn't as set on keeping things to themselves as Evie thinks. Someone mentioned the letters to a friend who was overcome by a sense of vigilante justice and happened to be a fan of our show. Or it's a very strange coincidence, which have been known to happen from time to time.

All compelling possibilities.

But you also can't prove it's not ghosts.

Acknowledgments

Of all the craft books I've consumed and classes I've taken, not a single resource covered how to write your acknowledgments. Gap in the market honestly, because this is *hard*. How am I supposed to string together a few paltry words to somehow convey what everyone's support has meant to me?

Thank you doesn't even begin to cover it. But it's as good a place to start as any.

To Bayley—your creativity inspires me. This book wouldn't be what it is without your gorgeous art and keen eye for detail. You've brought my story to life so beautifully and I'm forever grateful.

To Caitlin—this book would be all misplaced semicolons, no em dashes if not for your sharp skills. Thank you for your friendship, your cheerleading, and all of your unhinged comments in my doc as you edited.

To Lindsey, Stephanie, and Adrianna—I absolutely wouldn't be the writer I am today without you three, and I mean that genuinely. Thank you for always pushing me, never letting me take the easy way out, and your tireless dedication to making sure my interiority works. I hope every writer is lucky enough to find critique partners (and friends) like you three.

Thank you to every beta reader who told me this book *did* have a place in the genre, that the story it told was worth sharing, even if I was worried it wasn't.

To Kelsey—thank you for sending me the TikTok that spurred this idea in the first place, your fierce, unwavering support. I love you at your unhinged Stella and also at your sad girl Mel. You are the sort of friend every girl deserves.

To Lindsay—thank you for being a beautiful genius. I'd clone your brain and steal it if I could. You're so wise and giving and always have the right insight to solve whatever plot problem is making me suffer. Thank you for matching the fire in my chart and saying "actually, yeah, do it" when I sent a voice note asking if I should publish this book in an eight-week time frame on an impulse decision. You're stuck with me for this lifetime and all the next ones too.

To Aleshka—I actually don't even know where to start. You've been with me since the very beginning of this journey, and I'm so glad you have. Thank you for everything. For always being willing to read my pages (even when I'm being a line cook and not a chef). For keeping me from losing my mind. For offering valuable insight when I need it, about book stuff or life stuff. For keeping me grounded. Your tireless belief in me has kept me going through some hard days. I love you so much! You have the key to my safe.

To my train girls—Alice, Allissa, Brenna, Katie G, Liz, Emily, Haley, Isabelle, Katie J, Lex, Makayla, and Megan—thank you endlessly for championing me through everything. I love each of you dearly, and I absolutely would not be where I am without y'all. Full stop.

To Maggie North, Jessica Joyce, Maggie Eckersley, Letizia Lorini, Zarin Madiyha, and Rebecca Thorne—your guidance and mentorship has been invaluable for me and my career. I'm in awe of every author who has paved the way before me, and is kind enough to pass down their wisdom.

Shout-out to The Mid-List on Discord for being one of the most helpful, down-to-earth group of writers I've ever found online.

To Jenny and Brittney—thank you for being the kind of friends that make it easy to write about friendship. I love you both so much!

And to S—I couldn't do any of this without your support. I'm sorry I fall off the face of the earth when I'm in the thick of things, but thank you for understanding and for believing in me so deeply that you've never once questioned a single thing I've taken on. It's easier to write about love when you get to live it every day.

Last but certainly not least, thank you to every reader who has taken a chance on a new author and picked up this book. I write for myself, but I publish for *you*. Your support means more to me than I can ever explain. Not only have you made this author's dreams come true, you've reminded me why I started doing this in the first place. More than anything, I hope I can keep writing tender love stories and I hope they can keep finding their readers.

About the Author

Cara Calloway writes heartfelt, character-driven romance with depth and a whole lot of banter (and usually a weird job thrown in for good measure). Her stories embrace the messy, challenging authenticity of what it means to be human while centering the belief that we all deserve a happy ending, no matter how flawed we think we are.

She lives and writes in the heart of Houston, TX with her husband. When she's not writing, you can find her designing websites, making messes in the kitchen, and deep diving topics that have absolutely no bearing on her life.

caracalloway.com | @caracallowaywrites